EMP: SAN ANTONIO

J.S DONOVAN

❀ Created with Vellum

THE SOWER

*E*yes like chips of dirty ice and a heart to match, Jose Martinez leaned his grizzly forearms on the chrome railing, overlooking the techno-nightmare.

Massive light racks on the ceiling shot waves of green lasers across the crowd of sweaty dancers. The music, a rage-induced pulse, shook the walls and pillars. In the dark recesses of the dance floor, dealers of the latest synthesized drug practiced their trade. Elsewhere, women of the night lured in clueless prey, wrapping them in a web of lies to later drain their life. On the crisscrossing walkways high above, gang-bangers, armed and deadly, patrolled and used earpieces to point out suspicious parties.

Jose sipped his champagne, a hint of apricot and pear. He swished the drink between his rotting, golden teeth. "He's late."

Wearing designer clothes and painted with face tattoos, one of his lackeys nodded and hurried out of the VIP area.

On the floor below, sixteen-year-old Abigail Martinez ground against a patron. The pretty boy brushed his hands down Jose's daughter's figure. She laughed, enjoying the attention she never got at home.

Jose's scarred knuckles turned white around his glass flute. "Tako."

"Yes, sir," the trusted triggerman said, appearing next to him.

Jose pointed with his glass-holding hand. "Him."

"Understood." Tako started for the door.

Jose took a sip. "Make it quiet."

Now alone in his little throne room, Jose refilled his glass. The phone in his pocket buzzed. The caller: Gregory Swinestain.

"*Tsk.*" Jose's lip twitched. He pressed end.

To Jose, lording over a pocket of San Antonio's underground was less cumbersome than dealing with his wife's attorney.

Tako weaved his way through the crowd and put his arm around the pretty boy. He whispered something into the man's ear that caused the color to leave his face. Abigail yelled at the triggerman, but the music flushed out her voice. Tako escorted the patron through the crowd and out of sight.

Jose smirked. He glanced back at his daughter.

Mascara tears marred her tan cheeks. She gave him the finger and stormed outside.

Jose waved at her as she went. "Bye, now."

The VIP door opened. The lackey in designer clothes peaked in his head. "He's here."

"Bring him up." Setting aside his glass, Jose leaned his rear against the railing and awaited his guest. His silvery-gray hair and glossy steel blazer reflected the ceiling light. *Tink, tink, tink.* The back of his pinkie ring tapped on the rail.

He thought of his father's farm. Under the merciless sun's striking rays, little green leaves sprouted across the acres of Mexican dryland.

Father squatted by one of the little plants. *"This is yours."*

"The field?" five-year-old Jose asked.

Father chuckled. *"The field, he says... No, not even close, my son. Just this plant."*

"But it's nothing," the boy complained.

Father held his son's scrawny arms. *"Learn to steward one and you can steward all. Understand?"*

The memory ceased as the bald man entered. Square jawed, boxed shoulders, and a head taller than anyone in the room, he was a mass of muscle, a gorilla in a suit.

Jose's lackey followed and sealed the door behind him.

"I was expecting Mr. Woo," Jose remarked, annoyed.

"My client is a busy man," replied the muscular man.

Jose stopped tapping his pinky finger. "So am I."

The men exchanged glares.

The muscular man broke his silence. "These are Mr. Woo's terms: you buy from us and only us. Cash and Crypto only—"

"This is business. I buy from whoever the hell I want," Jose interrupted.

"No loyalty, no deal. Those are Mr. Woo's terms," the muscular man stated.

Slighted, Jose gestured for the man to continue.

"We'll drop the product at locations of your choosing. You'll pay half before delivery and half on site. Once the product is in your possession, outfit your people as you see fit and prep them for future assignments."

"Prep them—?"

"Let me finish, please," the muscular man replied. "My client promises to make you a very wealthy man, Mr. Martinez. Wealthy and powerful. To do so, however, he has certain expectations about our future relations together. Don't take my words lightly: something big is coming. You can either thrive in the new or die with the old."

Jose didn't understand. "Is that a threat?"

"It's however you interpret it, but before you get your panties in a bunch, let me show you a demo product." The man pulled out a burner phone and made a quick call. He simply said the word "now" and hung up.

Jose set his jaw and crossed his arms.

A moment later, a knock. Jose nodded at his lackey, who opened the door.

Two men holding a heavy-duty plastic crate entered. They set it down on the table without Jose's permission and popped the latches. Stoic, they stepped to either side of the crate and let Jose do the honors.

Hesitant, he approached and opened the lid. Inside, the military-grade assault rifle rested in black foam. He lifted the weapon. It weighed more than he expected. The ergonomic grip fit nicely into his palm. The magazine was currently absent. "Quite the piece of machinery."

"Tried, tested, reliable, and fully automatic," the muscular man said.

There was a certain power one felt holding such a weapon. "Any one of my people get caught with this, and we all go away for a long time."

"With all due respect, Mr. Woo chose you because of your discrete nature."

"These weapons are anything but that…. What sort of *assignments* does Mr. Woo have in mind?"

"You'll know in time," the man said cryptically.

Jose lowered the gun back to the crate. "How many of these you got?"

The man smiled. "Enough to turn San Antonio into your personal playground."

2

DISTRESS CALL

*T*he mid-summer seven am sun climbed behind heaven-reaching skyscrapers, packed streets, and a million-and-a-half residents beginning their Monday morning rush. San Antonio, also known as Alamo City, was alive and well on the flat plains of Texas.

Inside the outdated police squad car, the dispatch radio crackled to life. *"Control to 233."*

Twenty-four-year-old officer, Kora Clark, swiftly answered. "223 speaking!"

In the passenger seat, the dried-up Officer Kensley smirked at the novice. "You don't have to sound so damn chipper. This isn't food service."

Balding and out of shape, the former detective had been put on rookie duty after showing up at the department intoxicated two months ago. This morning, he reeked of booze and body odor, and his uniform was wrinkled.

"Respond to Villa De San for a 10-59. Proceed with caution."

"10-4." Kora put the corded mic back in place. Like a deer in the headlights, she looked at her partner. "What's wrong with food service?"

"Oh, we are so screwed." Kensley looked out the window.

Kora cracked a smile and punched him in the arm. "I'm playing. Geez."

"Keep your eyes on the road."

"I'd have you know I graduated in the top fifty of my class," Kora replied as she navigated through traffic.

"Wow, top fifty out of two hundred cadets? You must've at least had a *C* average." Kensley's sarcasm cracked up Kora.

"*C*s and two *B*s, actually."

Kensley cursed under his breath, but Kora saw the beginnings of a grin.

"There it is. There's that *widdle* smile." Kora poked him in his side.

"Stop, woman," the old officer grumbled.

"Stop, what? This?" Kora tickled him with her free hand.

Chuckling, Kensley swatted at her hand. "Dammit, Clark! You're going to give me an ulcer—look out!"

A homeless man stepped off-sidewalk and onto the road. Sucking air through her teeth, Kora jerked the wheel. The cruiser swerved around the man before straightening out. The bum shouted at her in the rearview, shrinking the farther away they got.

Kora slowly turned to her mentor, her lips parted, and her teeth clenched together.

"Oh, ho, ho, ho," Kensley laughed wickedly. "Chief's gonna tear you a new one when he hears about that."

The amateur directed her attention back to the road and said sheepishly. "*If* he hears about it… I mean, he doesn't have to."

"Tough luck, Clark. Tough. Luck." Kensley enjoyed the power trip.

They turned into the Villa De San neighborhood. The run-down homes, the suspicious locals, and an air of danger, the setting quickly sobered up the officers.

"Have you ever been to this hell hole?" Kensley asked.

Kora shook her head.

"Highest crime rate in Alamo. Some bad *hombres*. Don't give them an inch. Force is the only thing these spics understand," Kensley warned.

"Mildly racist, but okay," Kora replied.

"Oh, save that liberal BS for your book club."

"Don't have a book club." Kora winked. "And who said I was a liberal?"

Their cruiser rolled to a stop outside of the dive bar. It was nothing but decrepit houses boasting broken fences that flanked the property. Around the side of the bar and near the back, they spotted a gathering of suspicious individuals on a dusty gravel road. Near the gathering, multiple vehicles were parked facing the three exit roads behind the bar. *Do-rags, matching gang colors, a typical gangbanger profile*, Kora concluded.

Still in the cruiser, Kensley grumbled, "There's your *10-59.*"

"Suspicious individuals, indeed," Kora remarked, switching off the engine. She noticed one man with face tattoos wearing designer clothes. "Who's Abercrombie?"

"Gabriel Puru, one of Jose Martinez's bottom boys," Kensley said incredulously. "I've been trying to nail the bastard for years."

"Is he really gay?"

Kensley gawked at her. "No, Clark, it's an expression. He's just a bad dude, all right? One we need to keep an eye on. Man, you're dense."

"Bad dude, got it." Kora felt her blood pumping. Policing was a drug, and she was waiting for her first real hit. The westerns she had watched as a kid were becoming a reality before her eyes.

"What's the play?" she asked.

"By the book." Kensley waved at Gabriel.

The gangbanger cursed and said something to his half-dozen friends.

"Protect and serve," quoted Kora.

"Law enforcement. That's the job."

The officers exited the cruiser.

Kora took in the cool, summer morning air. Her short ponytail and bangs swayed in the gentle breeze. Despite academy training, the bullet-resistant armor and utility belt weighed on her. She kept her posture straight and her Glock 22 ready to draw. *Don't-mess-with-me* .40-caliber rounds were loaded the pistol's fifteen-round magazine.

Limping slightly, the out-of-shape former detective led. The two of them passed through the dirt road between the dive and the decrepit house.

"Gentlemen!" Kensley said to the strangers. "Am I too late for the shindig?"

They glared at him.

Kora stayed a pace behind. "They likely don't know what that word means, Kensley."

She got a better look at the T-shaped road. The hairs on the back of her neck rose. The crossroads where they stood left them exposed. Without thinking, her hand found her pistol. It stayed in its holster.

"Gabriel Puru," Kensley grinned wickedly. "How's your boyfriend, Martinez, these days? I haven't heard much."

Gabriel, annoyed and anxious, asked, "What seems to be the problem, Officer? Is it a crime to practice our freedom of assembly?"

"Oh, the big man knows his rights." Kensley's eyebrows drew together. "Take a hike."

"We've not done anything—"

"A report of suspicious activity says otherwise. Now walk before I'm tempted to do a routine cavity search."

A lowrider crept from the east road and another other from the west.

"Kensley," Kora called out.

The older officer saw the incoming traffic and glanced back at Gabriel. "Friends of yours?"

Gabriel's men tensed and started shouting at each other in Spanish. A metal gun barrel poked out of the passenger-side window of one of the moving vehicles. Officer Kensley's eyes went wide. Before he could speak, the Uzi unleashed a swarm of bullets.

He jumped on Kora, slamming them both onto the dusty gravel. Bullets zipped overhead as Gabriel's men shot blindly and scurried for cover behind their parked cars.

A shot punched through the glass off the lowrider's windshield and hit the driver. Blood splashed across the splintered glass, and the vehicle accelerated rapidly. Its nose smashed into Gabriel's car, disabling both vehicles.

Kensley yanked up Kora by her arm. "To the car! Go!" He hurled her forward.

The green officer sprinted and baseball slid behind one of the parked cars. A bullet punctured the tire next to her. Yelping, she peered around the bullet hole-littered feeder as Kensley ran to her. A yard away, a stray shot hit him in the back of the thigh.

"Motherf—" he crashed to the earth.

11

"Kensley!" Kora moved out of cover the moment she was able and pulled him under the armpits.

Bam-bam-bam-bam! Deafening machine gun fire thundered nearby.

Pulling her partner, she glanced over, seeing Gabriel unload a military-grade assault rifle into the crashed lowrider. Every curse flowing from her lips was masked by the horrifying sound. Pressed against the vehicle's side panel, she covered Kensley with her body and put her hands over his ears, shielding her superior from the firefight.

Two more vehicles raced down the side roads. One came from the way where the officers had entered

"Clark, radio back-up!" Kensley yelled through his pain.

Blood pooled in the gravel around his thigh.

Trembling, she yanked her shoulder mic and picked the button. "This is Officer Clark, we need—"

Boooooooosh!

A massive bright light flashed across the cloudless, blue sky. The rival gangs stopped their shooting, looking at the strange phenomenon. The light vanished as quickly as it had appeared.

The vehicle racing Kora's way suddenly lost control, fish-tailed, and smashed into the dive bar. Bricks crumbled over its hood, kicking up a cloud of dust. The other vehicles skidded their breaks and crashed into each other at the center of the battleground.

"This is Officer Clark. We need backup immediately. I repeat—" There was no radio static. Kora clicked the button. Her mic was useless plastic. "The hell?"

Gabriel's voice sounded from out of view. "Try to steal from me again, huh?" He unleashed a storm of bullets at his crashed enemies. "Die, die, die!"

His three remaining allies scattered, routing the rival gang with their superior weaponry.

Still pressed behind cover, Kora said to Kensley. "The radio, it's—"

The older officer grimaced, hardly able to keep his eyes open. "Get out of here, Clark, while you have the chance."

"Not happening." Kora helped him sit up.

"Stupid girl. You have no clue how the real world works. If these people find you—"

Kora opened her mouth to reply when a shadow fell over her. She twisted back to Gabriel and the barrel of his gun.

"Get down!" Officer Kensley shoved Kora aside with the last of his strength. She landed on her back as Kensley pulled his weapon. Too late. A half-dozen holes blasted through his torso and chest, one clipping his jaw.

Kill-crazed, Gabriel jerked the rifle toward the younger officer.

Kora screamed. Her finger squeezed her trigger multiple times, blindly shooting at the gunman. Misty blood burst from his designer coat. He staggered back as each bullet hit, spit blood, and fell backward.

Shaky breath escaped Kora's parted lips as she kept her weapon trained on Gabriel's corpse.

The gunfire sounded down the two nearby streets. A massive plume of black smoke billowed from the car's engine lodged in the dive bar's wall.

Kora's heart beat faster and faster. She could not breathe right. Nothing in training had prepared her for—

One eye open, Kensley glared at her. He leaked everywhere.

"Oh, God…" the young cop mumbled.

The world turned upside, and the ground came up to hit Kora.

3

BROKEN ORDER

*G*raduating from the San Antonio Police Academy was one of the happiest days of Kora's life. Her parents had driven from Utah to applaud her from the crowd. Paul, her boyfriend, was there, too. He was the only person she was close to in her uneventful little world. Donning that blue uniform gave her purpose. The naïve pastor's daughter was blue-blooded now, and she swore to be one until the day she died.

A deep gasp!

Kora shot awake. One of her hands found her racing heart while the other rested limply at her side. The high-noon sun seared spots into her vision. A waft of smoke and cinder drifted before her eyes. She turned her head to the dive bar. Fire engulfed the little building. The hellish inferno twisted and roared, unleashing a tower of black smoke and dancing cinders. Other black spires grew in the distance—fires across Alamo City.

Bewildered, the officer sat up too quickly and got lightheaded.

Flies buzzed around Kensley and Gabriel. Their bodies hadn't been moved, but their weapons were gone. Looking around, Kora noticed her Glock was missing, too.

It was a strain to stand.

Her eyes scanned the unattended dead bodies and disabled cars where the shoot-out had occurred. Gabriel's corpse grabbed her attention. *I did that...* A few pulls of a trigger and a life—and all it could ever be —was snuffed out like a candle.

She walked among the dead, lost in the surreality of the moment. Her boot jammed a bullet shell casing into the gravelly dirt. A few spent ammo magazines littered the area, but someone had procured the weapons.

Crows cawed from nearby light posts. Their beady black eyes followed Kora as their heads jerked side to side. They were bad omens warning that the worst was yet to come.

A man slouched in the passenger seat of the rival's car. The windshield was shattered, and there was a bloody hole just below his shoulder.

Kora's shadow crossed over him, and he gasped. She backed up a few feet.

"W-water..." the man croaked. "Please."

Shards of glass littered the bottom of his shirt. Blood and dried spit crusted at the sides of his lips. The gravel crunched as Kora neared. She noticed a second bullet above his kidney.

Kora wrapped her trembling fingers around her corded mic and brought it to her lips. "Central? Hello?"

Dead.

"There's nothing I can do," she mumbled to the man.

"It was supposed to be a q-quick job..." the man said, attempting to clear his consciousness. "Something big was coming, and we knew... I had to... for my..." The light flickered out of dark eyes. He sat there, unmoving, unbreathing.

The mic fell from Kora's hand and dangled on its cord.

Unable to linger at the site of the massacre any longer, Kora took a few steps back before sprinting to her police cruiser. Someone had attempted to smash the windows but to no avail. She unlocked the door and slipped inside. She turned the key. Nothing. Not even a click. Another try. Same results. In her frustration, she threw open the laptop and dashed her fingers across the keys. Dead. There was no power anywhere. It was like the whole world had stopped.

The flash in the sky. If it were a nuke, she'd be pulverized or been hit with a wave of radiation. This different. *An electromagnetic pulse,* she thought. It was a doomsday scenario that the academy had barely briefed her on. If it could take out cars and radios, how powerful was the pulse? And how wide was its radius? Her mind went to a dark place. People on the operating tables, others with pacemakers, dementia wards, cars, planes, buses, the stock market, and a hundred and twenty years of electrical ingenuity just... gone.

Running to Paul was her first instinct. Her boyfriend had a decent-sized apartment, but he didn't have any canned food or water bottles. Most people their age ate out all the time. Hell, Kora couldn't remember the last time she had cooked. *"You burned grilled cheese,"* her boyfriend had teased her the other night. *"How does that even happen?"* What about her parents in Utah? How would she get a hold of them? A catastrophe this big wasn't going to get cleaned up anytime soon. It could take months or years to reverse the damages. Her parents had roughly a month's worth of supplies they kept around the pantry. It was mostly canned fruits and soups, some of which could be used long after the expiration date. In short, Kora wasn't ready for this disaster, and neither were her loved ones. She wondered how many millions would be starving soon.

America's dead. Her heart sank to her stomach. She wanted to hurl. Holding her gut, she peered down at her blue uniform. Light blood spatter dotted her chest and badge. Her vows to protect, serve, and maintain law and order hammered her conscience. *You made a promise. If you walk away now, does your word mean anything? What about your beliefs in God and country? In self-sacrifice? Officer Kensley died protecting you; are you just going to run and let his death be in vain?* Fighting back terror and self-doubt, Kora grabbed the pump shotgun from between seats.

You're not a little girl anymore. Your brothers and sisters need you. This city needs you. She brushed the tears from her eyes.

In her memories, she could hear the phantom sounds of bullets and screams from the shootout. Her brief run-in with death would stay with her, she knew. Gasping the weapon and not even bothering to close the cruiser's door, she jogged away from the scene of the crime and set her focus on returning to her fellow officers.

The ghetto backroads were ghostly and only had a few totaled cars. No one was on the streets. Either they had fled to someplace safer or hidden inside the deepest parts of their domiciles. It was to be expected. Even without the EMP, the firefight Kora survived sounded like a warzone. How Martinez's people got the weapons and for what purpose they needed them was unknown to Kora, but her working theory was simple: *they want power*.

Every gangster and his mother would want their hands on the highly illegal, fully automatic arsenal. Whoever has the biggest guns and the grit to pull the trigger would be king of the hill soon enough. If the San Antonio Police Department didn't get their forces together quickly, the city would be a battleground before the week was over. It could even happen sooner.

Gunshots popped in the distance. Some were closer than others. None were near enough to be seen by or to threaten Kora. By the infrequency of the *pops* and *bangs*, the city had not devolved into Afghanistan levels of anarchy… yet.

The next neighborhood was packed. Pedestrians—young, old, black, white, crippled, and able-bodied—gathered in the street between the rows of houses. Some bickered, others complained, most were just trying to figure out what had happened a few hours ago and what to do next.

An elderly woman spotted Kora and pointed her crooked finger. "Police! Ms. Policeman. Get… get on over here! We've been waiting for hours."

"About time someone showed up," a man remarked.

Another spit. "Great use of our tax dollars."

Kora slowed her jog as she neared them. She kept her weapon down and her eyes keen. She was not a natural killer, but she was paranoid and all jacked up, making her dangerous and alert.

A young mother holding a swaddled baby to her chest saw the blood on Kora's torso. "I think she's hurt."

The blood must've been Kensley's or Gabriel's, likely a little spatter from both. The thought made her woozy. She kept silent. Parts of the crowd slinked away from her while others advanced forward, demanding answers to questions Kora didn't know.

"Are we under attack?"

"Why aren't the phones working?"

"Where's the army?"

"Do you guys have a plan?"

"Are all the cops as useless as you?"

"Why is she staring like that?"

"Ma'am? Hello? Do you have anything in that brain of yours?"

"Answer our questions, darn it!"

Bam! The shotgun blasted in the air.

The crowd recoiled, cursing and hysterical. A wisp of smoke snaked out of Kora's hot barrel.

She lowered the weapon. "I need everyone inside. Now."

The neighborhood crowd exchanged looks and grumbled amongst themselves.

"I said, now!" *Bam!* She fired off another shot to the sky.

Like roaches, the people scattered and vanished into their homes. Doors slammed. Locks clicked. The street was silent again.

She removed her hand from the shotgun's pump and opened and closed her palm, hoping it would stop it from shaking. It didn't. She put it back on the gun and started through the neighborhood. Curious and terrified gazes followed her from behind closed windows. Halfway down the streets, her walk evolved into a jog and finally into a sprint. Miles of urban terrain separated her from the police station.

The EMP had exploded at the beginning of rush hour, and the devastating effect was clear. Cars were wrapped around light posts, jutted out from buildings, and crammed into each other like crushed soda cans.

Injured parties gathered on the sidewalks. A group of parents marched to the local school, looking to bring their children home. Businessmen lingered outside unlit offices, smoking cigarettes to medicate the stress. One such man sat on a curb outside of a bank. He had pulled out tufts of hair from his already-thin head of hair. He must've been one of the few unfortunate souls who understood the gravity of the situation. The United States dollar, the world's leading currency, was worthless in a moment. Years of labor, retirement funds, pensions, *poof.* Those who had sold time with their family for an extra check or prestige in the business world were hurled back to the Stone Age at the snap of a finger. Their sacrifices, their material value… wasted.

We can find a way to turn this around. Kora grappled with hope, fighting to keep it strong.

A group of fast-food workers lingered in the parking lot, laughing and tossing around a joint. *Clueless.* To them, this was just a way to get out of their dead-end jobs. Kora wondered what mindset they'd have in six months when every store was looted and every city was a graveyard. Perhaps flipping burgers was a better fate than killing zoo animals for a meal or slaying your fellow man over canned beets and Spam.

The lonely souls who only delighted in the electronic pleasures of the modern world would be the most interesting to observe. Would they claim the earth like their forefathers, learning the oldest trades of hunting and gathering, community and self-governance, or would they wither away in self-pity, unable to grasp the reality of the here and now once the matrix had been destroyed?

How about the media-consuming drones? The ones who believe everything "experts" and "scientists" told them, rarely able to conjure a thought of their own because of fear of societal rejection or "moral" failure—morals that, by the way, were established by the self-proclaimed arbiters of truth who propagate the minds of "sheep" and "simple."

Kora had God, and God set the standard. She glanced up at the calm blue sky. Was this part of the divine plan or righteous retribution against the idolaters of society? Would a phoenix rise from the ashes of the world's great nation, or would the crucible of change lead man back down the path of barbarism? The questions plighted Kora's mind. Only time would tell.

A young man wearing a muscle shirt and shorts ran past Kora, holding boxed Mac laptops.

"Hey!" she shouted.

The man didn't even turn back. He vanished into an alley. Kora let him go.

The nearby Mac Store's glass windows and doors

were shattered. *That didn't take long.* The opportunistic thieves were robbing the wrong places, though. *Gun stores, pawnshops, and outdoor outlets are the only places that hold value.*

Two women called Kora over. A friend of theirs was still trapped inside a totaled car. The jaws of life were needed to open the crushed door, but Kora didn't have access to it. She kicked the door a few times. Useless. She directed them to the nearest fire department. They were visibly distraught, but Kora was neither the strongest nor the most equipped to help their friend. She was becoming more aware of her limits with every unsolvable conundrum.

Passing by the mall, she spotted her first wave of active looters. Alamo City had spewed forth its worst opportunists at the mega-complex, and they were stripping the mall of everything of worth. Desperately holding handfuls of stolen items and pushing carts overflowing with shoes and clothes, the crowd flowed in and out of the smashed doors and busted windows.

Shouting. Cursing. Chaotic laughter.

A fight broke out over a smart TV.

Shady figures watched the distance. Their shifty eyes tracked lone looters they could jump on the way out the parking lot.

Nearby, a security guard lay trampled on the sidewalk. His arm and neck were twisted in strange positions. It was hard to tell if he had been killed intentionally or just marched over too many times.

Moving across the lot, Kora shouted at the crowd to disperse. A few kids listened. Most adults ignored her.

"Police! Stand down!" she yelled again, her voice going hoarse.

The looters knew she was young, alone, and unable to arrest all of them. In swarms, the burglars dashed by her. They weren't threatened by her gun. One even blew her a kiss. Another knocked her over, and her shotgun spun out of reach.

On the ground, a couple stepped on her during their escape. Then another person. And then more. Kora curled up into a ball. The moment she could stand, she snatched her weapon and retreated. Dirty shoe prints stamped her uniform. Bruises throbbed across her back, side, and torso. She rested her palm on the alley wall and caught her breath. The shady figures approached.

Kora's venomous glance fell on them. "Back off."

They obeyed.

Defeated, she traveled through the alleyways and backroads. In her wake were thousands of unresolved conflicts, injured people, and a city turned upside down.

Winded and weary from the hour-long journey, she arrived outside the Alamo Heights Police Department.

The small police station was one of few in the city. It was single story and made of brick and bulletproof glass; it was far from a fortress. Multiple crashed vehicles obstructed the street. A small group of people lingered outside the steps leading to its front door. Multiple law enforcement officers kept them at bay, giving empty promises and urging them to go home.

One officer spotted Kora. "Officer Clark? Hurry, get in here!"

She hiked up the steps and entered the glass doors. Thick tension hung over the bullpen. Groups of officers huddled in cliques around the office space. Some were donning riot gear while others slumped at their desks, speaking quietly about what to do. A few lingered by the windows. Cigarette smoke hovered around the fluorescent ceiling lights. *Looks like no one is enforcing the no smoking indoors law.*

"It's only getting worse." The officer stood by the parted blinds.

Another replied, "I ain't going back out there. This is the national guard's mess now."

They noticed Kora's harrowing expression and went quiet. Officers Garrick, Shultz, and McAlister drew toward her.

Previously a firefighter, handsome and only curbed by his lack of ambition, Garrick was the leader of their little bunch of amateurs. Shultz was short and squat, and though he was just shy of thirty, he looked twenty years older. Lastly was McAlister, an unremarkable African American man wearing a cowboy hat and prone to following the crowd wherever it took him.

The blood on her uniform alarmed them.

Officer Garrick ushered her to a nearby chair.

"Man, Clark, we've been worried sick about you. Where is Kensley?"

"Gone," Kora mumbled. She glanced around the bullpen. "Why is everyone just hanging out? We need people in the streets. The whole city is going to hell."

Shultz traded a look with McAlister before saying, "We've been waiting on orders, but…"

"But what?" Kora asked.

McAlister answered. "Chief has locked himself in his office since the power died."

Garrick interrupted. "Wait. What do you mean Kensley's gone? Like, *gone* gone?"

With darkness behind her bloodshot eyes, Kora glared at him. "Dead."

Shultz cursed under his breath.

"Martinez's boys," Kora explained, reliving the firefight in her imagination. "They were doing some sort of arms deal when a rival gang showed up. It went south real quick. That was when the EMP exploded. Kensley was shot soon after, and the preps fled. I, uh, couldn't do anything."

Silence lingered among the small group of friends.

McAlister asked stupidly, "You really think it's an EMP?"

"Radios are dead. Cars are dead. There's no power anywhere," Kora replied.

Shultz shook his head. "Then what are we doing here? I should be back with Andrea and the baby."

Kora glared at him. "We have a job to do."

Shultz waved her off. "Yeah, okay. Like I'm going to give up my family's safety for a *job*. Since that BLM malarky, no one respects the badge anymore. Do you expect them to start now?"

McAlister lit up a cigarette and took a drag, holding it between his dark fingers. "Shultz is right. We've been underfunded and understaffed, just to get spit on and called traitors. This whole situation is fubar. I got my mother-in-law at home, anyway. She's probably worried sick. I do more good looking after her and the young ones."

"Exactly," Shultz agreed.

Blood rushed to Kora's face. "We joined the force to help people. Backing out now is an insult to every cop everywhere."

Short and squat, Shultz smiled mockingly. "Your idealism might've gotten you through training, Clark, but it means nothing out in the field. I say we get our stuff and go. If this EMP is as bad as we think it is, we aren't getting paid enough to get ourselves involved."

"No one is going anywhere," Garrick said, eyes still wet from hearing the news about Kensley. "Not until we hear orders from Chief. Got it?"

The other officers quieted down. Shultz took McAlister's cigarette, causing the other officer to eyeball him before lighting up another.

Chewing the inside of her cheek, Kora stared at Chief Winslow's door. The long blinds were closed over the frosted glass. The tension in the ballpen grew thicker.

McAlister put an arm around her shoulder. "He'll come out. We just have to be patient."

Kora removed his arm. "We don't have time."

She made her way to the chief's door and took a deep breath. The hierarchy was sacred in the police department, but if the head was poisoned or corrupted, what was to become of the body?

Kora knocked.

Getting no reply, she entered anyway.

Chief Winslow watched a burning building through his window. Gray hair formed a crown around his oddly shaped skull. His uniform was neatly tucked. He didn't turn back to Kora. "I said I didn't want to be bothered."

"Sir, I—"

The chief twisted around to face her. His droopy eyes were bloodshot. Wrinkles etched his face. The man had aged since the morning. "Office Clark, you were supposed to be on patrol."

"I was, sir, but—"

"I gave you an assignment." His tone sucked the life out of the room.

"Yes, I understand. However—"

"If you're on patrol, I expect you to stay on patrol. If you were called for office duty, I'd expect you to keep doing office duty. Is that too complicated? Kensley was right about you cadets. You get dumber and dumber

every year." The chief turned back to the window."
You're dismissed."

A weight pressed on her shoulders, but Kora kept her cool. Nothing was worse than the shoot-out this morning. "Officer Kensley is dead, sir."

Chief didn't reply.

Kora continued, "By the looks of it, we have dozens of other officers unaccounted for, and the ones who are here are openly discussing desertion. We need orders, sir. Your orders."

"And you have them. From this morning. Or do I need to repeat myself?" Chief replied.

"Sir, there are riots in the streets. People are dying. And—"

Chief shouted over her. "I said *dismissed!*" His command carried into the bullpen.

Kora's hand trembled, and her heartbeat quickened. *Just turn back. This is a lost cause.*

She didn't listen to the discouraging voice, choosing to march toward her superior's desk. *For Kensley.* "No. I'm not going anywhere until you do your job."

Chief twisted around and talked down to her. "And what do you know about my job? You think you know better than me? Go ahead, tell me what I should do. C'mon. Do it. What's wrong? Haven't thought that far ahead?"

"I'm not going to play stupid games," Kora replied before pointing back at the bullpen. "We need a plan. New orders. New ways of communication. Something, anything, to get us moving forward before more is lost!"

Chief put his palms on his desk, dominating the room. Hatred burned behind his gaze. "You want my job? Is that it?"

Kora put her hand above her chest. "What? No, I—"

"Power-climbing rookie using this as an opportunity to show off? To humiliate me? I know your type," he sneered.

"Chief, that's not—"

The chief yanked off his badge and slammed on his desk. "There. Have it."

"Wha—"

He took his gun—*smash!*—and slammed it on the desk as well, cracking the glass. "That, too. Good luck, rookie."

The display of rage stunned Kora.

The chief walked around the desk and stopped next to her. "Congratulations on your promotion," he spat. "If you want my advice, burn your uniform and get out of Dodge."

Kora was left speechless as the chief walked out of the office.

His booming voice sounded behind her. "I quit, and I suggest any of you with a half of a brain do the same! Oh, and Clark is in charge now! Have fun!"

4

THE LAW

*W*ith sweat glistening on his brow, Shultz stuffed his gym bag full of clothes. "I'm out." He walked by Kora at the locker room door.

She sidestepped, blocking the short man. "Not you, too, Shultz."

"Yes, me. Now get out of my way." Shultz pushed past her.

"We need you," Kora pleaded, blocking him again.

"If you stay, you're going to get yourself killed. Go home, Clark." With that final remark, her friend shouldered past her and left the building.

A third of the other officers had exited with the chief ten minutes ago. Some made excuses—their first duty was to family, this was the national guards' problem, they were fighting an uphill battle, etc. Whatever they said, Kora ground her teeth. *Cowards*. Others bore their shame quietly. They simply grabbed their belongings and left as if their vows to uphold the law meant nothing.

Don't take it personally. They're just saving their own skin. Logic didn't deflate the feeling of betrayal.

Kora returned to the bullpen where McAlister was burning through another cigarette. That was the third within the hour. Stoic and handsome, Garrick leaned on the nearby desk. His mind was lost in deep thought.

"What are you thinking?" Kora asked, taking a seat in a rolling chair.

"Nothing important," Garrick lied.

Kora leaned forward, arms crossed and her expression tired. "You're going to leave, too. Aren't you?"

Garrick shrugged. "I don't know... I mean, what choice do we have?"

Three other officers returned to the room, wearing riot gear. They gave Kora and her colleagues a nod before leaving the building. *Strip us of our assets and quit... very classy.*

She glanced around the bullpen. There were only about twenty officers left.

"We should head to North Station," McAlister suggested. "We could team up with their officers."

"And what if they are deserting, too?" Garrick asked.

"We won't know until we try," McAllister mumbled.

"What we really need is to figure out a clear chain of command," Garrick thought aloud.

And in the meantime, more people die. Kora tasted bile.

A blistering headache caused her to shut her eyes. Thinking passed her feelings, she felt a plan forming. It wasn't complex, but it seemed reasonable enough. *It might work.* "I... I got an idea."

Garrick raised a brow.

Kora said, "We get civies to help us."

"How so?" Garrick asked.

"We deputize any able-bodied person and place them under the command of one or two officers. We'll split the city into sectors and secure one at a time—"

As she spoke, the other officers turned their attention to her.

The vision of a citywide conquest formed in her mind's eye. "We'll keep some of the deputies in charge of their home sector. Arm them if we have to. If we see anyone breaking the law, we cuff them and leave them on the curb. The public needs to know we're still doing our job, and criminals need to know they won't be tolerated. Everyone else, we'll send them into their homes until we can work out a food situation. Right now, we just need to establish a lawful presence in the chaos."

By the time Kora finished speaking, everyone in the bullpen was listening. She didn't know how she had gotten the courage to lead, but perhaps the fiery trial was needed for her to claim her destiny.

Continuing, she said, "We'll go as a single unit at first. Securing a quick win in the first few sectors will be paramount to further success."

It felt like she was playing one of the imaginary war games she played as a kid. She had her armies and a loose plan. She didn't need perfection, just efficiency. Much to her surprise, none of the other officers contested her plan. *Desperate times, drastic solutions.* Her average grades in the academy, along with her lack of experience, tempted her to disqualify herself. *No. Kensley died for you to be here. Make it worth something.*

They donned Kevlar vests, shin guards, and arm protectors. They tightened their ballistic helmets and dropped the plastic face protector. Some officers equipped their tactical rifles, others shotguns, and a few had pistols. They kept tear gas at their side, along with a spare gas mask. Each officer also grabbed a few magazines full of rubber bullets. Though they were few in number, their well-equipped militia would rouse hope for the helpless and fear in their enemies. Dozens of handcuffs dangled from their belts. They knocked together like wind chimes. Justice was coming.

They kept five officers in the bullpen. Their job was to fortify the building and look for a place to store food. With every sector secured, they would bring back supplies. Once their needs were covered, they'd have some food to give up away to upstanding citizens, AKA those who were loyal to the police.

Kora led her squad outside. The number of lingering civilians had doubled since she'd last seen them.

"Listen up!" Kora shouted from the top of the stairs.

35

"Until further notice, no one will be allowed outside of their homes."

The crowd bickered.

Kora kept talking. "If we see you, we will not hesitate to detain you."

"That's not fair!" one man spat.

"Yeah! We have rights!"

Kora glanced at the other officers and then back to the crowd. "However, anyone who wishes to join us will swiftly be deputized. If not, this is your final warning—return indoors, or we will use force."

A few men raised their hands. Kora placed them under Garrick's control. He would give them their tasks and outfit them as he saw fit. They wouldn't arm someone too hastily. Those who seemed trustworthy, they'd send with the officers as watchmen and supply gatherers. The plan wasn't complicated: anyone who helped would be helped. Everyone who wasted space would be temporarily sequestered into their homes until Kora established order in the area surrounding the station.

The four blocks around the station were secured rather awkwardly. The officers weren't flowing in rhythm, a few looters got away, and one gang had to be dispersed through the use of rubber bullets. Kora's heart went out of the people, but she needed to be unflinching. Aiming for the torso and the back of the legs, she popped a teenager a few times. The teenager ran away, screaming with bleeding welts.

They ended up cuffing two robbers and sitting them on the curbs. Two officers were put in charge of the sector. They could deputize whoever they wished. If things turned sour, however, they would be responsible.

By the time they'd taken a few blocks surrounding the station, Kora's team had developed a pretty good method. They didn't hesitate to toss tear gas into hostile crowds, pinpoint civilians who would make good allies, and move through the mass of disabled cars with finesse and ease. They placed deputies on rooftops and gave them binoculars. They put others on the corners of streets to ward off travelers. Within the secure sectors, they had more deputies cleaning out gas stations and shopping centers, moving the supplies back to the police station. Locals accused them of looting and hypocrisy. *A week from now, you'll be thanking us.*

Kora bet that the rival gangs in the city lacked long-term solutions. They were likely stealing but not saving. Kora wanted the police to monopolize. She wasn't sure exactly how that would look yet, but in theory, the people would be more likely to follow and obey if given food. *I feel like a communist.* Kora hated that thought. *Fascist might be the better term.* She promised to return the people's rights the moment she had the opportunity. Anyone who didn't like her way of doing things was free to leave. Honestly, that was the best solution. They're going to be many mouths to feed as it was, and she didn't need every officer and civilian, just those who were loyal to the cause.

Barricades were placed on the streets around the station. Crash cars were pushed to curbs to make a clear walkway. Shopping carts were ushered in and out. Kora returned with a few officers to get a thirty-minute nap and a quick meal. She didn't bother removing her gear. Leaning back in the chief's chair, she listened to the officers speaking on the other side of the cracked office door.

"Officer Clark is good, but I think we got a handle on this now," one officer said.

Another agreed. "We need someone with more experience. The chief put her in charge as a joke anyway."

Kora shut her eyes. *Don't let it get to you. Actions speak louder than words.*

She dreamed about the firefight, but this time she didn't survive. Bullets bombarded her like they had Kensley, and she spent her dying moments wondering if her efforts had made a difference.

Jerking awake, she sat up in the office chair. Her eyes fell on the gun and badge on the splintered glass desk. *I just have to own the moment.* The badge clipped nicely to her belt. The gun was a 1911 with a custom grip. It felt good in her hands. She closed an eye and aimed the weapon around the office. She kept her shotgun as her primary weapon, though.

"Okay, everybody, time to get back out there,"

Kora announced as she stepped into the bullpen. "We need to get done with as much as we can before nightfall."

"Clark," one officer said.

"What's up?" she asked.

"When does my shift end? My wife is going to kill me if I don't stop by."

Kora thought for a few moments. "Uh, how about… Yeah, set her up in one of the surrounding buildings. Anyone who wants to bring their loved ones into this sector can do so freely. Set up an evacuated house or office for the women and children."

"And if there are none available?"

"Find another sector," Kora said curtly. She wasn't going to start dragging people out of their homes.

She teamed up with McAlister, Garrick, and seven other officers to move into another sector.

San Antonio was getting rougher by the moment. More fires burned in the distance. A dead body or two occasionally spotted the street. Doors to various places were smashed in. Jewelry, designer clothes, and food were robbed. Restaurants were completely abandoned. Groups of people wandered the streets. They fled at the sight of Kora and her army.

"Looks like word is spreading," Kora remarked.

Garrick replied, "I hope they know we're not the bad guys."

McAlister said, a cig hanging from his lips, "Their opinions don't matter much. We do our job regardless."

Kora cracked a smile. "You're going to get lung cancer before the day is out."

"Are you my mother-in-law now?"

They turned a corner. A prison bus—tipped on its side—was crashed outside of a bank. The officers stopped joking and fanned out across the street. Keeping their weapons ready, they moved closer to the bus.

Gentle steps. Steady breathing. Kora moved to the busted front windshield. The driver's seat was empty. The cage beyond was not.

Two dozen prisoners, a few dead and many injured, packed the cushion seats. Chains bound them to the floor. None had escaped. They leaned sideways, gravity pushing them into each other. A horrible stench caused Kora to wrinkle her nose.

"Hey! Hey! Get us out of here!" They screamed and fought against their chains. "We've been in here for hours, man!"

"Lamar crapped himself!"

"You got to go when you got to go," the stinky prisoner replied.

"This ain't right, man!"

McAlister stood next to Kora and lowered his weapon. "Leave 'em."

Kora's jaw dropped.

"Useless eaters," McAlister explained. "Guys like this ruined the last world. We shouldn't allow them to ruin this one, too."

Garrick flanked Kora's other side. "I'll leave it up to you, but McAlister makes a good point. These guys were on the way to the federal penitentiary. Murders, rapists, pedos, the worst of the worst. It might be best to let the Lord decide their fate."

"I ain't got a problem with that," another officer remarked.

As the bound criminals screamed for help, the brown eyes of a scruffy-bearded man with a buzz-cut locked onto hers. He seemed to maintain his cool despite having a dead body leaning against him. Her gut told her to trust him. *That makes no sense.* She contested the feeling. Nevertheless, something about the man allured her. It was almost spiritual. *That shootout must've really messed me up.*

"They come with us," Kora announced.

McAlister shook his head. "Okay, Clark. That's on you, though."

"Everyone shut up and stay put!" Garrick command.

Desperate, the criminals listened.

Kora kept watch outside while a few officers climbed through the broken windshield and used bolt cutters to get open the bus's cage door. They released two criminals at a time and ordered them to sit on the sidewalk. One tried to run. They shot him with rubber bullets until he dropped, and then Kora personally cuffed him. It took about fifteen minutes to get everyone out.

Though the sector wasn't secure, Kora ordered everyone back to the station. They had officers surrounding the criminals from three sides—right, left, and back. Possible runners were given a single warning and the promise that they wouldn't use rubber bullets to drop them.

Kora walked next to the bearded man.

"Psst," he said. "You. Listen up."

Kora kept her eyes forward.

The bearded man glanced around as he walked and spoke quietly. "I got a place a few hours south of here. No people. Secure. You let me out, and I'll show you the way."

Kora stayed silent.

"I've been preparing for something like this. I got food. Weapons. I'm not playing around. It's a lot better than this city," the bearded man explained.

"Keep walking," Kora commanded.

"Come to me when you change your mind."

The man had a certain survival instinct that Kora had picked up instantly. She couldn't trust him, though, and likely wouldn't have time to mine his head for knowledge.

The police station was active. Multiple citizens lingered at the sidewalks. An officer was stationed on the roof of the building. His scoped rifle captured the glint of the sun. *We're only ten hours into the powerless world, and it's already completely unfamiliar.* Mankind was pliable when pressured. Most heroes rise out of necessity, not by choice.

Officers Terry Lee and Jennette Harold hiked down the steps. The women were hardy in appearance and could bench two times the amount of weight as Kora. Lee, in particular, had mannish qualities. Her spiked gray hair added to the look. Jennette's hair was pulled back into a tight bun, revealing her serpent-like facial structure.

Kora smiled at them. "I've been missing y'all! Glad you could make it!"

Lee shifted her jaw as if chewing gravel. "What's all that?"

Garrick answered. "Prisoners. We need to get them changed and put in the temporary holding cells until we figure out our next step."

Jennette crossed her arms. "We didn't travel halfway across the city just to have this place flooded with lowlife scum."

Kora lifted the chief badge. "That's not up to you."

"Let me see that." Lee hiked down the steps.

A few other cops gathered around. Their fingers were near their triggers. Their dagger-eyed gazes fell on the prisoners. When Lee was close, Kora tossed her the badge. Lee caught it effortlessly.

Kora said, "Winslow put me in charge before he quit."

"And your first plan was to pack this place with killers? Yeah, not happening." Lee pocketed the badge.

Kora put her hand on her hip. "Real mature. Now hand it back."

Lee addressed the other officers. "We can all agree that Kora's done a great job getting us going, but it's time for the professionals to take over."

Kora scoffed. "Okay, Lee. Whatever you say. Just because I don't have the badge doesn't mean my words are not law."

Lee pointed at her. "See that, everyone? Look at the mouth on this rookie. *My word is law.* Give me a break. How old are you? Twenty-one?"

Twenty-four.

Kora turned to Garrick for support. He shrugged. McAlister was silent, too.

"What the hell, guys?" she barked at them.

Garrick replied, "We really can't take care of these prisoners, Kora...."

McAlister nodded in agreement.

Jennette spoke up. "We'll make you a deal, Clark. Deal with the prisoners and come back, and we'll make sure you're looked after."

One of the prisoners mumbled. "Just let us go. Everyone wins."

The bearded one remained silently, waiting to see what Kora would do.

"You're not in charge," Kora replied to Lee, holding back her frustration.

Lee said smugly. "Chain of command dictates otherwise. Fall in line, Officer."

Kora exclaimed, "You want to release these criminals into the wild?"

Jennette answers. "No, I said *deal* with them."

Kora's eyes widened. "You can't be serious."

Lee said, "It's them or us."

Kora turned to the other officers. No one made eye contact. No one was on their side.

She spoke to the officers around her. "It has been a horrible day for everyone, but today is only the beginning of our troubles. If we lose our principles now, who will we be in a week, a month, a year? None of us know how long we're going to be without power. Now, this morning, we established some order out of the craziness. Let's not stop now. Guys, please. For our fallen brothers and sisters, don't lose yourselves."

Lee interrupted her speech with a gunshot into the clouds. Kora flinched at the *pop*.

Lee lowered her pistol. "Anyone who wants to support rapists and killers is not welcome in this station. Kora, last chance. Us or them?"

Kora's heart thumped behind her ears. She balled her fists. *Actions speak louder than words.* "Keep the station, Lee. Any officer still interested in honoring their commitment to the people, follow me."

"Where?" one deputized citizen asked.

A thought came to Kora. "The Alamo."

5

NIGHT FIRE

*S*even officers and five deputies followed Kora and her prisoners away from the police station. The prisoners outnumbered them by six.

The sunset over the historical Alamo site in a sector of the city they hadn't secured. Looters scattered at the sight of Kora and the other well-armed cops. No one was inside of the old fort. Aside from a wealth of history, there wasn't anything valuable inside. That worked in Kora's favor. Strategically, the site was near the heart of the city. If they could successfully hold it, they'd have an easy landmark to point deputies toward and bring supplies to and fro. The surrounding walls were shorter than she remembered.

"You'll need razor wire," the bearded prisoner remarked. "I'll give you a list of a few places."

"Thanks," Kora said coldly.

"The name is Glen, by the way."

"Kora Clark."

They shook hands.

Glen grinned, further etching his crows' feet and wrinkled brow. "You should've listened to your friends and left us."

"Is there something I should know about?" Kora asked, annoyed.

"Nothing that you haven't already heard before. Killers and cops. Not a great mix."

Kora pursed her lips. "I'm not about to give another speech. I get, like, one of those every two years or so."

"Justice, fairness. They're good ideas, but application-wise… eh."

The cops in front forced open the courtyard gate and began marching in the prisoners.

Kora walked alongside Glen. "The true measure of someone's character is not how they treat their friends but how they teach their enemies."

Glen pondered the words.

"My dad told me that," Kora clarified.

"Wise man, but I can't say I agree with him."

Kora shrugged. *And now I trust you even less.*

Time had worn down the old stone buildings. The iconic chapel would be where they'd set up their base, while the large lawn could be a good place for tents. The prison and guardhouse would store the prisoners. Garrick and McAlister kicked in the doors and gestured for the prisoners.

"Don't kill each other," McAlister replied as he sealed the door.

Two cops guarded the cell while the rest headed inside the chapel building. The boots clacked on the stone floor. Flags were placed on the walls. They formed a circle.

Garrick stretched. "What's the plan now?"

Kora replied, "We set up a new base."

McAlister said, yawning, "I saw a hardware store on the way over. We can get some tents, tools, and chairs."

"Perfect," Kora replied. "That'll be our last run of the day."

The tired officers nodded and started for the door.

"Hey, everyone, hold up," Kora stopped them.

Fatigued, they turned back to her.

Kora smiled. "Thank you all. We're on the right side of history. You'll see."

The officers mumbled agreeing words.

They split into three different groups of four. The first went for food, the second for tents and sleeping necessities, and Kora's group went for the razor wire.

Garrick led them. McAlister, Kora, and a deputy named Hank Marshal followed. The old cowboy had a strong sense of patriotism and his own gun—a custom AR-15. He was first to follow Kora when she had left the police.

"They have uniforms, but they ain't real cops," he had said. "This here—us—we are the real lawmen. Hell,

I hate taxes, but I'd pay for our guys double if it means a fair shake for everyone."

Kora was glad to have him on her side. People burning with the American spirit would fight for their neighbors. Ideas don't always lead to action, but powerful principles always do. They'd fall in line with orders and even sacrifice themselves for a righteous cause. However, those who despise the USA and all it stands for will revel in its destruction. They'd join the rioters, burn the flags, and hunt the cops. *San Francisco or New York City must be hellscapes by now.... Never mind, they were always hellscapes.*

Shouts and screams sounded in the distance. Kora and her crew dashed through a series of alleys before arriving at the source of the sound.

Masses of people packed the downtown, stealing from bars, breaking windows, and starting small fires. They flipped over cars. A couple of the youth playfully tossed glass bottles across the street. A group of women danced in their drunken, intoxicated haze, cursing society and laughing hysterically.

Hank stood behind Kora in the alleyway. "There are hundreds of 'em, at least."

Garrick said, "Not worth the trouble."

"Yep," McAlister agreed. "We'll find another way to the hardware store."

Kora pulled a canister of tear gas from her belt. Her finger slid into the pull ring.

"Uh, Kora, what are you doing?" Garrick asked.

The young officer kept her focus on the chaotic mass stripping the city like vultures on a corpse. "If we let this type of behavior slide now, how will we keep them from coming back night after night?"

McAlister disagreed. "Let them enjoy their party. Tomorrow, when they have horrible hangovers, we can send them on their way. We're exhausted anyway."

Hank shook his head. "Kora's right. Tonight, they'll burn *this* street. Tomorrow, it will be the next one over. Hard justice. Right now."

"Garrick, thoughts?" Kora asked.

"They vastly outnumber us, Kora. I get you want to do the right thing, but... how?" Garrick asked hopelessly.

Kora put on her gas mask. "One can of tear gas at a time."

Things might get nasty, but if they could cause enough of a bang, the people would scatter.

Her little group put on their masks and got ready. Still, in the shadows of the alley, Kora counted back with her fingers.

Three.

Two.

One.

She stepped out of the alley and—

Bam-Bam-Bam! Machine gun fire roared in the distance.

Kora and the rest of the crowd turned toward the noise.

At the end of the road, a half-dozen machine gunners climbed on the tops of cars. Bandana masks covered their faces. Green and gold, their outfit colors matched Martinez's gang. The gunman standing on the center cop car was Tako Perez, Jose Martinez's main triggerman.

He lowered the machine gun barrel down from the sky. "*Adios.*" And trained the military-issued assault rifle on the crowd.

The scream that followed came straight from hell. In a mass of rolling flesh, the pedestrians piled into each other, crawling, punching, and shoving their way away from the shooters. Whole bodies were swallowed up in the chaos. A volley of bullets zipped over the hysterical masses. Like a tentacle, a branch of people smacked into the alley. They rolled over Kora. The sudden impact sent her to the ground and her gas mask skidding away.

She heard Garrick's shout when a boot stomped her head.

Black.

Bad eggs and rotting meat, a horrid stench assaulted Kora's senses. She awoke in a dark place on a bed of squishy plastic. *Trash bags*. She didn't remember how she had gotten into the dumpster.

She pushed open the flap above, revealing the starry night sky. A fire on the nearby, silent street spilled light across the asphalt path. Groaning, Kora climbed out of the heap of garbage and flopped face-first to the earth.

Pain throbbed across her body. A boot print had stamped her bruised face. She couldn't bring herself to move. Her busted lip smeared blood across her cheek and chin. *You're not dead. That's something, at least.*

A woman in yoga pants and tank top stuck to the alley floor. Her half-open eyes displayed no life. A bloody clot stained her blond hair. What was her story? What events had led her to this moment? Only God knew.

"G-Garrick?" The cry seeped from Kora's broken lips.

The soft crackling fire replied.

Pressing her palms against the coarse ground, she started to push herself up. Her elbows trembled. Throbbing bruises across her back and side caused her to fall back to her face. She rolled over. The chief's pistol and the various cans of tear gas remained attached to her belt. A long three minutes ticked by before Kora used the dumpster to pull herself to her feet.

Holding her bruised side, she limped to the mouth of the alley. The horde of pedestrians was long gone. A handful of neglected corpses dotted the glass-littered streets. A cursory glance revealed their cause of death to be trampling, not bullet wounds. *Tako's goal wasn't to kill. It was to get them running.*

"Over there!" someone yelled.

Kora flattened herself on the alley wall, hiding. At the end of the street, Tako directed his gunman to push shopping carts from building to building. They secured jewelry, booze, and non-perishable food from the restaurant kitchens.

Martinez is planning ahead, too.

The gangsters hadn't seen her.

By striking fear in the people around the area, he'll do a much better job keeping them inside than I could.

Alone and injured, there wasn't anything she could do to stop them. She dipped back into the alley and limped her way toward the Alamo.

Burning buildings and random fires illuminated the path; all else was in complete darkness. Spotting a *Walgreens*, Kora crossed the empty street and entered the store. The shelves were completely stripped of goods. *So much for painkillers.* The day and all its stresses hit her at once. She leaned against a crosswalk pole. The heavy vest made it hard to breathe, but taking it off would be idiotic. *Endure*, she told herself. Her father had preached many sermons on longsuffering. Though undervalued at the time of his sharing, his words kindled a fire in her.

There was hope for this city, Kora believed. If she just worked hard enough, her efforts wouldn't go unrewarded. Glen, her boss, Shultz, and the cowards on the force gave up too soon. *It's only day one. There is time to turn this around.*

Like rats, a small group of homeless junkies darted

across the streets. They saw Kora's uniform and ran away.

That's what I thought, she thought proudly. The uniform and badge still meant something. Until that changed, she wouldn't give up.

A woman screamed.

Kora froze.

Silence.

She quickly drew the 1911 pistol from its holster. Holding the weapon low and in both hands, she waited for another scream.

More silence.

Crap.

"Help!" The cry was cut short.

Enduring her pain, Kora ran to the source—a diner-style restaurant. Chairs had smashed in the windows, and the door lay flat on the ground. Illuminated by candlelight, two sleazy middle-aged men had pinned the waitress to a table while a third hiked up her skirt.

"Police! Back off, hands in the air!" Kora shouted from the entrance.

One of the men yanked a revolver out of the back of his jeans.

"Drop it!" Kora threatened.

"Run along now, or you'll be next," the armed man warned, his eyes wide with cocaine and lust.

The waitress used the brief opportunity to fight against the other two men. They overpowered her within seconds, keeping her on the table.

"*Please*!" Her horrifying cry shook Kora's head.

Chaos working in his favor, the armed man swiftly turned the revolver on the waitress and hissed at Kora. "Leave."

Tears welled in the young officer's eyes. "Okay."

"Okay?" the armed man repeated, confused.

He glanced at his partners, who shrugged.

A wicked grin grew on the armed man's face. "O-kay!" he celebrated.

Bam!

A bullet shattered part of his skull, and he smacked the ground.

The waitress fainted, and the other two rapists ran out the back exit, cursing up a storm.

Lowering her weapon, Kora approached the woman. Unhealthy curiosity drove her to look at the rapist's corpse. *The second person I killed today.* The gore seared her imagination. Bile climbed to her tongue. She swallowed it down. *God, that one was justified, I swear.* She claimed the revolver from the tiled floor before blood could pool around it. Her adrenaline was going crazy. The high was intoxicating. She hadn't felt this strong since the morning. It was like there was a beast inside her that hungered for death and dominance. Her reasoning center told her never to feed it. Her limbic brain tempted her otherwise. *In the old world, you're a rookie. In this new world, you are so much more.*

Kensley's words echoed in her mind. *"Force is all they understand."*

Knocking her elbow against her arm, Kora awoke the waitress. The terrified ginger rolled off the table and smacked on the dead body. She screamed and crawled away backward as fast as she could. The back of her head hit the rim of another table.

"Ow-ee" She rubbed her head.

Kora twirled the revolver around in her hand and extended it to the woman. "You're going to need this."

Trembling, the waitress took the gun. She held it clumsily. "Is… is it loaded?"

"Yep. When in trouble, aim and shoot… Use both hands and never put your finger on the trigger without the intent to kill."

Still shaken by the experience, the waitress nodded.

Kora helped her stand. "My name is Officer Clark. You can call me Kora."

"Katie," the waitress replied.

"What are you doing out here, Katie?"

"I…" she lowered her head in shame. "I was cleaning out the register."

"Money won't do you any good. Food and shelter, on the other hand…"

Katie's face contorted, and she started crying.

Shocked, Kora wrapped her arms around the weeping woman. "It's okay. You're fine now," Kora said comfortingly.

"I took the test this morning, and…"

"What test?" Kora asked softly.

Katie moaned. "How can I bring a baby into a world like this?"

I can't even imagine raising a child in this mess, Kora thought. She rubbed the woman's back. "How far along are you?"

"A few weeks."

Kora smiled. "You have plenty of time."

Katie pulled away far enough to look at the officer's damaged face. "You think so?"

"Absolutely," Kora replied confidently. "We're going to turn this whole situation around."

Katie started to smile. "I almost believe you."

Me too.

The waitress appeared to be a few years older than Kora and didn't have a wedding ring. She had a curious beauty about her that could be a hindrance in this new chaotic world.

Kora put an arm around her. "Come on. Let's get going. You got anyone you can go back to?"

Katie sniffled. "A few friends."

"Well, bring them to the Alamo historical site if you'd like. The police are setting up a secondary base there, and we could use all the help we can get."

"O-o-okay," she stammered.

Leaving the restaurant, Kora spotted two cops moving in her direction. Darkness obscured their faces, but Kora recognized their shape.

"Garrick?"

"Clark? You're awake?" Garrick replied.

"Yeah, and no thanks to the guy who tossed me into the dumpster."

McAlister apologized. "Once you went down, we had to act quickly. Too many people. A lot of them are out for blood. It seemed like the safest place until we could make our way back to you… You look horrible, by the way."

"Aw, thanks. I feel it, too."

The four of them congregated in the middle of the street.

"Is Hank okay?" Kora asked, her hand still around Katie's side.

Garrick nodded. "He's back at the base as we speak."

"We were waiting until the coast was clear before coming out again," McAlister added.

Garrick surveyed the area with his eyes. "We also had to take care of some other problems."

Kora waited for them to clarify.

Garrick continued, "Some of the prisoners broke out. They attack a few of us on the way over the wall."

"We let them run," McAlister said unabashedly. "No one was seriously hurt."

The news infuriated Kora. "How could this happen? Who was on guard duty? Do you know where they went?"

McAlister glared. "We're not spending our energy chasing after those lowlifes, Kora. Sorry. We still have another ten in the cage."

"Ten? Ten! We had almost two dozen."

Garrick said, "One of the cages busted open. The lock was faulty, we think."

"Someone let them out..." Kora thought aloud. "Maybe one of the deputies. I want the names of the guards in charge."

Garrick and McAlister exchanged looks.

"Don't tell me..." Kora said.

"They left, too," McAlister admitted.

Garrick nodded. "Shortly after the prisoners."

"Faulty lock... Sure, Garrick."

Garrick put up his hands. "Hey, don't blame me. I was on the other side of the camp, planning your rescue."

Kora let go of Katie. She told the woman, "Go home. Get your friends... And don't lose that gun."

Katie nodded dutifully and ran into the darkness.

Kora turned back to her allies. "If we can't keep prisoners detained for a few hours, how are we supposed to get anything done?"

The other cops said nothing. A wave of vertigo passed over Kora. She stumbled into Garrick's arms.

"Easy," the stoic cop replied.

Kora let out an exasperated sigh. "Let's head back, okay? I feel like I'm about to pass out."

Garrick helped keep Kora balanced while McAlister kept an eye out for any unsavory characters. The journey back took longer than Kora expected. She longed for a hot shower and some ice cream. Instead, she'd likely get a disposable wash pad and whatever soap they had lying around.

A group of armed men stood on the strip mall's roof, burning a fire. They waved at the police as they passed by. Farther along the journey, a family of four carried travel bags and torches as they navigated their way out of the city. Apart from the occasional gunshot, there was very little noise. The relative silence was not peaceful, however. Everyone had limited vision, and thus the evils committed in the dark corners, unmanaged hotels, and unguarded buildings spurred the imagination. The unknown, the darkness, the unsettling feeling of hostility and desperation, the lightless world, kept Kora squeezing her partner more than she realized.

Small fires danced inside wood-stuffed trashcans outside of the Alamo's walls. The flames blackened the edges and cast their shallow glow in a little pool around them. A few deputies tirelessly fixed the razor wire across the wall's tops.

"You were able to get the razor wire," Kora remarked.

"A different team did," Garrick admitted. "One of the prisoners, Glen, I think, pointed them to a nearby store. The stuff is not easy to come by."

He pointed to plastic orange barricades blocking the walkways. "We plan on putting more barbed wire there, too."

"I suggested spikes," McAlister chimed in.

"Very medieval. I like it," Kora replied.

Almost thirty tents dotted the courtyard. A larger medical tent was being staked into the earth nearby. A few civilians busied themselves by the fire by organizing tools, building defenses, and cataloging supplies. It may have felt like the day had gone on forever, but it was only 10 pm-ish.

"Pretty good for day one, huh?" Kora remarked.

McAlister replied, "I still have yet to convince my mother-in-law to come over."

"As long as she stays inside the next few days, she won't have many problems," Kora stated.

McAlister raised a brow. "When did you become the survivor aficionado?"

"I'm not. I'm just good at guessing... sometimes." Kora glanced around the courtyard. "Which tent is mine?"

"Those are for the others. We're inside," Garrick said.

They entered the old chapel. Large square tents were set up to form little "bedrooms."

Garrick led her to the one in the back. It had candles, a cot, a fold-out table, a collapsible chair, a stack of water bottles, packs of beef jerky/Slim Jims, and a hamper full of folded clothes.

Kora took one of the Slim Jims. "You know the way to my heart, Garrick."

Too tired for the quip, he said, "I wasn't sure your

clothes size, so they just picked up a bunch of different stuff from the nearby thrift store."

McAlister replied, "Someone robbed Forever 21, sorry."

"That's too bad," Kora said sarcastically. She lowered herself to the cot. "Thank you, guys. I'm crashing for the night. I'll see you bright and early."

"Night, Clark."

"Rest up, Kora. We'll get some first aid for you in the morning."

When she was alone, Kora made the flap to the tent secure and stripped off her uniform. Her body ached at the simple action. She rested her police shirt and pants on the table and washed with a bottle of water, soap, and a rag. Bruises blossomed across the chest and torso. She checked her ribs. Nothing was broken. She could touch her toes, so her spine was fine. She was happy to get the boot print off her cheek. Her busted lip would make the next few meals a chore, but she'd manage. *I'm very lucky.*

Suddenly, her knees gave out, and she started weeping. Silent screams tore out of her soul. Tears flushed her injured facade. Pent-up fear and emotions hit her like a bus. The death of Kensley, being excommunicated from the force, the killings, everything that she bore without complaint for the last twelve hours roared awake. Alone, she couldn't hide behind her forced optimism. The unspoken pressures of leadership put her in a chokehold. She felt small. Insignificant. *You're doing the best you can,* she told herself, but her heart refused to believe it.

She curled into a ball on the cold floor and allowed herself to cry. She would have to manage people in a lose-lose situation. *Technically, you don't* have *to do anything...* That's what her boyfriend Paul would tell her. She missed him. Having a friend she could express her true worries to would be an answered prayer. She feared that being transparent in front of an already weak-minded crowd could cause morale to plummet further. *That's why we have structure.*

Police protocol was designed for times of trial. However, due to fractured leadership and misplaced personal priorities of fellow cops, she had to improvise everything. Wisdom told her to get out of town. If she prioritized her personal well-being, she might get through this crisis with little harm. Nevertheless, she despised losing. She knew she wasn't the best, the brightest, or the fittest for the job, but her grit prompted her to stay put. If she would not fight for San Antonio, who would? Martinez and other gangsters aimed to make the city into their sandbox. Her rival officers had turned the police into their self-serving faction. Fear would drive looters and the panicked masses down the road of evil. She had to be the hero. It was for this moment she was created. That was her conviction, a conviction she chose to believe. Holding firm to destiny could steer her in the right direction. *Endure.*

A deep sigh escaped her lips. She shut her eyes and breathed from her diaphragm. The purge of emotions drained her, but when she had risen, she had a newfound acceptance of the situation.

Dressed in warm black sweats and a slightly over-sized hoodie to hide her bullet-proof vest, Kora outfitted herself for one final evening run.

6

HALFWAY HOUSE

*K*ora was too tired to jog, so she limped down the sidewalk, reminding herself that danger could be lurking around any corner. The pistol in her hoodie's front pocket flapped against her stomach. Her left hand grasped a makeshift torch.

All around, skyscrapers stood like black monoliths against the skyline. They were empty of people. Their doors were locked. All the expansion plans were abandoned, and millions of digital files were wiped. The city's business sector was vacant of life.

Crashed luxury sedans and electric cars obstructed the road. Kora took a moment to rest her legs in the leather front seat of a totaled Mercedes. She drank from her water bottle and tongued a loose tooth. McAlister had warned her not to go. *"I'll be back within the hour,"* she had promised him.

Tossing her spent water bottle into the backseat, she continued her journey.

Crunching glass beneath her boot, Kora reached the bicycle shop. The front door was chained shut, but the display window had been pulverized by bricks. Inside, more than half of the bikes remained.

"Awesome," she mumbled.

She grabbed the fastest one she could find, carried it out the broken window, and mounted up. Racing against the wind, she lost her torch. Getting off her feet, however, was worth the sacrifice. She didn't want to end the day without getting to Paul, and if she had to reach him in the dark, so be it.

As speed increased, her surroundings blurred. Opportunistic thieves stalked about. Anarchists and graffiti artists trashed cars and buildings. Without her uniform and badge, she was invisible to most people. Her quick speed also kept anyone from getting a good look at her.

Paul's apartment was two and a half miles away. On her way there, Kora witnessed a few muggings, a biker gang shootout, a group of local fathers guarding their neighborhood, and a whole ton of people boarding up their homes from the inside.

Tucked away in the low-income area of the city, the apartment complex had been ransacked. Embers drifted a section of charred units. Cars were flipped. Doors had been kicked in. There were dead in the streets.

Too terrified to stop, Kora biked around a half-dressed woman marinating in a pool of blood. She was one of the multiple victims rotting outside of various apartment units. The nightmarish complex appeared to be empty. Whoever wasn't butchered had fled, and quickly, too. The attackers, likely a gang, hit hard with their only aim to cause harm. She biked down the winding streets toward her boyfriend's building.

A body bobbed in the pool where Kora and Paul spent their weekends. Their favorite ice cream truck had been set ablaze for no discernible reason. A man with a self-inflicted gunshot wound leaned against the glass wall of the window-lined shared gym.

Wiping a tear, Kora left the bike at the bottom of the one building's exterior stairs. Pistol drawn, she ascended to the second floor and moved her way to the last door on the left. It was ajar by an inch. The splintered wood around the lock alluded to a break-in.

"Paul?" Kora said, her voice scratching.

The door creaked as she pushed it open slowly. Every fear imaginable crept into her mind, suffocating her hope and causing her to regret coming this far alone.

Moonlight spilled across the floor. Kora aimed in the darkness. "Paul, it's me."

Apart from the TV face down on the carpet floor, the living room was relatively untouched. Whoever had invaded the one-bed, one-bath apartment had moved in and out quickly. The top drawer of the dresser was dislodged and its contents sifted through.

There was a small black ring box resting on a disheveled shirt. Kora knelt and opened it. Empty. *Was Paul meaning to propose?* Kora felt woozy. Still fresh in the police department, she wasn't ready for that type of commitment. The current state of the world didn't boost her confidence. She left the box, pretending she had never seen it.

She entered the bathroom, seeing that the shower curtain was closed. "Baby?" She grabbed the edge of the curtain.

Her breathing quickened.

The gun trembled in her hands.

The curtain rings screeched as she pulled it aside. The shower was empty. Her boyfriend wasn't there.

Leaving the apartment behind, she decided to head to her place. She and Paul didn't live together, but they were only a few blocks apart. Call her traditional, but Kora had no intention of sharing a bed until marriage. Their furthest line of intimacy they'd cross in their relationship was a kiss on the lips and playful wrestling. The values her parents instilled kept her from a lot of heartbreak, shame, and dead-end relationships.

Unlike Paul's complex, the neighborhood containing Kora's duplex had been untouched by violence. Its proximity from any major shaping center or strip mall kept it isolated from the surrounding horrors. Candlelight flickered behind glass windows. Her neighbor's garage door was open. The 1971 Range Rover was missing. *I've never seen him drive it. I wonder if older cars were unaffected by the EMP?* If so, Kora would have to keep her eyes open. Having a functional vehicle would expedite her plan to secure the city.

She hiked across her little lawn and toward her front door.

"That's far enough!" a woman yelled.

Kora twisted to the duplex's other door and the woman standing in its frame. She had messy gray hair, a half-lit cigarette hanging out of the corner of her chapped lips, and a shotgun held at her waist.

"Dana, it's me," Kora said, lowering her pistol.

"Kora? The hell happened to you?"

"If I told you, we'd be here all night," Kora told her landlord/neighbor. "Have you seen Paul?"

"Nope. The whole blackout has got everyone on edge. The government has finally decided to screw us. Well, I say bring it. I got enough shells to bring down a small army and food to last me six months," Dana boasted.

Kora smiled sadly. "Are you sure you didn't see him?"

"I'd know, sweetie, trust me."

Kora's shoulder's deflated. *Oh, Paul, why couldn't you make this easy?*

Dana asked, "You ain't got your uniform. The police turn on us, too?"

"I'm off duty now, but we're doing our best to keep things together. If you want to help, we could use keen eyes at the Alamo," Kora suggested.

Dana shook her head. "I've owned this house back when San Antonio was still considered country. Forty-three years I've stayed here. I'm not going anywhere."

Kora could use the ammo and food for her people but was too tired to beg or persuade anyone.

"Stay safe, Dana." She mounted back on her bike.

"You just got here. You're not coming inside?"

"I've got to find Paul."

Dana said, "I got my gas stove going if you want to tea for the road."

"I appreciate it, Dana, but tomorrow is going to be a long day. Lots of bad guys to stop."

The older lady rested the shotgun against her shoulder. "Choose your battles, girl. Some you just won't win. That's life."

Kora waved her goodbye and pumped the pedals, distancing herself from her little studio living space. All she was leaving behind was a basket of unwashed clothes, worthless electronics, a few plants, and a half-eaten pizza in the fridge. These were the staples of her simple life. She wasn't a materialistic person. That would be one of the traits that would work in her favor. The new world had no place for sentimentality and useless babbles. Her love for Paul may have to go, too. Her destiny was bigger than the butterflies in her stomach and the pleasant times they had spent together. It was a cold, pragmatic thought, but if she succumbed to her selfish, *wanting-to-feel-good* nature, she'd be just like everyone else. The world didn't need the same. It needed better.

She stopped at the entrance to the neighborhood after almost crashing into a telephone pole. The second wind she'd gotten after her cry back at the base had come to an end. Her energy was depleted, and her wounds were starting to ache again. *One more stop,* she convinced herself. *If he's not there, move on.*

Heading back through the city, Kora wondered what her day would've looked like without the EMP. The shootout between Martinez's guys and the rival gang would've been the same. There was a chance that neither Kora nor Kensley would've survived it, but if they had, they'd have to report the biggest gun bust in San Antonio history. She'd likely be put on the *beat* while more experienced detectives sought out the origins of the various firearms. In the later part of the day, she would've come home from her shift, called up Paul, watched a rom-com, and gone to bed. Perhaps three or four years down the line, they'd get married. Kora would have a higher rank in the force and get paid something she'd consider fair. Simple. Predictable... well, as predictable as police work could be.

The halfway house was surrounded by fencing on a street with multiple storage unit places. The blinds behind the barred windows were closed. *Here goes nothing.* Kora climbed over the fence and landed roughly on the other side. She stumbled and caught herself on a tree in the front yard. Limping, she sucked air through her teeth and knocked on the front door. Large long metal bars secured it, as well.

"C'mon, Paul. Open up," she mumbled.

Someone ruffled the blinds on the nearby window, but only for a moment. A lock clicked, and the door opened an inch, revealing an eye.

"You have three seconds to tell me who you are or else…" the teenage boy threatened.

"Terrell? T, it's me." Kora drew back her hood.

"Officer Clark?" the fourteen-year-old exclaimed.

"The one and only. I'm surprised you've not run off somewhere."

"This is the safest place in the city," the boy replied confidently.

Kora attempted to get a look past him but couldn't. "Hey, I'm looking for Paul. Is he here?"

Terrell reared back his head. "Yo!"

Footsteps sounded behind the mostly closed door. It opened the rest of the way, revealing the man with square glasses, light stubble, a cardigan, slacks, and business shoes.

"Holy crap," Paul exclaimed. He pushed open the metal barred door and wrapped himself around Kora.

He wasn't the buffest nor fluffiest, but his hugs were always sincere and heartfelt. She melted into him.

"Thank God…" Paul whispered, kissing the top of

her head. "I was terrified. I wasn't sure when I'd see you again."

Kora nestled against his chest. "Me too."

She wanted to spill all that was on her heart. Her boyfriend was a good listener; it was one of his most admirable qualities. But, she thought it best to stay quiet. Neither one of them wanted to let go. All the problems in the world hadn't vanished, but at this moment, all that mattered was that they had each other.

"I almost forgot how much I loved you," Kora admitted softly.

"Wow, I'm glad you didn't forget that," Paul replied with a little sarcastic grin.

Still holding him, Kora asked, "I thought you were off today?"

"I was, but when I saw what had happened… Someone had to be here with the kids. I was going to go looking for you in the morning."

"Duty calls," Kora replied.

"If I neglected my responsibilities when the crap hit the fan, I wouldn't be much of a role model. These kids don't have anyone. A few already ran away. The rest stayed because of me," Paul said, sadness in his tone.

Kora gently released him and was quickly reminded of the chilly wind. She buried her hands in the hoodie pocket, next to the cold gun. "So, what are you thinking?"

"About?"

"Staying? Going? Have you made any plans?" Kora asked.

Paul's mouth formed a line on his face, and he shook his head. "At this point, my only goal is to stay alive and help these kids do the same. C'mon in. I can get a bed set up for you."

"No, I..." she sighed. "Fine, just for a minute?"

A little confused, Paul escorted her inside. Seven delinquent teens, between the ages of eleven and seventeen, packed the candle-lit living room. One was reading a book, a few were playing a game of Risk, and the final two were wrestling on the floor. Terrell jumped back into the game of Risk.

"My turn yet?"

Bags of chips and soda bottles stood on foldable trays. Blankets and pillows were in a stack in the corner. All the unlit candles were in a cluster on the dining room table, along with a few matchboxes and a tall, lopsided stack of board games.

"We've been busy, as you can see." Paul grinned.

"I'm glad someone is having fun." Kora lowered to the couch. It felt a million times better than the bike seat. If she wasn't careful, she'd pass out.

Paul scooted in next to her, reaching an arm around her back and shoulder and pulling her close. "Tell me everything."

"*SparkNotes* version or..."

"That's probably a good place to start."

It was not the *SparkNotes* version.

She started from when dispatch reported the suspicious persons and ended with what she saw at Paul's apartment complex. By the time she was finished, all the kids were listening with sobering fear.

"A-are we in danger?" the eleven-year-old girl asked.

"Everyone is," Kora said, unable to lie to the little girl.

Face pale, Paul pushed his glasses back to the bridge of his nose with a quaking finger.

Terrell looked at him. "Uh, why are we still here? We should be running."

Most of the other kids agreed, filling the room with noise.

"Hey, everyone, chill out," Paul demanded.

Respecting their counselor, the kids quieted down.

He turned to Kora. "They have a point. This Alamo business, Kora, I don't see it ending well."

A frown sunk Kora's face.

"I'm just saying, we should have an escape strategy," Paul corrected, very diplomatically.

"I'm not a coward, Paul."

"And I never said you were, sweetie. But in your own words, everything is F'd."

"And I plan to un-F it," Kora said defiantly. "And you can either help me or..."

Paul withdrew into himself. "Please, do not make this ultimatum. There's always a middle ground; it just takes time to find it."

"How is this for a middle ground: if no one does their job, children will be starving, women will be raped, and our home will be overcome by gangbangers and killers." Her grim description silenced the room.

She rose from the couch. "I've been trampled, disowned, shot at. I'm pissed off, tired, and got an impossible task ahead of me. I need you on my side... please."

Paul chose his words carefully. "I'm just trying to look at this from all angles, okay?"

Kora squinted her eyes at him.

He sighed deeply. "God, help us... If you really think you can turn this around, I'll back you up, all right? But I need you to run when it's time to run. Is that fair? Or am I being completely unreasonable?"

"There is nothing reasonable about anything that happened today, but to answer your question, no, you're not. I just..." Kora's eyes watered. "I just can't stand by while I watch the world burn around me. I can't."

Here are the waterworks. Kora averted her gaze while fresh tears flowed. She hated looking weak, especially around those she cared about.

Paul took her hands. "Look at me."

She did so.

He spoke with sincerity. "I'm with you, baby. Okay? Always." He kissed the top of her hand. "Forever."

Kora wrapped herself around him. He held her

tighter than he had when they first had seen each other.

He spoke into her ear. "We'll save this city… together."

Kora grabbed his cheeks and kissed him as if he were the only man alive.

Maybe marriage wasn't completely off the table.

7

MOVING FORWARD

s it wrong to fight a losing battle?
Holding candles in little stands, the two
of them lead the procession of teenagers through the
quiet city. Terrell stayed on Kora's bike while the rest
of them walked in sync toward the bicycle shops. It
reminded Kora of a vigil. The horror stories she had
told the kids kept them quiet and alert. She took no
pleasure in scaring them straight, but it would keep
them vigilant and ready.

The long day was drawing to a close. For the first
time in hours, there weren't any gunshots or distance
screams. Many of the fires had dwindled. Sobering
darkness hung over their nation. Only God knew what
the second day had in store.

"Kora," Paul whispered, grabbing her arm.

She looked at him, head slightly cocked. She turned

to where he was looking. Fire light and shadows danced across the wall of a nearby building.

Kora whistled at the kids.

They quickly blew out their candles as they had discussed before leaving. Splitting up and taking cover behind the many vehicles obstructing the road, they trained their eye on the incoming invaders.

Paul put his finger over his lips, making sure the kids got the message. Just like in the *Art of War:* the best battle is on the one you don't have to fight.

Holding lanterns in gloved hands, the strangers entered view.

Green and yellow outfits. Martinez's colors. Kora gave her boyfriend a telling look.

His hand found the little 9mm pistol he had concealed under his shirt.

The twenty armed men moved with tactical precision across the street. They were trained for this and in their palms were assault rifles just like from the morning. In the middle and guarded on all sides was the gray-haired, gray-eyed man himself: Jose Martinez. He wore a black bulletproof vest under his flashy blazer. In his hands was a tactical shotgun boasting a massive drum magazine.

He must be finding a new place to bed down for the night. All around them were abandoned office buildings and clothing stores. *Not here, though, thank God.*

As the outfitted gangsters made it just over halfway across the street, Kora spotted movement in an opposite building. A window quietly opened and the barrel of the hunting rifle poked out.

Kora whispered to Paul. "Tell the kids to hide under the vehicles. Now."

Nodding, her boyfriend darted from car to car, staying hunched over and silent.

More shadow figures moved within the sniper's building.

It's going to get really nasty, really soon—Before she could finish the thought, one of Martinez's men shouted something in Spanish.

Scattering, the gangbangers ducked behind cars and trucks as the firefight began. Deadly bullets zipped across the street. Kora stayed low and out of sight.

Using their superior arsenal, Martinez's men routed the snipers and cleaned out the office building. Muzzles flashed behind broken windows. The skirmish was over in minutes. Martinez took no survivors. His people collected the enemies' armory. He spoke to Tako, the machine gunner who had previously chased away the crowd of people.

"Good call," Martinez put his hand on the man's shoulder.

"I told you they would be here," Tako replied. "Latin Kings next?"

Martinez thought about it. "All right, before word gets out."

Tako shouted a command at his men.

Only suffering one casualty, the hardened gangster took their bounty and left the corpses to rot.

Paul returned to Kora. "Who are those guys?"

"Enemy number one," she replied. "Get the kids. We're not far."

Relighting their candles, they grabbed bikes at the shop and used the moon and stars to guide them back to the Alamo.

The deputies on the night shift allowed them inside. A cop patrolling the tents ushered the kids into a shared camping canopy. Paul wished them a good night, reminded them to find him if they needed anything, and left. Kora waited for him in her tent.

"Crazy, huh?" he said, rolling out a sleeping bag next to the cot.

"What?" Kora asked.

"Everything." Paul proceeded to share his thoughts, but Kora heard nothing. She'd fallen asleep seconds after shutting her eyes.

There were no dreams, just a restless black void. She awoke before dawn about to vomit. Sitting up, she took deep breaths and mumbled affirmations over herself.

"You're a good leader. You are confident. You can do this." The stress sickness started to subside.

She overheard hushed voices outside her tent flap. Stepping over Paul, she peeked outside. McAlister, Garrick, and the other cops were gathered around a table quietly discussing the day over a large map of the city.

Peeved, Kora put on her uniform, utility belt, and boots. She let Paul sleep and joined the others.

"You started without me." She took a seat at the table.

Garrick said, "We thought you'd want to get some rest."

"I'm fine," Kora said defiantly. "I saw Martinez's men last night."

She pointed at the city map on the table. "Sector C."

Her allies traded worried looks.

"They're hunting down rival gangs, taking no prisoners," Kora explained.

Leaning back in his fold chair, McAlister sipped an energy drink. "Good. They can do our job for us."

Kora said, "If we don't put a stop to them quickly, they'll keep growing."

Garrick rubbed his hand up through his greasy hair. "We're cops."

"Okay?" Kora asked, missing his point.

Garrick clarified, "None of us are trained for war."

"None of us are trained for any of this, but that doesn't mean we quit," Kora reminded them all.

The table was silent.

Kora took a breath. "All I'm saying is that if we don't deal with this threat now, it may come back to bite us later."

McAlister fixed his posture. "Kora, the only reason

why he followed you was to look out for the little man. The civies. That's what I'm sworn to do. If we're not making that number one priority, I have no reason to stick around."

The other cops nodded in agreement.

Garrick said, "I say we put it to a vote: raise your hand if you track down Jose Martinez?"

Only Kora raised her hand.

"All right, raise your hand if you want to focus on securing sectors like we planned."

Everyone else put up their hand.

Kora crossed her arms.

Garrick gave her a pity-based smile. "Sorry, Kora."

Kora said, "Well, we need to deputize more guys and get more guns. Up our defense ASAP."

"Sounds like a plan," Garrick said agreeably before turning his focus toward the map. "Okay, so where to start..."

Kora sat silently while the rest of the allies discussed supply routes, establishing messengers to go from sector to sector and diversifying their stockpiles. If the Alamo site were to be attacked, they'd have secondary supplies on the top floor of a nearby office building that only those in the inner circle would know about.

Garrick, who had previously had a personality of a follower, took charge. With the looks, voice, and charm to match, he was a better face for their little unit than Kora. Just like with the cops who sent them out of the department, Kora's friends had taken her ideas and owned them, pushing her aside. *Maybe leadership isn't about control but empowering others to fulfill the cause themselves.* There was too big of a task ahead to take any of this personally.

She teamed up with Garrick, Hank, and a few other deputies. McAlister commanded his own unit.

Paul awoke just as Kora was setting out. "You're not leaving without me," he said.

"I thought you'd want to look after the kids."

"I've already put them to work helping set up tents. They'll be fine as long as they stay within the walls."

Kora didn't show it, but she was glad he was joining her. Having him at her side boosted her confidence. Their small squadron of five marched through the sectors they'd already secured. They told the pedestrians to stay indoors, promising to have a food pantry and medical supplies available soon.

"How long is *soon?*" one woman asked.

The cops didn't reply, not having a solid answer themselves.

Kora got an idea. Anyone who didn't want to stay inside could help clean up the streets. Cars needed to be pushed to the sides of the road, allowing a clear bike path for the cops. Little by little, San Antonio might start looking like itself again.

Moving into an unsecured sector, the police made headway toward Methodist Hospital. Hundreds of injured people crowded the front entrance. Armed civilians patrolled the outskirts, playing their part in protecting the hurting.

They parted at the sight of Kora and her crew. Moving through the tight gap between loads of people, they arrived at the front doors and pulled them open. The waiting area was so packed that half of the people were standing while others lay on the floor. Blood, bandages, and vomit stained the tile. No one had time to clean it. Nurses ran to and fro, calling anyone who needed emergency assistance. If you didn't have a broken bone or bleeding wound, you were sent away immediately.

The receptionist at the counter had bloodshot eyes and wrinkles across her forehead. It was obvious she hadn't gotten any sleep in the last twenty-four hours. "If you want to see the doctor, you need a ticket," she said flatly.

Garrick smiled. "We were actually hoping to help. Can we talk to whoever is in charge?"

"Show your badges and hurry up. I've already dealt with too many imposters."

Kora and Garrick showed their badges. Hank, Paul, and the other deputy they brought along didn't have anything.

"They stay back," the receptionist glared at the deputies. "The two of you—" she pointed at the door.

Paul gave Kora a thumbs up as she and Garrick entered the hallway. Nurses bustled about, shouting orders and pushing moaning patients on stretchers.

Without power and windows, candles in topless glass beakers lined the bottom edge of the wall. A nurse led the cops into the employee lounge and left them alone.

"This place… boy, I can't see how they can get anything done," Garrick lamented.

"Yeah, I don't think we're going to get any medical supplies here," Kora replied.

Garrick nodded. "We'll have to trade. The question is, what do we have that they need?"

The door opened, and in stepped Dr. Lambert, a fit man in his late fifties. Blood smeared the front of his scrubs. He put on his frameless glasses and said, "You got two minutes. Talk."

"I'm Officer Clark, and this is—"

"I don't care about your names," Lambert interrupted. "One minute, fifty seconds."

Anxious, Garrick gestured to Kora.

"We are establishing order across the city and need supplies," Kora said as quickly as possible. "Can you help us?"

"No," Lambert said bluntly. "If that's it, I gotta get going."

Garrick pleaded, "Doctor, we know you're doing your best, but if we plan to keep on doing our job, we need access to pain killers, first aid—"

"Rob a pharmacy," Lambert replied. He glanced at his watch. "One minute."

Kora stepped forward. "One of our cops for one of your nurses."

Lambert raised a brow. Even Garrick was shocked by the bargain.

Kora continued, "You need someone to keep you safe. We need someone to look after our injured. Is that fair?"

"One cop will do nothing against this mob," Lambert said cynically.

"That's why we're giving you your best: Officer Garrick," Kora replied.

Garrick opened his mouth to protest but stopped. Straightening his back, he nodded dutifully. "I'll be your point-person between the police and you. If you need quick evacuation or any supplies, talk to me and I'll work it out."

Lambert saw someone pass by the door window. He quickly opened it and yelled, "Dr. Lowry!"

His fast-moving colleague rushed inside. "Yes, Doctor?"

Lambert took off his lanyard and gave it to him. "The police need me. You're in charge when I'm absent. Officer—"

"Garrick."

"Officer Garrick will look after you. If you need to find me, talk to him."

Doctor Lowry nodded rapidly, absorbing the information.

Lambert asked, "Keep him close, you understand?"

"Yes, Doctor," Lee replied.

"Great. Now get moving."

"Yes, Doctor."

Lowry vanished into the hallway.

Kora said, "I wasn't expecting—"

"If I spend one more moment in this place, I'll eat a cyanide pill," the doctor replied. He turned to Garrick. "You best catch up with Lee. The bastard is quick."

Officer Garrick nodded dutifully and rushed out the door. He turned back to Kora a final time before disappearing down the hallway.

Lambert sighed deeply. "Finally. Freedom."

"Doctor, are you sure you don't just want to send a nurse or…"

Sniff. Lambert sniffed a bead of coke from a little vial. He glanced at her, his eyes wired but uncaring. "Are we going to do this or what?"

Kora closed her gaping jaw and gestured for him to lead the way. The doctor led her to the changing room, unashamedly stripped naked, and put on a T-shirt and running pants.

"Don't look so dreary," he said as he tied his tennis shoe on the bench. "I can handle my crap, not like the junkies that come through here."

"Right," Kora said doubtfully.

She questioned her decision to trade Garrick. *What's done is done.* The choice was made in the heat of the moment, and her partner didn't protest. They'd all have to live with the consequences now. As selfish as it sounded, she'd also have one less opinion to worry about, too.

Dr. Lambert finished tying his other shoe. "We'll take the back exit. Less fanfare. Some of the people aren't happy that I let their loved ones die on the table."

"I'll get my team and meet you out there," Kora replied.

"Suit yourself."

Picking up Paul, Hank, and the other deputy, Kora rejoined Lambert behind the hospital.

"Where's Garrick?" Hank asked.

"He decided to stay and help," Kora said, keeping her voice kind and chipper. "It's best for everyone."

"Yeah, but wasn't he one of our leaders?" Hank asked.

"Good leaders always take the hardest jobs. Teach by example, you know," Kora said, slightly insincere.

They returned to Alamo without issue.

Kora provided Lambert with a living tent inside of the church as well as an outdoor medical tent to look after patients.

When no one else was around, Kora pulled him aside. "Keep a lid on your vices."

"Are you going to arrest me?" Lambert asked smugly.

Kora said, "Not if I don't have to."

"Remember one thing, lady—you need me. I don't need you. If it weren't for the Hippocratic Oath, I would have ditched this city yesterday…. So, anything else you need from me?"

Kora shook her head.

"Then leave," Lambert said, waving his hand at her while he settled behind the desk one of the deputies got them.

She separated herself from the rest of the camp, hoping to collect her thoughts. *You gave up Garrick because you felt threatened,* her conscience told her. Truthfully, Kora wasn't sure why she had made the split-second decision. Was it truly to remove her competition? They were a team, though. *It was either the cop or doctor... the choice was obvious.* Making value calls on human life ate at her. Throwing herself at her mission was the only way to clear her head.

Gathering a few volunteers, she went to a local gun store. The owner had boarded the doors and window and positioned himself on the roof. High-powered rifle in hand and his pre-teen daughters at his side, the owner aimed at Kora and her band of law enforcers.

Kora put up her hands, walking down the ransacked streets. Every other building had been looted, stripped, or burned. Judging by the two corpses at the front of the gun shop, the owner wasn't taking any chances.

"Officer Kora Clark, can we talk?" Kora held out her badge.

On his belly, the owner pulled at the side of his gray handlebar mustache. "Here to arrest me? I'd have you know that I was defending my property."

"I can see that," Kora replied, lowering her arms. "Cute kids."

"Bella." The owner hiked his thumb at one and then the other. "Nancy. Say hi, girls."

Also prone, the two girls looked up from their scoped rifles and said "hi" at the same time.

The owner asked, "So, are you buying?"

"Recruiting, actually," Kora answered. "The streets are getting more dangerous, and my people need weapons to enforce the law."

The owner chuckled. "What law? Girls, you see any law?"

"No, Pa," one replied.

The owner said to Kora, "From the mouth of babes…"

Paul spoke up. "Look, man. We're trying, but this is a community effort."

The owner darted his eyes from Paul to Kora. "Is he a cop? He doesn't look like a cop."

"He's one of many concerned citizens playing their part," Kora replied diplomatically.

Paul nodded. "There are a lot of kids out there who need help. Many are your daughters' age. Without the police, the same bastards who turned this street upside down will be in their homes before the week is up. There's going to be a lot of evil stuff happening and no one to stop it—"

"Unless you help," Kora chimed in.

The girls looked at their father, waiting for his response. The owner sighed deeply. "How many guns do you need?"

Kora replied, "Any you can spare. If you're looking for a safe community, come to the Alamo site."

"I'd prefer to stay here," the owner grumbled. "Now, give me an exact number."

Kora huddled with her team and discussed it. When they finished, they ended up with a number roughly equal to half of the owner's stock.

Begrudgingly obliging, he honored their requests. Kora's team walked away with bags full of weapons— shotguns, pistols, rifles, etc. Ammo, too. The owner's girls waved at them as they vanished down the street.

Confident with the trade, Kora spent the rest of the day outfitting the deputies, finishing the razor-wire fencing around the gate, and creating a system of rotating guards to watch the remaining prisoners. Glen was one of the unlucky convicts who hadn't escaped the previous night. Like a caged animal, he kept his eyes peeled for any opportunity out.

"This whole thing is going to go tits up," he told Kora as she passed by.

"We'll see," she teased.

Grabbing the bars, he said, "My offer still stands."

Kora kept walking.

Glen cursed under his breath.

She joined Paul in the chapel. They wrote out various task lists for the following day. Each of the six remaining officers was assigned ten deputies and given a code name: Alpha, Beta, Charlie, etc. Kora's was Alpha. She had Paul, Hank, and eight other men. Each group had jobs ranging from gathering supplies, securing sectors, and building base camp. It was by no means perfect, but their government was well underway. Just like solving any conflict, the faster she could develop *modus operandi*, the quicker she'd move out of damage-control and into productivity.

Not all was well, however.

McAlister was pissed at Kora's decision to trade Garrick. He was also against the idea of arming the deputies so suddenly after Kora had warned about it yesterday and had concerns over the ever-expanding camp.

"We have tents everywhere," he complained. "It's like a maze."

"Then re-organize it," Paul said bluntly.

"Kora, I like your boyfriend, but he's not one of us," McAlister said, despite Paul sitting next to him at the table.

"The chief put me in charge," Kora asserted.

"Yeah, but—"

"You have full autonomy over your team, McAlister. Same as every other sworn officer. But I have the final say. Paul is on the team," Kora interrupted.

"Nepotism, great…" McAlister mumbled sarcastically.

There was a knock on the chapel door.

"Come in!" Kora yelled.

A deputy peeked his head inside. "Uh, we have police outside."

Kora and the others around the table traded looks before bursting from their chairs.

In full riot gear, Officers Terry Lee and Jennette Harold, as well as a dozen other officers, gathered outside of the east gate. Above them, the sun cast its dying crimson rays across the darkening sky.

Lee kept her gloved hands firmly on her shotgun. She eyed the razor wire across the walls and tent village beyond. "What the hell is all this mess, Clark?"

"San Antonio Police Department," Kora replied.

Her people gathered behind her, holding their mismatched armaments in standby positions.

Lee replied. "Don't think so."

"Impersonating a police officer is a crime," Jeanette added.

"Oh, give me a break," McAlister interrupted. "Y'all come all this way just to cause trouble?"

"To enforce the law," Lee said condescendingly.

Kora said, "You have your side of town; we have ours. Let's keep it at that."

"You have no right to wear that uniform," Lee said. "You left us, remember? Not the other way around."

"Hear that!" Jeanette yelled to Kora's people. "These aren't real officers! They're liars! Opportunists! No better than the looters on the streets!"

The corner of Kora's lip twitched. "I think it's best you left."

"Is that a threat?" Lee asked, looking for a fight.

Kora replied, "All I'm saying is that if you don't walk away, I can't guarantee your safety."

Kora's army of sixty silently stared down the fourteen armored cops.

Lee boiled.

Jeanette said to her partner. "Maybe we should… give them some space."

Struggling to stuff her rage, Lee said, "Disband this… this… whatever, all right? Or we're going to have a real problem."

"Right to form a militia," Hank said. "Cops or no, we follow the Constitution of this nation."

Lee appeared to be ready to shoot the old patriot. She opted to pull back her people instead. "This isn't over, Clark."

Kora had a list of foul things she wanted to say but held her tongue.

They waited by the gate until the cops had vanished before lowering their guard.

Kora turned back to the crowd and told the deputies. "We're the police. Not them. Not anymore. It's up to us to save this city. No one else will. No one else wants to. We have to look out for each other. The person to your left and right is your new best friend. Don't let them down… Everyone stays in for the night. We'll get a fire going and cook a good meal. We've all been working hard. Let's rest. We have a long road ahead."

8

THREAT LEVEL

*P*aul massaged Kora's shoulders. She leaned against him on the little cot, trying to forget about the tasks ahead of her. They needed better communication between sectors, weapons training, a functional jailing system, bartering rules... the list was endless.

"You're tense," Paul commented.

"Everyone is." Kora shut her eyes.

"The people won't be able to handle this type of pressure for long. Honestly, it's a miracle we're not seeing more fights."

"My father used to say, *'Nothing unites people like a crisis,'*" Kora quoted.

"In the short term, yeah. But... burnout is a real thing," Paul replied.

Anxiousness squeezed Kora's heart. "They're just going to have to deal with it."

"I'm on your side. I want to take as much ground as possible before it's too late. We need to pace ourselves, is all."

Kora pulled away from him. Hunched over, she rubbed her temples. "We just had a massive bonfire and burned through half of our food to keep everyone happy. What more should we do?"

"I don't know," Paul admitted.

"If you don't have a solution, why bring it up?"

Paul replied, "I... Look, it's a thought."

The conversation lulled.

"Sorry, I didn't mean to frustrate you," Paul apologized.

"Let's just get some rest, okay?."

"Okay," Paul mumbled and blew out the candle.

Worries robbed her of sleep. Were there enough guards patrolling? What if the prisoners escaped? What was Martinez's plan? Would officer Lee try to attack them?

In the morning before everyone else awoke, she went around the back of the chapel and vomited. Her head felt light, and her now-empty stomach curled in on itself. She wiped a few tears from her eyes and glanced at the heavens.

"Help. Please. Thanks." She couldn't bring herself to pray more than that.

Dragging her feet, she returned to her tent and threw on her uniform. She tucked in her slightly stained shirt, tied on her boots, and headed to the meeting table. This time she was the first person there. She put out note cards for each of the six teams with their mission assignments. Two would stay at home base, further fortifying the area and managing the incoming supplies. Two other teams would patrol the already secured sectors. The last two teams would gather supplies and try to secure another block or two. Kora put herself on sector patrol, believing it would be less stressful. *Like Paul said, pacing.*

McAlister arrived at the table. He reviewed the Beta team. "Keeping me at the base, huh?"

"I thought you'd want to reorganize tents and welcome our new doctor friend."

"Ah, the resident coke fiend?"

"You know about that?"

"The guy is not even trying to hide it. Man, we've got a real motley crew here."

"We'll have to make the best of it."

"I just hope it's enough."

A tired smile formed on Kora's glossy face. "I appreciate you, McAlister."

"Don't start getting all emotional on me."

"No, seriously. We're in this together."

McAlister grumbled. "Come hell or high water."

"Hoo-rah."

Their breakfast consisted of protein bars and luke-warm water. The teams collected their assignments and went about their duties.

Patrolling the secured sectors proved more challenging than expected. The pedestrians were sick of staying inside, but many didn't want to help clean the roads, either. Kora's hostile glare and scary arsenal kept them from doing anything stupid. Most people were just bored; however, that didn't make them any less dangerous. Torturers developed new ways of hurting people when they were bored. Dictators planned their dynasties when they were bored, too.

A few blocks away, Kora noticed a crowd of people and a familiar face.

"Katie?" Kora called out, blocking the mid-day sun with her hand.

"Officer Clark!" the waitress exclaimed and ran to her.

The sudden hug almost caused Hank to shoot the woman. "You know this vixen?"

Kora smiled. "I helped her out the other night."

Katie gestured to the crowd of people. "You said to bring friends, well. Here they are!"

The mishmash of hippies, stoners, strippers, and orphans was not what Kora was expecting. She got an idea. Keeping half of her team on patrol, she returned to the Alamo and had the new flock of survivors build a tent camp around the outer walls. They were also allowed to set up in the surrounding buildings. McAlister came outside of the base at the sound of many voices.

"Uh, Clark, what are you doing?"

"Increasing our defense," Kora said.

"But they are outside of the walls."

"Exactly."

"So if we're attacked…" her officer put two and two together. "Very Machiavellian."

Kora playfully bowed. "Also, strength in numbers and all that jazz."

She met up with Katie in an alley where the woman was placing her tent.

The waitress tucked her jingle hair behind her ear. "I was under the impression we'd be inside the walls…."

Kora replied, "It's too crowded. We need your people to start building a border out there. Use cars, debris, whatever you find."

"M-me?" the waitress stuttered.

"If you could convince all these people to come here, you can prompt them to do this," Kora smiled wide. She took both of the woman's hands in her own. "You got this, girl."

"Well, I'll try my best," Katie's voice cracked with uncertainty.

Kora noticed Terrell and the other kids hanging around outside of the wall. "They can help. T, get over here!"

As the kids jogged to Kora, Katie mustered her courage. "Where should we start?"

"Finish getting the tents set up and start building a wall of junk at the cross sections. We want to make it as difficult as possible for strangers to come inside. Leave one section of the road open. We'll assign guards to that area and funnel our supply traffic through there. It may slow us down but make it easier to track supply intake."

Katie looked at her blankly. "Yeah, I missed all that."

Kora's shoulder sank. "Just follow my lead."

It was a long afternoon but productive. They secured the area around the Alamo, helped the supply teams unload, and served soup for dinner. The good American people in her little bubble looked out for one another. There was a feeling of hope among their budding community. *A city within a city*, Kora thought happily. Would their lives have intersected if not for the disaster? Could what wrecked the old world be the catalyst to bind people together? *Were we not unified before?* Kora wondered.

There was a sense of societal peace in the modern world, but much was superficial. *"What do you do for a living? How much money do you make? How are you today? Please don't tell me too much; I'm not interested in having a conversation."* Superficial. Commensal. It was like they were to follow a script all their life. Every man followed the talking points for strangers with big titles. They repeated them to friends and family across social platforms until the talking points became everyday reality, and questioning it was heresy. That which was a lie or slogan, after much repetition, became a program, a way of behavior to follow, a ritual to be protected. But who were the sheep without guidance? Did Kora have any right to be a shepherd?

Self-governance must be the end game. We must learn to own our actions, uphold tested traditions, and look after our fellow man. If Kora could only teach the people... would her words be enough, though? *No, action; only action. Action changes the environment. Action makes theory a reality. We can be better than before. We just need to see this as the beginning, not the end.*

The thoughts sparked a fire in her belly. Her self-radicalization stirred her to save her nation. The *everyman*'s sole focus is to protect what he has—his comfortability, stability, etc.—but a leader sees the future they desire and steers their present until it becomes the norm.

"You good?" Paul asked, breaking her train of thought.

They sat around the table as the sun fell.

"The day went by fast," Kora replied and returned to her stew.

"Tell me about it," Paul replied, stretching his arms above his head. "Oh, the supply team is back."

The two teams on supply duty rolled in shopping carts full of canned goods, tools, and books. The books pertained to gardening, manual engineering, and other useful troves of information to help them survive in a powerless world. The teams also brought bad news: shopping markets were taken over by another faction.

"Martinez's men?" Kora inquired.

The cop ruining Delta team shook his head. "No, someone else. We couldn't get close. They had snipers."

Before daybreak, Kora and her team headed out to the nearest Walmart.

The unsecured sectors on day four were hellish. Every unviolated building was heavily boarded, but still, the vast majority were abandoned. Small gangs of scavengers scurried at the sight of strangers. They welded simple melee weapons and were unbathed and dirty. If Kora had to guess, a solid third of the city had evacuated on foot and more were trying to leave every hour.

Kora's team happened upon a group of police officers on the way to the superstore. The rogue cops were harassing a group of women, frisking them and threatening to arrest them if they tried to resist. Their lecherous gazes were fueled by the realization of their power fantasy.

Ready to shoot, Kora's group got the jump on them. Threats were exchanged. Kora had them surrender their weapons. When the rogues were on their knees, Kora ordered her deputies to strip off their badges. She left them cuffed on the side of the road. Their cries of mercy echoed through the streets, but Kora kept moving. A cocktail of rage and sorrow caused her to grit her teeth. *Those men are worse than gangster scum. Treacherous oath breakers.* She spat in disgust.

The Walmart parking lot was a legitimate graveyard. Kora and her people took cover behind vehicles. Crows and buzzards picked at the dozen-plus bodies on the pavement. Strips of tattered flesh dangled from their bloodied beaks.

Staying out of sight, Kora lifted her binoculars and surveyed the area. There was a common theme among the scattered corpses: a bullet to the head.

"Double-tapped," Kora whispered and handed Paul the binocular.

He put up his palm in protest. "I'd rather not look, thanks."

"Chicken," Kora teased, unsure how else to cope with the horror.

Half crouched, Hank moved behind the truck with them. "This looks like the work of Soviets."

Kora agreed. "I'm thinking military. Why else would they shoot them again in the head?"

The idea offended the old patriot. "Our people wouldn't do this. The people behind the EMP maybe."

"That's what I meant," Kora corrected.

"Here?" Paul asked, the color draining from his face. "But I didn't see any planes or vehicles."

"Sleeper cells," Hank theorized. "An attack like this takes years of planning. They probably crossed the Southern border a long time ago. ICE is practically useless these days. Just about anyone can come over. We might just be seeing the beginning of Phase 2."

"You mean a full-scale takeover," Paul replied.

"Think about it. You've just crippled the most influential nation on the planet. What would you do?" Hank asked rhetorically.

Kora scrunched her mouth to the side as she continued scoping out the superstore. There was only darkness beyond the broken electric doors. "We should leave." She gestured to the rest of them.

No one protested.

They returned to headquarters and informed the other leaders of their discovery. After much deliberation, it was agreed that they would slow down their expansion plan and ensure every sector was secured. Kora was unsure of the verdict but agreed it was better to stay safe. Her original idea of taking over the city had been quickly kicked to the curb. Now it was a slow and steady climb to the top. There were benefits, though.

Firstly, the people would be less stressed. Moving into new sectors always placed the teams on edge. Even though they'd avoided shootouts and major gangsters, the fear of the unknown plagued every cop.

Secondly, they'd have to time properly train their deputies. Thanks to action movies and video games, most of the younger generation had a decent idea of how to hold and aim a gun. They needed to get used to the weapon's weight, reloading, and cleaning their firearm. Kora wished the gun shop owner and his daughters would've joined them. He would've done a lot better job at teaching the newbies.

Thirdly, they could set up a food delivery system. By this point, most of the food in people's fridges had soiled. Kora estimated the average American likely had a week's worth of canned goods. It would be necessary to start feeding the people. That would also establish their police force as a philanthropic organization. With trust levels at an all-time low, maintaining a good reputation would be paramount to keeping the peace. Her people needed to believe that they were the good guys and act accordingly.

Lastly, Kora had time to plug any leaks in the leadership. Since she had let Garrick go, it was much easier to control the others. Kora's goal wasn't to lord over her peers, but once you get the taste of power, it's hard to stay humble. Authority and power were a drug that had tempted Kora since she joined the force. *Guard your heart*, she told herself.

Thinking long term, she put the cops who seemed the most rebellious on scouting duty. If they were focused on the outside threats, they would have no time to sow descent among the people. Kora never liked the idea of keeping her enemy's close. She couldn't babysit all day and had discovered in her brief years of that life that people seem to forget about problems if they aren't right in front of their faces.

McAlister and others sold out to the cause were kept close to the camp, encouraging the people and reminding them that their hard work was not in vain.

She gave Terrell and other kids paint and had them write on the sidewalks and walls. Naming the different parts of their camp and having arrows to point toward key areas would allow for easier supply movement.

They were also encouraged to paint warnings. *Anyone caught stealing would be excommunicated. If a dispute is minor, solve it amongst yourselves, or both parties will be removed. If you draw a weapon on someone, you will be locked up indefinitely.* They needed real consequences to keep people from anarchy.

Toward the evening, another mass of survivors approached their community. Bandages wrapped around their heads and parts of their body. A few had their arms in slings. One was being pushed in a wheelchair. Kora stopped them at the edge of their farthest sector. Wearing a wrinkled scrub, a nurse stepped in front of the mass of people. Kora estimated at least one hundred.

"Office Clark, right?" the nurse asked.

"You know me," Kora replied, keeping her weapon at her waist.

"Dr. Lowry told me to find you," the nurse replied. By her tone, something was seriously wrong.

"What happened?"

The nurse nervously chewed the inside of her cheek. "Some soldiers—at least I thought they were soldiers—arrived at the hospital and just started... just started... shooting. We tried to seal the doors, but the waiting room was too crowded. When they got inside —it was a massacre."

The sleeper cells, Kora assumed. Martinez was dangerous, but Kora couldn't even wrap her head around this type of evil.

The nurse continued, "Dr. Lowry, he stayed back to hold them off, but…"

"What about Officer Garrick?"

The nurse seemed confused.

"The cop we exchanged for Lambert. Surely you saw him around."

"Oh, him."

Kora did not like the sound of that. She waited on the woman to say something but her sorrowful expression said it all.

"He got the children out when the attack first started," the nurse said. "But when he heard the gunfire, he ran back inside. I warned him not to, but he wouldn't listen. He said he had to fulfill his duty…. The rest of us ran. I don't think he made it."

It was like a chunk of Kora's heart had been yanked out. One of her best friends was dead in the place of a cocaine-snorting doctor. *And it's all my fault.* Kora wanted to bury the guilt. She wanted to believe her actions did not affect his fate, but that would be a lie. Now more than ever, everyone's choices created a domino effect: who would eat, who would starve, who would live, and who would die. The belief that one's action or inaction didn't affect the world around us was a myth. The main difference was that now it was in everyone's face. *And bringing the sick and injured into the middle of camp could cause an even more harmful chain reaction.*

Kora gestured to the buildings around the sector.

"Set up anywhere that's abandoned. The innermost part of headquarters is already overcapacity, but you'll be able to travel to and for."

"But we won't be safe out here!" the nurse exclaimed. "I have injured people who need attention."

Kora felt sickened by her own actions. "I know, but this is what we have right now. I'll get a few armed deputies to stay on patrol and—"

"No," the nurse replied. "We aren't going to come here and be treated like second-class citizens."

"No one is forcing you to do anything. You can go anywhere, but I can't risk putting more people in danger."

"So, we're a liability to you?" the nurse replied.

"Yes," Kora replied stoically. "You're injured, and you can't work. Moreover, you might've alerted the sleeper cells to this location. If you want to be under our protection, you have to follow our rules."

"Then I guess we'll go elsewhere."

"...Okay," Kora washed her hands of the situation.

Paul stood silently by as the nurse and the other people left.

"If you have something to say, say it," Kora kept her eyes ahead.

"Are you sure we couldn't have helped them?"

"Maybe," Kora admitted. "But we'd have to throw hard-working people out of their tents, give away the food we gathered, and focus the bulk of our attention on tending their wounds."

"I see your point..." Paul said half-heartedly.

"We'll just have to hope someone else can help them." Ending the discussion, Kora returned to work.

As choices became harder, she felt less like a cop and more like a dictator. *Whatever it takes to get us through this,* Kora told herself.

She grabbed a rifle from their ever-growing stash and made it her focus to train the people for war.

The following days were hellish. Scouting parties yielded less food, water, and bullets. The gangs throughout the city had consolidated. There were only a dozen or so power players, but they owned large swaths of territories. Unlike Kora, though, they didn't care about stopping crime. Pleasure, riches, and food were their main prerogative. Rumors of children being taken or shot circulated, but the sources were not reliable. Moreover, the sleepers had been silent. Some theorized that they had moved to another city. Kora feared they were planning something big.

Expansion plans were halted by the rising threat levels. They managed to take a few more blocks, but her people were too scared to advance forward. Unbathed and underfed, they reeked and acted skittish around anything new. Kora's goals were curbed; the lack of her people's ambition and peacemaking within her community became the main concern. In-fighting, bitterness, petty disputes plighted their little headquarters. It seemed that without motivation to fight their real enemies, the people channeled their hate on each other.

Near the center of the city, Kora had hoped the Alamo would be a great central location to maintain order. Instead, it was becoming a cage.

9

A MAN OF PRINCIPLES

*H*iding the candle light behind the cup of her hand, Kora moved through a maze of tents. Her quiet steps wouldn't wake anyone, and she knew there were a few more minutes before the night guard patrolled this side courtyard.

She arrived outside of the jail cell. The ten remaining prisoners were under blankets or in sleeping bags. Flies buzzed around their heads. In the darkness, Kora couldn't tell who was who.

"Glen?" she whispered. "Glen, wake up."

"I'm already up," a deep voice said nearby.

She glanced at the shadowy figure seated against the cell wall. The bearded man looked rugged in his dirtied orange jumpsuit.

"Ready to ditch this joint?" he asked, a weak smile growing on his wrinkled face.

"Just after advice. You're a prepper, right?"

Glen smirked.

"Something funny," Kora asked.

Glen glanced around the crowded camp. "You're little social experiment not turning out the way you hoped?"

"Something like that. I found that being flanked on all sides doesn't bode well for expansion."

"You ever played the game of Risk?"

"Once when I was a kid. I saw some others playing it recently."

"It's a game of world domination. However, every time you want to take land from someone, you roll the dice. Sometimes you get lucky. Other times... not so much."

"I don't believe in luck. Hard work and devotion get things done," Kora replied harshly.

Glen replied, "Good for you, but back to my analogy. When you're playing Risk, and your enemy has the upper hand, surrounding you from all sides, you have a hard choice to make. The first option is to continue defending your borders. Hopefully, you'll get lucky enough on your rolls to weaken his assault so you can advance."

"And the second option?"

"You launch a counter-offensive. You usher all your troops through the border of least resistance."

Kora visualized the city map in her mind. "But that leaves you unguarded."

"Yes, the enemy will sweep hard, but you will take

their land and force them to defend instead of attack."

"And if the counter-offense fails?"

"You're trapped in your own lands again, only this time you have fewer troops to defend against the next assault," Glen explained.

Kora chewed the inside of her cheek. She processed the information. She could lose the Alamo. However, if she kept her enemies on the run, they could take a lot of sectors in one fell swoop.

"Is there a third option?" Kora asked.

"You're the leader; you tell me."

"Hmmm," Kora thought aloud, unsure. "If I leave this place unguarded, who is going to watch after you?"

Glen shrugged. "You could always let me go."

"Not happening."

"I could be innocent for all you know. Besides, my only ambition is to get the hell out of this city," Glen replied.

"What about your friends?" Kora glanced at the rest of the sleeping prisoners.

"They are not my friends," Glen replied.

"I started this encampment to restore law and order. You guys are living examples that I'm serious," Kora admitted.

"It's all about appearance, huh?"

"How is this for appearance? You're in a cage and I'm not."

Glen glared at her.

Kora smiled at him. "Thanks for the advice. I'll take it under consideration."

"Before you go, tell me something."

"Hmm?"

Glen moved closer to the cell's bars, revealing the dark circles under his eyes and dirt smudging his forehead. "Are the rumors about the sleeper cells true?"

"I'm not at liberty to say."

"Very political of you, but seriously, are we going to get wrecked or what?"

The question terrified Kora. She didn't have an answer. She went with what she knew. "We have strength in numbers."

"But if you've not seen them, how do you know they don't have more people, more soldiers, better weapons. Counter-offense or not, if you face off against them, you die. And if you fall, this whole place goes under."

"That's why I'm building systems of government and productivity. Things will continue moving if something happens to me," Kora replied.

Glen was skeptical. "You say that, but how old is this system? Has it been tested? How long do you think it takes to train someone in it?"

"I created it in days," Kora bragged.

"Yeah, because you're not everyone, Kora. Most people don't want to lead. They hate risk-taking. They want Mommy and Daddy to make decisions for them so they don't have to bear the responsibility of failure.

When one parent goes away, they want to plug their umbilical cord into another. And I can guarantee they won't be as kind or caring as you. You're the diamond in the rough. That one person in a million who has integrity and genuinely loves. They won't find that in the world."

"I appreciate the compliment, but you underestimate people. They'll rise up. They'll have to or die."

"Have you studied people? We self-destruct all the time. Most people choose death every day. Porn, cigarettes, drinking, bad habits, laziness, I could go on, but you get the point. Without you, these little children are going to scatter."

Kora squeezed her fists closed, perturbed by this discussion. "Then I'll train them to be leaders, self-sufficient; we're already doing it."

"True, but how long will that take when they've been conditioned their whole life to follow the person with the brightest idea or fanciest title?"

Kora frowned.

Glen eyed her. "You know it's true."

"Goodnight, Glen." Kora turned to walk away.

Glen chuckled. "Okay, see ya later, Captain. Good luck. Oh, and don't forget. This vision to save San Antonio isn't theirs; it's yours, and it will end with you."

Quickening her pace, Kora returned to the chapel and snuffed out her candle. Her conversation continued in her mind as she thought of new rebuttals to his statements. Nevertheless, if the masses didn't learn to govern themselves, they would be slaughtered. *I'll have to teach them, but am I ready? I'm making up everything as I go. What if it's all wrong? What if I'm just getting lucky and all this comes crashing down."*

She stepped over Paul sleeping on the floor and climbed onto her cot. The mattress felt extra hard tonight. She could tell from the onset of the evening she would get no sleep.

In the morning, one of the deputized scouts reported a shoot-out in a nearby sector. Things had gotten messy. The shooters had used high-powered weaponry and left no survivors.

At the planning table, McAlister asked as he lit a cigarette, "Could it be the sleepers?"

"We only heard the shots and saw the aftermath, sir," the scout replied. He had a wired look, and his skin was losing color. "It looks like they shot every person twice to confirm the kill."

Kora told him, "Get some rest today. That's an order."

The scout nodded and left.

McAlister blew smoke out of the side of his lip. "Well, that's not good."

One of the cops replied, "These are the same guys who took out Officer Garrick, too."

The table turned to Kora, awaiting her command.

Kora took a breath. "It's too risky to attack them without knowing their numbers."

Paul said, "And remember, Kora, our deputies are regular people. Volunteers. They aren't going to rush into battle against an army of trained soldiers."

McAlister raised a brow. "*Our* deputies? Oh, ho, ho, boy. You're cocky. Last time I checked, you have no right to deputize anyone."

"I'm just trying to help, man. What's your deal?" Paul replied.

"You're not a cop. You shouldn't be in here."

"Cut it out," Kora growled. "We need to focus. It could be a matter of days before we're hit."

"Hours," McAlister mumbled cynically.

Kora gave him a look before addressing the table. "If we can't attack, do we think we can defend?"

"We have weapons, but we can't waste too much more ammo training," the cop in charge of the Delta team replied. "I don't think the people are ready."

A few others agreed.

Kora summarized. "So we can't attack and we can't defend…."

Paul suggested, "We could always leave the city."

"If we run, we lose," Kora replied.

"And if we stay, we die," McAlister added. "I'd rather be a living loser than a dead winner."

Kora spoke through a false smile. "That's very noble of you."

McAlister addressed the table. "We have to be honest with ourselves. We've fought the good fight, but now we're stuck. There is no shame in that."

Zeal rose up in Kora. "If we can't defend one city, our nation is screwed. Do you want that? I don't."

McAlister said, "The moment the EMP bomb dropped, we lost, Kora. Garrick is gone. Chief is gone. When the sleepers show up at our doorstep, how many more are going to die all because we couldn't let of our pride?"

"It's not pride; it's principles," Kora argued. "Mankind doesn't need to be selfish animals. We can fight for those who can't fight for themselves, but we have to want to. If you don't have the conviction to die for this cause, then leave now because things are about really frickin' scary."

The cop in charge of Delta stood from his chair. "I'm sorry, but I have kids and an ex-wife in Dallas. I'm not dying in this city."

"Thanks for your service, Officer," Kora replied, stuffing her spite as far down as she could and remembering the man's hard work over the last few days. "We'll tell your team. Leave quietly. We don't want to damage morale."

"Understandable," the cop replied and headed to his tent.

"Anyone else?" Kora asked.

The rest of the table stayed, though seemingly unwillingly.

Kora said, "We can't do this alone, that's for certain."

"So we wait on the national guard?" Paul asked.

"There is still no word from them," McAlister

remarked.

Kora said, "I believe there is an air force base not far from the city, right?"

The others nodded.

"We'll ask for help. Perhaps if they see what we are doing, they'll want to join us or invite us to join them," Kora replied.

McAlister said, "It's too risky to go as a group."

"Then just take your team," Kora suggested.

McAlister signed deeply. "Fine. I don't know how long it will take me to get there and back."

"Can you do it in forty-eight hours?" Kora replied.

McAlister looked over the map. "That should be enough time. You guys just going to wait here?"

The table waited for Kora's response.

Kora replied, "I'll take my squad into the city to see if I can recruit any more help. Everyone else will fortify and train the people. We won't take any more sectors until we have support. Will that work for you guys?"

The table agreed.

"Great," Kora said, exhausted. "Everyone is dismissed."

The leaders left their chairs and started on their duties. Kora remained at the table until all were gone. She sank into her seat and rubbed her temples. Paul stood by her side.

"Your dad would be very proud of you," he said kindly.

"You think so? What if I get all these people killed?"

"Everyone here, barring the prisoners, are here by choice, Kora. Just like us, they have nowhere else to go," Paul reminded her.

"I may have a solution, but I don't like it," Kora said, staring at the map.

"Uh, what do you mean?"

"We can't fight the sleepers. Our people are too soft. Heck, I might be too soft, but…" Kora hated what she was about to say. "There is one man. Ambitious. Dangerous. And has access to a lot of good weapons."

"Wait, you're not talking about—"

"Jose Martinez," Kora said, almost sickened.

"That's a deal with the devil," Paul remarked.

"I know, but with his forces and our forces combined, we might just stand a chance."

"What do you think he'll want in return?"

Kora shrugged. "Supplies, immunity, I'm not sure. He might just shoot us the moment we approach him."

"I said I'd follow your lead, and I meant it. If you think this is the best way, you have my support, but we both saw what he did to the rival gangs. This guy is a killer."

"That's why we need him," Kora replied. It felt like her ideals of justice grew more hypocritical with every tribulation. *We just need to survive. Then we can rebuild.*

Kora dressed in her riot gear and loaded her shotgun. She kept her chief's pistol at her side and his badge clipped to her belt. When the other officers heard her plan, they protested. Kora told them she was just exploring her options. When they realized they could not sway her, they told her not to bring any gang-bangers back. Making no promises, Kora went to meet with Jose.

Hank, Paul, and the rest of the eight deputies joined her. They moved out of their secured sectors and into the lawless city.

Debris and trash littered the streets. Mostly every building and home that wasn't boarded up had been smashed in and gutted. Gaggles of people roamed around, looking for food and water. Kora's crew stayed out of sight. Every man was in a dangerous predicament: risk escaping the city or join up with a horde of desperate people scavenging food to survive. Those who were undecided would starve in their homes. The water supply was off, and any hope of help coming quickly had faded. Your best friend and neighbor three days ago could be the same guy who robbed you of your last can of Chef Boyardee today. *If we don't start taking ground soon, we're doomed.* The anxious thought caused Kora to speed up her search for Jose.

Gangs monopolizing various parts of the city had set scouts on roofs, in alleys, and behind the windows of tall buildings. They were opportunists, waiting for weak prey to rob or worse. Not wanting to cause any trouble, Kora stayed hidden from them, too.

The team traveled to the location of the arms deal where Officer Kinsley had died and Kora was reborn. As they entered the neighborhood, they were met by a small squad of gangbangers. Judging by their colors and designer clothes, they were Martinez's men, and their weapon sparked fear.

"I want to talk to Martinez," Kora demanded.

Her crew stood behind her, ready to act.

The gangsters exchanged looks and chuckled. They exchanged a few words in Spanish. By their gestures, it was something perverted.

Kora cocked her shotgun. The mockers shut up.

"Bring me to Jose. I want to make a deal with him."

"How about this for a deal: you let us have a little fun with you, and then when we're done, we'll make sure the big man knows you stopped by." The gangster started laughing again.

Paul spoke up. "You talk to her like that again, and I'll shoot you in the face."

Kora gawked at her boyfriend. He winked at her. The gangsters eyed Kora's deputies, all of whom had been hardened by the events of the last few days.

"Who are you anyway?" one of the gangbangers asked.

"Someone with a lot of guns, people, and food. Get your boss before I bring the entirety of San Antonio's Police Force over here."

The gangsters sized her up.

"Wait here," one said.

Both factions stood silently while they waited. The sound of gunshots so frequent days ago was gone. Only a few pillars of smoke polluted the sky.

After a tense five minutes, the gangster returned and gestured to them to follow. *Last chance to turn back...* She moved forward, keeping her mind focused on her objective.

The neighborhood was not how she expected it. The elderly sat on their porches. Kids played in the streets. Adults played cards on tables moved to their front lawn. No one was hungry. No one was scared walking the streets and standing on the roofs that Martinez's men patrolled.

There was seemingly more peace in this neighborhood than all of Kora's sectors combined. She felt... jealous. Envious. Bitter. *How could Jose do a better job of retaining normalcy than us?* It didn't take long to realize there were Latinos only. *He was not helping everyone. Just his own people.*

Kora passed by the bar near where Kensley died. It had collapsed in on itself from the fire but no longer smoked. The corpses had been cleared from the alley, but the crashed cars and shell casings remained. Kora's pulse quickened as she relived the shoot-out. Memories of gunfire rumbled in her mind. *If not for the EMP, I'd be dead.* The final look on Kinsley's face reminded her to keep pressing forward. *Make this life count.*

The gangster took them to a fenced McMansion at the back of the neighborhood. A half a dozen gangsters kept watch. Two at the gate. Two more on recently constructed watchtowers. The last couple patrolled the outer wall. Their weapons were military-grade, fully automatic, and could easily mow down Kora's little posse. From a negotiation standpoint, she wasn't sure what she could offer the man that he couldn't take himself. *Ambition. Jose Martinez is a man who wants everything. I'll have to give him part of the city.*

The gates opened, and Kora and her team were ushered inside. The guards didn't bother fleecing their weapons as they knew they held the advantage already. Instead of going directly inside the mansion, they were led to the back. Another half-dozen armed gangster hung around the pool. Their scantily clad women snuggled up against them. Tako snorted a line of cocaine and let one of the women at his side do the same. On the second balcony overlooking the pool stood Abigail Martinez, Jose's sixteen-year-old daughter. She sipped champagne and had a sniper rifle propped up next to her.

The kingpin himself, Jose, swam laps. He finished his current circuit before turning his attention to the cops. "How do you like the place?" he asked.

Kora glanced around the well-manicured lawn, trimmed hedges, and well-outfitted guards. "It's all right."

Jose frowned. "You lack an eye for detail. What you are looking at is a sliver of heaven in the deepest depths of hell. An oasis for my people where children can still play outside and our elderly are tended to."

"Fine, it's impressive," Kora forced herself to admit.

Jose's icy-gray eyes fell on her, and it was like he

could see she was just a scared little girl in an oversized uniform. Kora waited for him to pick her part, demean her, tell her she was a worthless failure and be right about it all.

Instead, he rested his hairy forearms on the lip of the pool and said, "I was raised on this street, if you didn't already know. One of seven children. Immigrants. My father was an illegal. He married my mother for a green card and, after a few years of a bad marriage, strangled her to death before taking his own life in front of all of us."

"Sorry to hear that," Kora replied.

Jose tapped the side of his head. "That type of trauma can mess up a kid. My brothers, sisters, and I were left alone. They became crack whores, gang-bangers, tricks, conmen, whatever could earn them a few dollars to pay for their next fix. But not me. I refused to let my father's weakness define me. I worked hard, educated myself, learned about business, found mentors, and I made every necessary step to climb myself out of this gutter and become a king."

Paul remarked, "None of that matters now, I imagine."

Jose glared. "Every lesson I've learned, every mistake, every trial, *all of it* matters now. It shaped me into what I am, tempered me like a blade, and while the rest of the world burns, I sit among the gods. My people are happy, armed, fed. Their families are better off than they were before. I did that. All it cost me was a few nightclubs and auto shops. How about your people? What do they have?"

"Law and order," Kora replied. "We're rebuilding, Jose—"

Tako interrupted. "Address him properly."

Kora continued, "Sorry. Mr. Martinez, we are rebuilding the San Antonio Police Department."

A few of the guards chuckled. Jose silenced them with a look and gestured for Kora to continue.

"We want to preserve the old world and help get people back to their lives."

"Why?"

"To uphold the law. As chief of police, I've taken on that duty."

"What does the *old world* offer them? Dead-end jobs? False securities? Lying politicians? Petty squabbles? Stupid laws." Jose tapped the tile in front of him. "This new world —as you call it—offers them a chance to live free. Titles, rules, class, none of that matters. Only the law of the jungle—*for the strength of the pack is the wolf, and strength of the wolf is the pack.*"

Kora said, "Well, that's why I've come—there is a threat bigger than both of us. A foreign army is on our soil. A band of them in this city, clearing out block by block as we speak. As heavily armed as your people may be, these are trained killers who have been prepping their whole lives for this moment. If we don't team up, they will destroy us both."

"The Chinese, you mean?"

"You've seen them?" Kora asked.

Jose climbed out of the pool, and one of the women gave him a towel. "They were the ones who sold me the weapons."

Kora's heart sank. "What?"

"The hell?" Hank mumbled.

Jose dried his silvery hair. "They paid off your police chief, too. That's why the coward was quick to give up. It is also why he'd assigned someone as ill-fit as you to lead. The system was intended to fail."

"How do you know this?"

"I have people everywhere," Jose said threateningly.

Kora's hand tightened the choke of her shotgun. "So you're working with the sleepers?"

"Call it a momentary truce." Jose handed the towel back to the woman. "I'm sure they'll likely give me a nice reward if I squash what little remains of Alamo City's brave protectors."

Paul and Hank boxed their shoulders. The other deputies stayed quiet and hovered their fingers over their trigger.

"But," Jose continued, "I have a feeling that you might have a better deal for me."

"I do," Kora lied. "If we work together, you get full immunity for any crimes you commit against rival gangs, and we won't tell anyone about how you betrayed our nation."

"That's it? That's all?" Jose asked, insulted. He lifted his fully automatic shotgun from the table. "They gave me this and dozens of others. I could march into your police station and have it cleaned out in minutes, and you offer me immunity in a justice system that doesn't exist anymore?"

Beads of sweat formed on Kora's forehead. "Okay, how about half of San Antonio? We split together. 50/50. After the Chinese are gone, we'll mind each other's business."

"I can take half the city by myself. I don't need your help to do it. What else do you have, because right now, I'm not impressed."

Kora thought hard. She regretted coming here but had a feeling that walking away empty-handed wasn't an option. *One problem at a time. Until the sleepers are gone, nothing can get done. Whatever it takes.* She steeled her resolve.

"Joint-leadership," Kora offered. "We rule the city together. I help you stop your rivals. You help me stop mine. Our supplies are your supplies and vice-versa. If we have a conflict of interest, neither one of us proceeds until we've come to an agreement. The added pressure of our current situation will force us to work things out in a timely manner, I can guarantee that."

Tako looked to his master.

After a moment of thought, Jose asked, "Do you really think you can hold this city?"

"Without a doubt, and as long as you can give this city the same treatment as your neighborhood, we won't have many problems."

129

"And when the rest of the Chinese forces land? What makes you think we'll survive that?"

"By that point, the army will have organized enough to strike back."

Jose doubted, "Have you seen our army? The American empire isn't what it was a decade ago."

"Screw the army then; we'll defend ourselves," Kora replied. "We can outfit our people and begin a revolution that can change the nation... and you'll be the hero: businessman Jose Martinez from orphan boy to leader of the free world."

"You have big dreams." Jose laughed.

"What's so funny?" Kora asked. "We live in a moment in history where anything can change now. The playing field is level; it's not about who has the best education, money, or connections; it's about who is the strongest, as you said. You understood that before the collapse. Now is the time to maximize your efforts. Work with me, and we can not only lead but help a lot of people who need heroes."

"*Heroes. Change.*" Jose shook his head. "Naïve little girl."

Kora smiled. "I'll take that as a compliment. Is the world that I propose not better than the one we see? This is a come-to-Jesus moment, Jose. Everything in the past is gone. Let's go forward. Together."

She extended her hand.

TREACHERY

*T*ako and four of Martinez's thugs at her side, Kora, and half of her crew left Jose's domain. Hank and a few deputies stayed back to assist Jose's efforts and keep an eye on him. They weren't happy but knew speaking against Kora's decisions in front of their newest ally would make them appear weak. *"Strength, and the appearance of it, matters now more than ever,"* Kora told them privately before leaving.

"In forty-eight hours, we strike the sleepers. I'm here to make sure your people are ready," Tako explained.

"I'm happy Jose sent his best," Kora replied to the enforcer.

"From now on, you will refer to him as Mr. Martinez."

"But we're equals," Kora reminded him.

"Yeah, that's why he'll be calling you Chief Clark," Tako replied.

Kora liked that, despite it not feeling earned. *I've just made a deal with the most dangerous person in San Antonio. His man, Gabriel, killed Kinsley. Over the last few days, his body count must be in the double digits....* Kora felt sickened. She didn't let it show.

Tako slowed his pace to walk by his men. He spoke in Spanish under his breath. Neither side trusted the other. *Once we stop the sleepers, that will change. A shared battle will boost comradery. Or we'll go with Plan B...*

Paul moved up next to Kora.

"You don't approve?" she whispered.

"You didn't walk away with any assurances…" Paul looked over his shoulders at the gangsters before turning back to Kora.

"His men for our men," Kora replied.

"And what's to stop them from cutting Hank's throat as we speak?"

"He's probably thinking the same thoughts about us, but how would that benefit him? The size of his forces just doubled. We have access to each other's supplies if one or the other runs low. We're going to help him stop rival gangs. It's a good deal. And remember, he's also waging war on all fronts, just like us."

"Good deal or no, we have no leverage. Tako can easily put a bullet in our heads while we sleep. What if they betray us?"

Kora gritted her teeth.

Paul replied, "We need to be smart. Very smart. We're in a viper's nest, Kora."

"I know," Kora admitted. "Once the sleepers are gone, we'll have more options.

"Meaning?"

Kora gave him a look.

Paul rubbed the back of his neck. "Wow. That's… that's dangerous."

"What else is new?" Kora replied as they walked.

"One problem at a time, I guess."

She couldn't allow herself to get lost in too many "what-if" questions. She needed to focus on the immediate threats. Having Jose on her side, as morally gray as that might seem, was safer than having him as an enemy. Betraying him would cause a war she wasn't ready to fight. Nevertheless, Kora would have to pull the trigger if he got out of control. *What are you becoming?* she asked herself. *Your goal is to restore justice, not twist it.*

A few hundred yards out, Kora spotted a stirring in her sector. Deputies were moving through the streets and posting up on rooftops. Their weapons were in hand, and an atmosphere of panic caused Kora's heart rate to quicken. The mass of people gathered around what seemed to be a body.

Wasting no time, Kora unslung her shotgun and ran into the fray. She elbowed through the crowd and peered down at the teenager. "T?" she mumbled.

Two bullet holes spilled red across Terrell's shirt.

His lips were turning purple, and his eyes were half-open. The murder must've happened when Kora was negotiating. *Fourteen years old...*

"Who did this?" Kora asked.

"Those female cops," one of her people replied. "They marched in here and demanded that we surrender our weapons and supplies for the city of San Antonio."

Kora boiled. "Officers Lee and Harold."

Another witness nodded. "They said we were breaking the law and were considered terrorists by all accounts."

"There were a lot of them," the lady added. "The boy told them to back off. Things got out of hand. He pulled a fake gun to scare them, but they shot him. They retreated after."

Eyes red, Kora asked, "And you just let it happen?"

"They were cops; what were we supposed to do—"

"We are the cops. *Us!*" Kora interrupted, rage burning hot.

Paul and the rest of the team caught up to Kora. Awestruck, Paul froze at the gruesome sight. He slowly knelt next to the body and bit his fist to keep himself from crying.

Tako stared with cold indifference. "Does this happen often?"

Kora wanted to crack his nose. "No. And I'm going to make sure it doesn't happen again."

She directed the locals to move the body. Paul

helped them, not taking his eyes off the boy. There was a desire to comfort her lover, but Kora couldn't let Tako see her as a passive leader. She stuffed her emotions and pressed on. Tako and her team followed.

The rest of the leadership team rallied inside the chapel. Tako was allowed to join them while his gangster hung out in the courtyard. Their eyes fell on a few attractive women tending to the tents.

McAlister glared at Tako from across the table. "I busted you once."

"Twice," Tako said smugly.

"Guys, please, not now," Kora said. "We have to figure out our next moves and quickly."

McAlister offered Tako a cigarette. "Well, anyway, welcome to the party."

Tako put his hand up. "I don't smoke."

"A kid is dead," Kora spat, disgusted by their indifference.

The men gave her their attention.

"Ideas. Let's hear them," Kora said.

Leaning back in his chair, Tako spoke, "You won't have peace as long as there are two police forces, and they just proved your defenses suck.'

"They are traitors," Kora told him.

"Makes no difference. If I were them, I'd come back in the evening and strike again. Your people are distraught. Whatever training you've given them will matter little when emotions are high. That sort of chaos is easy to exploit. If attacked again, I'd guess half of your people run. The rest would fight but only if directly threatened. They'd carve into your little base like a pumpkin and walk away with the spoils. Such a defeat would destroy whatever trust these people have in you, and your little operation is over."

The council silently absorbed his words.

Kora asked the gangster, "You're suggesting a counteroffensive?"

Tako spoke nonchalantly, "The boss told me to follow your lead, but if I were in charge, I'd be outfitting my boys right now and marching to their front door, no warning." He made a gun with his fingers. "*Pow, pow, pow.* And everyone knows that you're the big dog."

"Not happening," McAlister said.

"Then lose," Tako replied.

The rest of the leaders grumbled, suggesting upping defenses, sending a warning message to the police, and more passive solutions.

Kora's mind drifted to Paul, and the grief cut into his soul. *I'm sorry I brought Terrell here, babe, but he was the idiot who pulled a gun.*

"Tako," Kora halted the discussion.

The gangster waited for her to say more.

"If we move against the sleepers as planned *and* strike Officer Lee, that's two direct attacks back to back. I don't think our people can handle that." It sounded like weakness, but it was true.

Tako's expression turned serious. "Then we have no use for you."

"Good," McAlister said under his breath.

Kora said to the gangster, "I believe that decision is your boss's to make, not yours."

"I know Martinez better than all of you. In forty-eight hours, he expects to see an army that can fight a death squad, but if you can't take care of a few rogue cops, we might just rob you ourselves and call it a day."

"Can I arrest him?" McAlister asked Kora.

"No," Kora said sternly. "Excuse us, Tako. I should've never gotten you involved in this cop business. You and your friends get settled in, and we'll meet tomorrow to discuss battle plans."

Without a word, Tako left the chapel.

Kora apologized to the rest of the leaders. "I should've never brought him in here so soon. I wasn't thinking. Sorry."

McAlister sighed. "I know the deal with Martinez was necessary, but man, Kora, that guy is going to get us killed."

"Like it or not, we need them," Kora replied. "And as much as I hate to admit it, he's right about Officers Lee and Harold. If they attack us before we can attack the sleepers, everything we've built could go bottoms-up. A threat won't do anything, either. We need absolute results…. Let's get our best people and march on the police station."

"Wait. What?" McAlister exclaimed.

"We will either arrest them or use force. If they choose to resist, whatever happens to them will be their choice," Kora justified.

"Kora, if you go down that road, there is no going back."

"They spilled first blood. If it were one of us at this table lying dead on that street, we'd hit with everything we got. As good leaders, we have to treat the lives of our people the same as our own. We have to strike."

For Terrell and for the battle soon to come.

The table fractured at the idea of attacking old colleagues. Two officers quit in the middle of the heated exchange. Battling rage, sorrow, and stress, Kora told them never to come back. *Cowards.* A third stepped down from leadership, wanting no part of the discussion. Kora put him on latrine duty. At least then, he would be useful. The remaining four split: two supporting McAlister and two backing Kora.

McAlister made his point. "One stupid kid's life, in the grand scheme of things, isn't much, and if the dykes want to attack again, we'll defend ourselves. But I'm not going to go all gangster on them because a.) it's dangerous, b.) we're not Jose Martinez."

Kora said, "Than let's make this simple: those in favor of arresting these traitors—"

"They will resist arrest, Kora, and you know it," McAlister spoke over her.

Kora continued anyway, "—head down there before sundown and deal with this mess. The rest stay here and keep the peace. Does that work for you, McAlister?"

The officer reached for a cigarette and found his box empty. He tossed it to the side. "Fine, Kora, fine, but know that we aren't cops anymore."

"Then what are we?" Kora asked facetiously.

"I don't know. Something. Maybe another gang. Maybe terrorists. But we've gone beyond the law now. It won't be long before we look like everyone else. Killin', takin', hell, Martinez might even be proud to call us friends."

"You're wrong. We're better. We will make a difference."

Kora sent her two allied officers to get their squads ready while she went to use the "restroom." Heading behind the chapel, she lost her lunch in the grass. Stress sickness was getting worse. A desire to hide from all the madness drove her to prayer. The world was indifferent to her struggles, and her chaotic thought-life entrapped her. She told herself, *You're fulfilling your destiny. You know this. Why are you so miserable?*

She closed her eyes and saw Terrell's corpse. She'd hardly processed the horror when she first gazed upon the blood staining his front. Rage and a strong sense of vengeance suddenly consumed her. *I'll give them one warning. If they don't surrender...*

Kora vomited again. Her belly was a hollow pit now. Her eyes seemed to sink into her head, and she trembled slightly. *I cannot show that I'm failing. If they know I'm out of control, all of this will be for naught.* The thought made her want to cry. *You can do this. You are strong. You are committed. McAlister was lying; we're the good guys. This is justice.*

A few long minutes went by, and Kora returned to her people. Without Hank, Paul, or McAlister, she felt alone in her conquest. The two officers at her side were devoted, but they weren't what she'd consider friends. Kora hardly knew their names, and she was even less aquatinted with their deputies.

"Make sure your weapons are loaded and your safeties off. Things could go nasty real quick," she told the small militia.

The homespun soldiers obeyed her orders. A mixture of determination and fear hung over them like a cloud. These men did not need Kora to justify the attack. They were fighting for their families and the future of this city, they were fighting for a dead kid, and they were fighting for a leader who had given them purpose when the rest of the nation lost hope.

Kora didn't promise them spoils, either. There would be no celebration until the traitors were gone and sleeper's bodies littered the streets.

"Clock is ticking, gentlemen. Time to move." Kora led them out of the camp.

The local survivors had sobering faces, Terrell's friends wept, Dr. Lambert prepared the operating tools inside his tent, and Tako watched with approving eyes.

Droplets of rain struck their Kevlar vests and

plastic masks. Steel clouds barred the skies. The tempest was upon them by the time they reached the police station. Sheets of rain pounded the orange street barricades. Crash cars had been moved in a way to form multiple consecutive walls. Shaking slightly from the cold downpour, Kora reached the first set of cars.

"Kora Clark!" Officer Jeanette Harold yelled.

The officer was stationed under a wall-less tent on a rooftop. She had binoculars around her neck and a rifle at her side. A handful of other cops lingered on the roof with her while more were stationed in the windows of various surrounding buildings. Advancing would put Kora and her people in a death box.

Staying behind cover, Kora yelled back to the short-haired woman. "I've come to arrest you for first-degree murder! Drop your weapons and put your hands in the air!"

"The boy drew on us! None of that would've happened if you hadn't armed those criminals!"

Kora replied. "We could've lived peacefully, you know, but you didn't want that!"

"I've had it up to here with your crap! Either surrender or leave!"

Kora swapped out her buckshot for slugs and loaded them into her shotgun. "I'm only going to offer this once! If you and Lee stand down, I'll pardon the rest of the officers! Anything less, and we will use force!"

"Go to hell, Clark!"

You first. Kora swung out of cover and pulled the trigger. The stock of the barrel punched her inner shoulder, and a spent shell burst out of the chamber. The deadly slug zipped through the air and obliterated part of Jeanette Harold's mannish face.

"Holy crap!" Kora shouted and pumped her shotgun.

In a horrific noise, her people opened fire.

Bullets shattered glass and blew off chunks of bricks. The enemy cops hid under windows, shouting commands and shooting blindly.

"Go forward!" Kora yelled and launched herself over the hood of the car. "Keep the pressure on!"

Crossing wall after wall of barricades, they advanced as the deluge distorted the environment. The sound of thunder was lost behind the constant gunfire. Kora had no time to think. There was only the moment. She dropped another two officers—guys she used to eat lunch with. She was the storm: unrelenting, ever-moving, and indiscriminate.

By an act of God, she reached the station's front door. Part of the glass was broken. Plywood and chairs blocked her from entering. Kora took a canister of tear gas from her waist and threw it through one of the holes. She retreated around the side of the building, feeding shells into the chamber. Buckshot was better for close quarters if you didn't care about damage. A few of the deputies followed up her flank. Kora shot the latches off one fire exit and gestured for the deputies to advance first.

The group of good ol' boys made it five feet inside before getting pumped full of bullets. The moment their bodies hit the floor, Kora bent her shotgun inside and pulled the trigger.

The loud boom of the weapon was followed by a horrific scream. Kora pumped the fore-end and shot again. Silence.

Controlling her breathing, she peeked around the corner. Three fresh bodies painted the dark corridor red. Kora moved inside, escaping the rain. Outside, her team continued exchanging fire with a few cops still in the windows.

Kora was alone. Her boot landed in a pool of fresh blood and left a crimson trail as she entered the bullpen. A cloud of faded tear gas lingered around the entrance. It had worked well to draw the cop into the corridor. She had to wonder if they were any left.

She crept between the desks. Water drained down the face mask and dripped on the floor. Her finger stayed on the trigger, and her eyes surveyed the surrounding offices.

"Drop it," Office Lee said from behind.

The hairs stood on Kora's neck. "Okay, I'm putting down the weapon."

"You better, you psycho."

Kora slowly lowered the shotgun. "I gave you a chance to surrender. This is on you."

"You know the worst type of evil is the type that doesn't know it's evil all along."

Kora let the shotgun drop and heard the jingling of handcuffs.

"Now, hold still."

In an instant, Kora pulled her pistol and fired behind her.

Lee gasped as multiple bullets punched her chest and caused her to drop. Winded, she reached for her weapon again, and Kora didn't hesitate to put a final bullet in her head.

11

ALL GOOD THINGS

*K*ora holstered her pistol after searching the police station. The shooting outside had ceased, and one of her people called her name from beyond the barricaded entrance. Removing one chair at a time, Kora cleared a way to the front door and opened it for her allies. Out of the twenty-five people she had brought, only three stood before her, and none were leaders.

"Where are the rest?" Kora asked, lifting her faceguard.

"Gone."

Kora thought she'd mourn. Instead, she felt nothing. "And the traitors?"

"Dead, too."

Around them, the storm had calmed, but darkening skies remained. Night was quickly approaching.

Kora looked at the deputies, realizing that she didn't

know their names. One appeared to be as young as seventeen. "Two of you head back to HQ and report that we've won. Get McAlister to send a supply team to gut this place. I want every weapon, vest, and bullet out of here before morning."

"What about the dead?" the young deputy asked.

"No time. Scavengers will be here in hours, and I want us only to take the essentials and go."

Kora sat at her boss's desk, waiting for McAlister to arrive. How long had it been since the EMP had erupted? Months? Weeks? Much less than that, but it felt like an eternity. Putting an end to Harold and Lee made Kora think of Kinsley's death differently. Previously, it was like losing a friend. Now, the casualty was just a number in a much larger game. A part of her humanity had died tonight, but she felt stronger, more able to lead. *There will be more necessary sacrifices when I attack the sleepers.* The thought didn't seem so scary. It was just a fact. *People will die, and I will be responsible.... I just have to accept it.... As long as we come out on top.*

When McAlister arrived, he could hardly look at Kora. *Be ashamed all you want, but we won.* She kept the remark to herself.

McAlister put his team to work while Kora and the few survivors returned to base.

She found Paul waiting for her in the tent. His eyes were bloodshot and puffy. At first sight, she embraced him, locking her lips with his and pushing him to the bed. Instinct took over. Working feverishly, she tore off her vest and tossed aside her gun belt.

"Kora, I—"

"Shut up," Kora whispered while she removed her pants. "I don't want to talk about anything right now." She fought against his belt.

Paul snatched her hand, preventing her from continuing. Kora looked at him dumbfounded. Her mood changed from shocked to annoyed.

Paul said sternly. "We promised we'd wait."

"I want to…. I swear we won't go too far," Kora pulled down his zipper. *I just need to feel something.*

"No." Paul gently but firmly lifted her off him, surprising her with his strength. "The last thing we need is to complicate things and have a bunch of remorse."

"Are you kidding me? Do you know how many people I sho—you know what, never mind." Kora stood up.

Paul held her hand. "I love you, Kora. And I want you, too. I do." He glanced up and down her body. "A lot. But we have to do this the right way…. besides, how many guys beg their girlfriend *not* to have sex with them?"

Kora rolled her eyes.

Paul sighed. "I wish you told me you went to the police station, though. I felt like a coward."

"You were mourning your friend."

"I should've been with you…. I should've—" Paul

147

stopped and collected himself. "The dead can bury their own. We need to fight for the living. I'll be there next time. I'll show I'm a man you can count on."

Darn it, Paul, now I really want to... Kora sat down next to him.

He put his arm around her, and she rested her head on his shoulder.

"I… I hurt a lot of people tonight," Kora confessed. "The moment the shooting started, it was like a switch flipped. All the hesitancy just left me. The fear was there; it always is, but when I saw the targets, I just went after them. I didn't even look back. I can't even remember how I got to the front door so fast. By the time it was over, twenty-two of our people were dead and all of theirs. Maybe fifty-ish people in total."

"I… I don't know what to say," Paul replied. "You were protecting us, right? They attacked first. You warned them. They could've surrendered…."

It seemed like he was trying to convince himself that everything was justified. Kora knew they wouldn't give up, but she had gone anyway.

"I feel nothing," Kora said. "It wasn't like that when I shot Gabriel or stopped that rapist from attacking Katie. Now, there is this… this... hole in my heart. It's like I can't even see them as people. There are just obstacles or assets now. I want to care. I really do. But… Harold and Lee. They're nothing to me."

Paul chose his words carefully. "You're a good woman, Kora. With a good heart. Things will get better. I know it. And when the sleepers are gone, the whole city will be like Martinez's neighborhood. We'll see children playing. People eating together and laughing. Life will be good. Don't lose yourself along the way."

"Martinez didn't get there because of his *good heart*."

"Who said you have to follow his path? What you did at that station tonight was necessary, but once we get established as the leading faction, we won't have much opposition."

"We lost half of our leaders today. The ones who weren't shot quit before the mission. And McAlister hates me, too."

"Let's just keep our eyes on the future. What is done is done," Paul assured her. He got off the bed.

"Where are you going?" Kora asked.

"Restroom." He left the tent.

Kora rested on her side and pulled the covers over her body. *He's just being nice. He knows I did the wrong thing... or did I? We are now the only police force in the city. We are the authority.* She shut her eyes and dreamed of fire. The flames lapped at her skin. Her flesh turned to wood and turned black before crumbling. In the rubble of ash was a shard of tarnished silver. Did it mean something? Was it just random?

Kora awoke, got dressed, and found the chapel empty of people. Light flooded through the windows. *It's mid-afternoon already.* She heard a commotion outside. She quickly pushed open the door and saw the camp in disorder. People were running to and fro. Some were packing. Others were arming themselves. The first familiar face she spotted was Dr. Lambert. He was in the process of stitching up a person's head wound.

"Ah, the great chief has awoken," the doctor remarked.

"What's going on?" *And why hasn't anyone told me?*

The doctor laced the hooked thread through the person's wound. "You should know."

"I don't," Kora was quickly losing patience.

"You're new friends moved in. A real lovely crew. Nice chains, big guns, really fond of the ladies."

"Martinez." *He must've sent in his forces for tomorrow's assault.*

"Let's just say some people aren't fond of having a bunch of criminals as their new neighbors and seem to believe it's their job to remove them if you won't. On top of that, yesterday's body count didn't have the best impact on public relations. A couple dozen people packed their bags, loaded up from the food stores, and ran away to greener pastures. But hey, there is a silver lining."

"And what might that be?"

"At least I'm not bored anymore."

"Thanks, Lambert," Kora replied sarcastically.

She left the courtyard and found Tako, Martinez, and another forty or so gangsters in the streets.

McAlister and Paul spoke to them, seemingly harshly, but Kora was too far away to hear the words.

When she approached, the men directed their attention to Kora.

"Finally awake?" McAlister asked.

Paul said, "Hey, that's on me; I let her sleep…. I thought you could use it, Kora."

Kora mouthed, *thank you*.

Martinez grinned. "I heard about your *altercation* yesterday. I got to say, I'm impressed. I didn't think you had it in you."

Kora replied, "Tako made a good point during our council meeting. This city can't have two competing police forces, especially if one is abusing the law. Now that we have consolidated and obtained their weaponry, it's just a matter of out-fitting our people and getting ready for battle. To be honest, I thought you would've stayed on your side of town until the morning."

Martinez said, "After I heard Tako's report about your victory, I thought it would be best if we sure up our defenses."

McAlister, seemingly peeved, interjected. "Yeah, and Paul and I were making sure they knew this is *our* place with *our* rules. A lot of folks aren't happy siding with this arrangement. Some claim that Martinez's boys robbed them a few days ago."

Martinez dismissed his concern. "We have the weapons. You have the numbers. The quicker everyone gets acclimated to each other's strengths and weaknesses, the better…. My people, too, need to know they can count their allies."

Kora replied, "We proved ourselves yesterday. If that's not enough, then take a hike."

Martinez met her gaze. "It is enough." He turned to McAlister. "And I'll make sure my people follow your rules."

"And stay away from our women," McAlister added.

Martinez nodded.

"Good," McAlister replied, surprised by the kingpin's compliance. "Then I'm going to get back to work. I have to prepare these people to die tomorrow." The cop started leaving.

"One second," Kora told the others before following after her partner.

Out of earshot from the others, Kora caught up with McAlister as they moved through the lively street. "Are you good?"

"Nah, but I'll get done what needs to be done," he said while keeping his focus forward.

Kora said, "What happened yesterday was necessary—"

"With all due respect, Clark, I don't want to hear it."

"But—"

McAlister halted and turned to her. "After this suicide mission tomorrow, we're finished."

"You're joking, right? We're down half the team as it is. I thought we were in this together?" Kora asked.

"We were, but you've changed. This isn't about helping the little guy anymore. Power plays, ends justifying the means, and Machiavellian BS; I'm not about that. And after walking among our dead brothers and sisters last night, I made a decision that I will never be about it, either."

"The people are still our top priority. We just have to stop our enemies first," Kora explained. "We won't be safe until—"

"Don't talk to me like a kid. I know what you're doing, and I know you think it's right. It might work: yours and Martinez's paradise. I just want no part of it, and no matter what you say, offer, or whatever, I'm not changing my mind. I'm done, Clark. Done." With nothing more to say, her friend vanished into the busy crowd leaving Kora to ponder her decisions.

She returned to Martinez, Tako, and Paul.

"Paul, could you get supplies ready? Make sure everyone has rations, bandages, and extra ammo for tomorrow," Kora asked.

"You got it, babe." Paul excused himself.

Kora said to Tako, "Settle your people in the outer sectors. If they want to stay here tonight, they have to play their part."

Tako replied, "They deserve better sleeping arrangements seeing how they'll be pulling most of the weight tomorrow."

Kora looked to Martinez.

"Do as she says," Martinez told his triggerman.

"As you wish," Tako replied and rallied his people.

"Are Hank and the others back?" Kora asked Martinez.

"Yes, I only have a small team stationed in my neighborhood and thought you'd want to have all your people here for the big day."

I'd prefer to have the leverage. Kora thought. *If you aim to betray us, we'd have nothing to deter you, but you probably know that.*

"Let's talk about tomorrow," Kora said.

Martinez followed her to the chapel, where they discussed battle plans. Scouts would be sent out in the morning to find the sleepers. Believing the death squad to be flighty if spotted, Kora and Martinez would only send in the bulk of their forces after hearing the scouts' report. Hopefully, they could catch the sleepers fleeing. Martinez said it was much easier to shoot a target in the back. Kora was okay with that. The sleepers had been killing civilians for days; it would be a waste of time to give them a fair trial. This was a war. A decisive strike would ensure victory. When the time came, they would have their people separated into different squadrons and travel various streets to avoid ambushes. As imposing as one giant mass of fighters could be, automatic weapons could mow them down if they stayed clumped up.

While they spoke, they had Dr. Lambert erect multiple medical tents as well as give a few key deputies basic first aid training. The civilians who proved to be inaccurate shooters were given ammo duty. Though armed, their main mission would be to make sure that Martinez's men stayed loaded at all times during the battle.

Kora matched every three of Martinez's men with ten of her own. Without much of a leadership team left, Kora would let Martinez's men take charge of their squads during the battle. They would be tasked to make sure no one retreated without consent. Desertion could destroy morale and had to be quenched as soon as it arose. Martinez opted to shoot any deserters that fled. Any other day, Kora would disallow that, but not tomorrow. If they lost against the sleepers, they could lose the city. Anyone that volunteered would be expressly told the consequences of fleeing.

"Anything else we're missing?" Kora asked Martinez.

"That about covers it," the kingpin replied.

"Tomorrow morning, we'll give a little pep-talk," Kora replied.

"My men don't need it."

"Mine do. Everyone needs to know that this operation is a righteous act for our nation and future. Also, that you are a repentant hero who is going to lead us to victory," Kora said.

A wry smile grew on Martinez's face.

"What?" Kora asked.

"I never took you for such a tactician."

"I am what I need to be at the moment," Kora replied.

"My daughter could learn a few things from you," Martinez replied. "When this fight is over, I want you to mentor her."

"Okay," Kora said suspiciously. "What are her qualifiers for leadership?"

"She's my daughter," Martinez replied sternly.

"That's not enough, sorry. I can't waste my time babysitting," Kora replied coldly.

Martinez set his jaw for a moment. He cooled his anger. "Nothing, nothing is as powerful as blood, you understand?"

"She could be my daughter, and it would make no difference. I need people who can get results today."

"You need loyalty," Martinez replied. "Many can follow an order, but there are very few who would voluntarily lay down their lives for yours. My people, I treat them like family. I give them rewards, feasts, the best clothes, the best women, we eat together, we mourn together, and they love me. I tell them to shoot, and they shoot. I tell them to steal, and they steal. I tell them to dance, and they—you get the picture. Your people listen because you are the boss but do they love you? Will they fight for you the same as you fight for them?"

"Right now, they know I'm their best shot at a better life. That's enough in my book."

Martinez let out an exasperated sigh. "For the short

term, yes, but when pressure wanes, and they don't need your protection, what will keep them around? "

"I'd rather them go back to their normal lives than follow me. Once the city is safe, I'll promote a few deputies into sheriffs and maintain the peace. As long as they're not breaking the law, I don't care where they go or what they do."

"And you? What are your plans?"

"I do my 7 am to 4 pm shift and go to sleep," Kora replied.

"Boring," Martinez commented.

"Good. I could get used to boring."

"What about outfitting our people for a nationwide revolution, as you stated in our first conversation?"

That was before I tasted war, Kora thought to herself. "We'll keep them armed and ready, but if we can't properly maintain order in one city, a revolution won't do us much good."

Martinez got up from his chair. "Very well then." He buttoned the front of his suit. "I'm going to prep Tako for tomorrow... I would really like it if you took my daughter under your wing."

"Not until she proves herself," Kora replied.

"You'll reconsider after the battle," Martinez said, almost like a threat before leaving Kora alone.

She pinched the bridge of her nose to quell a growing migraine. Despite having slept in, she felt exhausted. When the sleepers were gone, she promised herself a mini-vacation. Even if it were just a few days, she wanted to get away from everyone and clear her head. Perhaps she and Paul could do something fun like play mini-golf at one of the abandoned courses or go on a nature hike. *We'd have to get an armed escort to do such a thing. Perhaps Hank.* She wondered about the old patriot. The deputy had been gung-ho about her operation since they met up. Kora chewed her fingernail. *Will he leave me like McAlister?*

Her ever-shrinking friend's list made her consider Martinez's message about loyalty. *Isn't it enough that I'm making the hard choices? Do I need to be their mother, too? Most of these guys are double my age.* She knew she couldn't allow herself to get bitter. She had chosen to lead. Now she'd have to deal with all the consequences that followed.

Unmotivated to do any more work for the evening, Kora decided to visit her favorite prisoner. The commotion had ceased around the courtyard now that Martinez's men were in the outer sectors. Most people wanted to have a quiet meal with their families before the big day. They were reluctant warriors but knew that without action, they would never be safe.

Meanwhile, Glen and the rest of the convicts were as bitter as ever. They had been fed leftovers the last few evenings and had to defecate into a bucket. Unlike everyone else in this new world, they were the ones still bound by their past sins.

"I got good news for you, guys," Kora said as she approached the stinky cell.

Wearing dirty orange jumpsuits and looking like hell, the men eyed-balled her.

"If the battle goes well tomorrow, I'll be releasing you all," Kora promised.

The men mumbled to each other. Glen stayed silent.

Kora continued, "You'll be escorted out of the city under the conditions that you never return." *Mainly so we won't have to feed you or change your waste buckets anymore.*

"Yes, ma'am," one of the prisoners replied.

The rest of the men nodded. Everyone but Glen.

"I thought you'd be happy?" she asked him.

"You're friends with Jose Martinez," he replied.

"So what?"

"You should've left when I told you," Glen answered.

"I know how to handle myself."

"He'll drain you of all you got and then throw you out to the wolves."

"You're a bundle of joy, Glen. Keep it up," Kora said sarcastically.

"Avoid that battle tomorrow," Glen warned.

"Why?"

"Because if you die, Martinez will execute us. We're what he would call *useless eaters.*"

"Well, then you better start thinking of ways to make yourself more useful."

Glen grabbed the cell bars. "I'm serious, Clark. Don't throw away your life."

Wishing them a good night, Kora retrieved a few protein bars and a water bottle from the supply cache and returned to her tent. She would've killed for a real meal and hot shower. Going to bed early would have to suffice. Hands folded on her chest, she lay on her cot. Before dark, Paul entered and climbed into his sleeping bag.

"I got the kids packed up," Paul said in the dark. "They have food, water, and a crude map of the city. If we don't return, I told them to flee."

"Do they have any adults to supervise their retreat?"

"An elderly couple."

"That's something at least," Kora replied.

Paul spoke with sorrow in his tone. "None of the kids are taking Terrell's death well. They blame themselves, God, me, anything to make sense of it."

"Did you tell them that his killers are gone?"

"Yeah, but they'd much rather have their friend back. You don't know him like they did, Kora. He was like the big brother of the family."

"To be honest, I don't know a lot of people that are following us," Kora admitted. "There is Katie, Dr. Lambert, McAlister, Hank, you, and the other leaders, but... it's all surface level."

"You've not had time to form personal relationships, and who can blame you?"

Kora stayed silent for a moment.

"Paul?"

"Yeah?"

"I have a feeling that a lot of people are going to die tomorrow."

Her boyfriend sat up. In the darkness, she could only see his silhouette. "No matter what, we stick together."

"I'm scared."

"Scoot over." Paul climbed onto the little cot and held her. "Get some sleep. We're going to need it."

Kora clung to her man. She dozed in and out of sleep. Her nerves and fear of tomorrow kept her from peace. The confidence she had from defeating the traitorous cops was fleeting.

Suddenly, distant gunfire and shouting jerked her from her weak slumber.

"Clark!" McAlister yanked open the entrance flap of her tent in one hand and had a torch in the other. A sheen of sweat glistened on his forehead and trickled down his nose.

"Am I dreaming?" Kora mumbled, rubbing the sleep from her eyes.

"Get armored up. The outer sectors are being attacked."

Paul quickly got out of bed. "Is it the sleepers?"

"I don't know, but they have a lot of guns, and it doesn't appear they are in the mood to take any prisoners." Closing the flap, McAlister dashed through the church, yelling at the other few leaders to wake up.

"Not a dream," Kora realized.

Paul put on his pants and proceeded to put plates into one of the vests they got from the police station.

Heart racing, Kora took a moment to stretch and limber up. She donned her uniform, vest, and weapons, opting for an AR-15 instead of her shotgun. The chief's pistol sat snugly in her side holster, ready for any close encounters.

They joined McAlister in the courtyard. Firepits and torches had been lit beside various pathways and behind the razor-wire topped walls. Men and women crowded around the weapons cache to retrieve guns and ammo from trusted deputies. Meanwhile, the prisoners shouted from inside their cage. "Let us fight. Please. We'll help you."

"Ignore them," McAlister said coldly.

Gunfire thundered in the distance. The rapid bangs came from a fully automatic arsenal. Kora couldn't tell which shots were from Martinez's men and which shots were the enemy.

"What are we waiting on?" Paul asked McAlister.

"Them." McAlister pointed.

Hank and two other leaders jogged into the courtyard. "Clark, McAlister. We need a lot more people in the outer sectors!"

"What did you see?" Kora replied.

"Soldiers and a whole lot of them," Hank said, catching his breath. "They are certainly not American."

12

REMEMBER THE ALAMO

*T*he outermost sector had fallen before Kora could arrive. Screaming, disorganized, and hysterical, the survivors and Martinez's broken forces bolted down the streets. They tumbled in the darkness. Four carried an injured gangster by each limb. Blood spilled down his shirt as he cried to his mother.

"Fall back! Fall back!" they screamed as they darted past Kora's posse.

Suddenly, there was a commotion from another sector. More shooters. Another leg of the foreign army was advancing. From the east and south, there were similar shootings. *We're being boxed in.* The horrific revelation caused Kora's stomach to drop. *How many are there?*

Hank turned in her direction. McAlister was too preoccupied with the injured people down the street.

Kora said, "We set up in this sector. We cannot afford to lose any more ground."

She directed a few of the deputies to share the word around HQ.

"Only fall back to HQ if you lose a sector. Otherwise, no retreating."

The men nodded and vanished into the night.

Bile climbed up Kora's throat. *No retreating... I just killed these people.*

Paul put a hand on her shoulder, breaking her negative train of thought. "We need to get off the streets. That office building might provide good cover."

Kora agreed, happy it was a decision she didn't have to make. McAlister and Hank followed them into the building while the rest of the deputies and Martinez's scattered people took up vantage points up and down the street.

Hunkered by a window, Kora inspected her rifle. If there were any issues, now was the time to find them.

Paul stayed opposite of her, crouched as well. "You stay behind me, okay? I'll be a lookout."

"Thank you," Kora replied.

The cool calm she felt at the attack at the police station had evaporated. In that situation, she was in control; she was the one attacking. Tonight, horror and fear put her in a stranglehold.

How could this happen?

McAlister answered her unspoken question. He was stationed by another window. "We had fewer scouts out tonight. We wanted everyone rested for the battle. It looks like the battle came to us."

A flare shot up in the distance, lighting up the sky with orange and red light before landing in the middle of the street. More flares shot up around the various sectors. The light revealed hidden deputies and allied gangsters.

"Keep your head down," Paul commanded and peered out the window. He kept his rifle high and ready to shoot.

Like black specters, soldiers in dark uniforms tactically advanced down the street.

"How many do you see?" Kora whispered. "Paul? How many?"

"Dozens," he replied.

Hank remarked, "If we shoot now, they'll light us up to kingdom come."

McAlister lit a cigarette with trembling hands. "We got women and children just down the street. We can't let them pass. Period."

A deputy in the building across the street signaled to Kora, awaiting orders.

Below, the enemy soldiers were still a few hundred meters away. They were outfitted with top-of-the-line weaponry and body armor. There were too many to just be the sleepers. These were the soldiers the sleepers were clearing the way for. *The CCP is on American soil.*

Kora looked to McAlister. "Weapons free, whenever

you're ready."

Cigarette dangling out of the side of his mouth, he mumbled, "God help us." He signaled the deputies. "Open fire."

Paul and the others leaned out the windows and unloaded on the invaders. Shouting orders in Chinese, the foreign army scattered behind cover before returning fire.

Chunks of brick exploded by Kora's head.

Another flare illuminated the battleground as the warring factions exchanged bullets.

Kora noticed one of the foreign soldiers assembling a rocket launcher from behind a car.

"Get down—" Her cry was cut short by the shrieking rocket hitting the wall.

Boom!

A brief moment of darkness.

Kora tumbled.

Consciousness returned when she was a floor lower and three-fourths covered by debris. She hacked up chalky dust. The floor directly above had broken and was slanted sideways where the rocket had blown a massive hole in the wall. Groaning in pain, Kora pushed aside the broken fragments of floor and ceiling when she heard footsteps in the stairwell. She played dead as three soldiers reached her floor.

Speaking in Chinese, they fanned across the room.

Bam-bam-bam! McAlister's mussel flashed from a

dark corner, dropping two of the soldiers. The final soldier shot a few rounds McAlister's way before Kora could pull her pistol and shot multiple bullets in his back.

"Kora, you alive?" McAlister asked weakly.

Retching herself from the ruins, Kora limped to her partly covered partner on the side of the room. The black cop kept his cigarette between his dusty fingers. A teardrop of blood seeped from the corner of his lip. Kora noticed the holes in his stomach. The high-powered rounds make easy work of his bulletproof vest and the organs behind them.

"Oh, no, no, no," Kora mumbled. "Not you. Not you, too."

"Don't beat yourself up. This whole thing was doomed from the beginning. We're just a couple of cops. We weren't ready for this—*ack!*" He hacked up blood.

"I got to get you to Lambert. H-he'll—"

"It's over, Clark. Get out of here before more come. Go. Go!" He shoved her backward.

Kora hit her rump on the floor. By the time she got back to her feet, the light had left McAlister's eyes. Her friend was dead and gone, just like Kinsley and Garrick.

The nightmare was only beginning. Outside, soldiers shouted. Movement could be heard on the floor below. Boots thumped the hardwood floor.

Tears flushing her face, Kora grabbed McAlister's

rifle and hurried upstairs. She turned to the side, facing down a barrel of a gun.

Hank lowered his rifle. His eyes were wide and crazed. "I thought we lost ya."

"Paul here?" Kora asked desperately.

Hank hiked back his thumb. Her boyfriend leaned against the wall, half of his face annihilated from the explosion. His breathing was choppy and weak.

Kora rushed to him. Burned and blistered flesh marred his appearance. He moved his mouth to speak, but no words escaped.

"Help me with him," she commanded Hank.

The old patriot put Paul's good arm around his shoulder and lifted the man. "Can you walk, son?"

Paul nodded slightly. He scooted his feet in sync with Hank.

Kora glanced about the room, finding the fire escape. She ushered them in that direction. Keeping open the door, she aimed into the alley behind the building. A few troops jogged below, chasing down a fleeing gangster.

"Follow me." Kora gestured to Hank.

Keeping the rifle at the ready, she hurried down the metal steps and unlocked the suspended ladder. Descending the rungs, she reached the alley's floor far behind the soldiers.

Rifle holstered across his back, Hank guided Paul down the stairs and reached the ladder. The soldiers inside reached the upstairs fire exit.

Taking a knee, Kora shot at them, preventing them from opening the door again. She twisted back to the alley. The soldiers ahead of her were gone. Sighing in relief, she grabbed Paul as he reached the bottom of the ladder and helped him to the wall. When Hank arrived, he took the injured man again, and the three of them used the backroads to return toward HQ.

They passed through two fallen sectors with nerve-racking suspense. The soldiers only bothered to spare unarmed women and children. Every male, even those who openly surrendered, were mercilessly gunned down.

Kora and her two men hugged the shadows. Every time a flare cast its glow over the streets, they concealed themselves behind dumpsters, cars, and inside buildings.

The warfare was the hottest in the sectors just outside the Alamo. Those who remained fought tooth and nail for their families and loved ones. They positioned themselves in high places and hurled down Molotovs to create fires on the main road. While the fires blazed, they trained their guns on the allies and side streets. The insurgents mercilessly bombarded them with their full arsenals. Rocket launchers obliterated walls. Grenades were tossed into buildings. Fully automatic gunfire peppered windows. The reaper had taken to Kora's grassroots army, and his harvest was plentiful.

In the middle of chaos, Kora, Hank, and Paul

skirted around the friendly fire and crossed through the sector just in time to see Martinez, Tako, and the remaining gangsters flee with Kora's hard-earned supplies.

"Hey!" Kora shouted.

The sounds of war prevented the silver-haired kingpin from hearing her. He and his crew fled, leaving Kora to the wolves.

Kora aimed at Jose, but her shot was blocked by Katie and a few other women running across the street. The pregnant waitress and her hippy friends moved inside of the courtyard. By the time Kora had a clear shot, Martinez was gone. Cursing, she followed after Katie.

The Alamo historical site was the only sector untouched by battle. Within the tent-packed courtyard, twenty-plus injured people crowded in and around Dr. Lambert's medical tent. Another ten deputies guarded the various entrances and exits. The defenseless mothers, children, and elderly packed the center.

The color left Kora's face. *This is it? This is my last stand?*

Hank moved ahead of her. Shouting, he muscled his way through the crowd of injured people and brought Paul directly to Lambert.

"There's nothing I can do right now!" Lambert shouted as he removed a bullet from a man's shoulder. "You'll just have to wait in line!"

"Can't you see? Half of his face is gone!"

"Get back!" Lambert pointed his bloody scalpel at him.

The children previously under Paul's care rushed to Kora. They wore backpacks and were armed with knives. One had a pee-stain on his jeans.

"You're going to save us, right?" a little girl asked.

Kora looked at a nearby elderly couple. "Are you the ones Paul put in charge?"

The couple nodded soberly. The sound of gunfire caused the old man to flinch.

Kora said, "Take them out of here."

"That's suicide," the elderly woman replied.

"It'll be much worse for them if they stay. Now, go!" Kora demanded.

The elderly man took the little girl's hand and gestured for the others to follow. Kora shouted at the deputies guarding the back entrance to step aside. The older woman herded the kids out of the gate.

With the children gone, Kora said to the rest of the survivors. "Everyone, listen up! We're going to be swarmed soon. Our brothers and sisters on the outside have weakened their forces, but it doesn't change the fact that we are out-manned and out-gunned." A tear flowed down Kora's cheek. She quickly wiped it. "Holding this position is a losing battle, but we need to do so until we find their weakest front that the majority can escape by. We do this by drawing them in and hitting them hard. Once we see a break in their defense, we go. Pack light. Move fast. I, and any willing volunteers, will be the last ones out, that I promise you. Any questions?"

Aside from the groans of the injured, the crowd was silent. By their ghastly expressions, they were already defeated.

"We... we did a good thing here," Kora continued, trying to convince herself and the others. "When the rest of the nation crumbed, we unified, we built, and we stood our ground. Remember that."

The remaining women and elderly took up arms from the weapon tents and posted themselves among the various entrances. The razor wire would prevent wall-climbers. The four choke points were all they needed to hold. Once they had a clear route out, they would use it. Kora reloaded McAlister's AR-15. Katie stayed by her.

"You should gather with the others and get ready to run," Kora suggested.

"I'm staying with you, Kora," the woman said firmly.

Kora replied, "My friends don't tend to have a long life expectancy."

"You saved me once. Now, I'll do the same."

"But the baby—?"

Katie put her hand on her flat belly. "I know. But you need me now."

"Go away, Katie. Please. I can't lose you, too," Kora replied.

The pregnant waitress protested but could see Kora

wouldn't budge. Pouting, she folded into one of the crowds.

Glen called Kora to the cell. She ignored him. Releasing prisoners in their confined space spelled trouble. There were enough threats already.

The last of the surrounding sector's deputies retreated into the Alamo.

Trembling, Kora, and two lines of survivors formed by the various gates. Some were prone, some kneeling and others standing, but all ready to shoot their invaders.

A flare shot over the camp. It cast its orange, hellish glow over all Kora had built before tumbling among the tents.

The soldiers appeared quickly after, and the last stand began.

Gunfire held back the oppressors, and the battle seemed to slow. Defending only a small area made it much easier to keep the enemy at bay. The Chinese had suffered enough casualties to charge recklessly forward. Little by little, more soldiers appeared around the surrounding streets but were unable to press forward.

Then, an RPG blasted a hole in one of the historical site's walls.

Part of Kora's force relocated to the new blast zone, but a fourth of her remaining people were mowed down by gunfire. Another blast opened up another wall, further dispersing Kora's people.

Every tense minute felt like an hour, and every stray bullet reminded Kora of her fragile mortality. The helpless people she'd armed failed to handle the shock. A few fled before there was a confirmed clearing and were killed. Others threw down their weapons and accepted defeat. Kora yelled at them to rise up, but their minds were like soup and their morale long dead.

"Clear! Let's go! Let's go!" Hank's voice boomed when all hope seemed lost.

His small squad holding the northern exit shouted for the injured and elder to escape.

"Go in waves!" Kora commanded, but only a handful listened.

Most people abandoned their posts for a quick escape. Those still standing their ground quickly found themselves unable to peek around corners without catching a bullet to the neck.

"Kora, please!" Glen shouted from his cage.

"Hold the line," Kora told her people before rushing to the cell. She fished the keys out of her pocket and hastily unlocked the gate.

The instant it opened, the wave of prisoners ran over her and scurried out of the walls. Only one of them extended a hand.

"Glen?" Kora asked.

The bearded prepper lifted her off the ground. "Are you finally ready to go to that place I told you about?"

"Why would you help me?"

"You have a good heart," Glen replied.

Shouting could be heard outside of the walls. Kora gasped. "They're coming."

Glen grabbed a gun from the stockpile.

"Wait here!" Kora exclaimed and rushed to the medical tent.

Dr. Lambert was jamming supplies into his medical bag while Paul sat in a wheelchair. Bandages wrapped his face. Only one eye and a mouth-hole were visible.

"Time to go." Kora grabbed the wheelchair's handles.

"Do you have a plan?" Lambert asked.

"Get out of the city," Kora replied.

"Good enough for me."

She pushed Paul's wheelchair out of the broken wall as the last of her people dispersed. Hank, Katie, and Glen stayed close to her and Lambert. Running by dead and bleeding soldiers, Glen took charge.

"Keep up or get left behind!" the prisoner shouted.

Bullets zipped by, causing them to separate. After two blocks, Kora and Paul reconvened with the rest of their crew. They stayed bunched together and avoided main roads and open areas. The enemy was far behind them, but they needed to stay frosty. Kora didn't have it in her to keep fighting.

Hank stayed close to her and spoke softly. "Can we trust this Glen, fella?"

"He's our best shot at getting out of here," Kora whispered.

Hank grumbled, "When are we going to strike back?"

"Right now, let's just survive," Kora replied.

It was sunrise when they arrived at the city limits. A caravan of military Humvees drove parallel to the vehicle-obstructed road. More Chinese were moving into the city. Their full-scale invasion was only just beginning.

Glen led the team into an abandoned trailer park. The double-wides had been stripped of what little valuables they held, and the locals were either dead or long gone. Glen hiked up the steps of one of the messiest ones and entered. After a moment, he returned. "It's safe."

Hank and Lambert helped carry Paul's wheelchair up the steps. Though Kora's boyfriend could walk, the painkillers Lambert gave him kept him sedated. Katie, who had not spoken a word since they left, helped Glen close the various window blinds.

"Make yourselves comfortable," Glen said, heading into a bedroom. He said from inside. "We'll have to move in the evening if we want to avoid fanfare. I suggest you get some sleep. It's going to take a few days to get where we're going."

Kora took his advice and crashed into the guest bedroom. Removing her bulletproof vest and weapons made her feel one hundred pounds lighter. She crawled onto a twin bed and attempted to tally the losses in her head. It was not worth the time or effort to figure it out. All she had done to restore order had been destroyed in a few hours. The foreign invaders would continue to take, and she'd be powerless to stop it. She gritted her teeth. Jose Martinez was still out there, too. The Chinese wiped out most of his forces, too, but the traitor left when Kora needed his people most. She hoped to never see him again.

The day slowly passed by. Around lunch, the crew ate cold canned food around the little table. The mood of each survivor varied drastically.

Guilt ate at Kora to the point where she felt disgusted to lead anyone. Dr. Lambert openly partook in his addiction and made cynical quips about their horrible loss. Fuming, Hank kept his gun across his lap and talked of vengeance. Katie cleaned the trailer, attempting to keep her mind off the loss of her friends and loved ones. Paul said nothing. Maroon blotches stained inside of his face bandages. Lastly, Glen had traded his jumpsuit for camo and quietly enjoyed his newfound freedom.

Dr. Lambert said, "Tell us about this place of yours."

"It's a farm," Glen replied. "A hundred miles north of here, smack dab in the middle of nowhere."

"Once you get there, you plan to...?" the doctor rolled his hand.

Glen lowered his spoon. "I'm going to live off the land. Simple as that. If you want to join, I expect you to be useful."

"I'm a doctor," Lambert said flatly. "Anyway, is it big enough for all of us?"

"Yeah… but it will be tight. You can always go your own way."

"Rather not," Lambert answered.

Glen addressed the table, "I'm a simple man. You look out for me; I look out for you. I showed grace to Kora over here just cause I know she's trying her best. I don't know the rest of you, but if I see you acting out, I will remove you. Rules don't matter to me; respect does, though."

Hank grumbled. "All this talk of running… We should go back to the city. People need us."

"No one is stopping you," Glen replied.

"We're stronger together," Hank said.

"Well, I'm never going back." Glen continued eating.

"Me neither," Lambert added.

Hank looked at Kora. "What about you? There has to be more like us still out there. We gather up a militia and take back what they stole from us."

"I can't," she replied.

"And why not?"

"I'm tired, Hank. Very tired. I'm sorry," Kora said.

The old patriot was flabbergasted. "I shot eight men last night, and we're just going to give up?"

Katie broke her silence. "What is there to go back to?"

"With all due respect, ma'am, I'm talking to our leader," Hank said harshly.

Katie replied, "I promised to follow Kora, too, and if she says that we stop, we stop."

"Stopping ain't an option. This is a war. Hell, we were willing to team up with that psycho Martinez if it meant victory, but we aren't willing to go back after one defeat?"

Lambert said, "We weren't defeated. We were destroyed. Half the people I patched up are dead. The rest are scattered. The only guns we have are the ones we hold, and we have neither food nor water." He patted his medicine bag. "I have the equivalent of a first-aid kit with a few extra morphine shots in this bag. If anyone else gets shot or their face exploded—no offense, Paul—they are SOL. Unless you have a couple of tanks, planes, and heavy artillery you haven't told us about, this *war* is over. We now live in occupied territory, and if the Chinese know we resisted, they'll put us in front of a firing squad. Game over."

Hank mumbled a curse and left the table.

"Hank?" Kora asked.

"I'm going on a walk!" The man slammed the back door behind him.

Kora sighed deeply. She gently squeezed Paul's hand and looked at Glen. "How soon can we get moving?"

"Sundown," Glen replied. "And once we start, I'm not stopping."

13

THE LONG ROAD

*T*he brilliant starry sky and pregnant moon guided their path. Critters in nature chirped. The whispering wind caused their torches to dance and ruffled Kora's hair. I-10 was a vision from the apocalypse. Abandoned vehicles, garbage, and the occasional corpses marked the path.

Where had the people gone? The cities weren't safe. The country was full of unknowns. The only place that seemed logical would be their home. Would it be much different from the rest of the nation? Likely not, but loved ones in the time of the disaster were like lights in the darkness. Kora's parents were states away, though. If they survived the dark winter and the establishment of a new Chinese-American government, maybe they'd reunite. She didn't allow herself to hope. Hope dangerous. It had cost her the lives of many people.

I should've died in that arms bust, she thought as she

pushed Paul's wheelchair. Somehow, Hank still believed in her, but he despised her decision to leave. Out of all the people in that final battle, she'd thought he would get a heroic death or run away to the family he never talked about. Instead, the old man survived and would have to live through the hell that followed the downfall of his nation. Kora knew full well that the Chinese soldiers were raping and killing anyone they'd like tonight. No one would stop them. Without Martinez or Kora, San Antonio would become a circus for the evil and deranged. If history was any indicator, there would be no white knights or happy endings. *Judgment Day will sort them out... me too.* The fates of all the people Kora couldn't save were added to her lists of woes. *Hundreds, Lord? Hundreds of souls I sent up?*

She mindlessly pushed her disfigured boyfriend. His scarred flesh was a monument to her failure. There was an argument in her mind: was hope a snare or a propeller? Murphy's Law stated, "Anything that can go wrong will go wrong." Once again, history showed this principle time and time again. The cycle was broken by courageous individuals who dared to hope for a better tomorrow and paid the highest price for it under God's guiding hand. Controversy, everything eventually dies, and nothing on this mortal plane is free from failure. If all died, then raging against failure was like raging the elements themselves. Yet, there were victories in the areas of innovation, government, morals, etc. *Those cycles can die too. Will a phoenix rise from the ashes, or will death beget death?*

A flare shot overhead, followed by shouting. By the time Kora grabbed her weapon, she had realized how hopeless she was. Two dozen men and women encircled the portion of the highway where they stood, in their hands, full-automatic weapons. Leading their pact, Jose Martinez.

The flare landed on the hood of a nearby pick-up truck. Sizzling, the ball of burning light flickered like a fallen star.

"Chief Clark," Jose smiled. "Fate is a curious thing."

Blood spatter marked his wrinkled silver suit and bulletproof vest. He kept his large, drum-magazine shotgun level at his waist. His daughter, Tako, and the remainder of his gang aimed at Kora's allies.

Kora kept her finger over the trigger. "You left us when we needed you."

"First rule of business: know when to cut your losses," the kingpin replied.

"And your little neighborhood? What about the people there?"

Jose ignored the question. "I'm going to ask you to hand over your weapon and armor."

"Like hell!" Hank barked.

Glen lowered his firearm to the ground and put up his arms.

"What are you doing?" Hank exclaimed.

"Complying." Glen dropped to his knees and rested his hands on top of his head.

Dr. Lambert smiled and shook his head as if the situation were a big joke. He mimicked the convict and got to his knees.

Frozen in fear, Katie waited for Kora to act.

"Really? You're going to do this to us? What happened to loyalty?" Kora asked.

"Just hand over the weapons. Don't die for nothing," Martinez replied.

His daughter was the only one who showed sympathy for Kora. The rest of the gangsters were apathetic or angry.

"You blame me, that's it," Kora concluded. "You thought that by joining me, you'd have the world, but now you have nothing. Even the Chinese will kill you on sight."

"You're testing my patience," Martinez growled.

Kora scoffed and tossed her AR in front of her. She pulled her pistol from her side and did the same. Wasting no time, she unstrapped her vest and lifted it over her head. She looked at the police insignia at the front before throwing it to him.

"Anything else?" Kora asked, too exhausted to give him any lip.

"His too," Martinez glanced at Hank.

"Over my dead body—"

"Hank! Just do it!" Kora's command shook him.

The patriot hocked a globe of spit on the road

before surrendering his weapon. The gangsters rushed in and claimed the armaments, vests, and medical bag.

"See you in hell, Kora Clark," Martinez said.

The flare fizzled out. Martinez and his people melded into the darkness.

Stripped of their most precious belongings, Katie wept. Hank held the pregnant woman, deep-seated anger burning his eyes.

Glen got off his knees and offered a hand to the doctor.

Lambert refused the help. "I'm not that old."

Displaying no emotion, the prepper said to Kora. "C'mon. We can get another six miles before daybreak."

"You screwed us, Glen. We could've taken them," Hank said, still holding Katie.

"If you want to survive, get used to losing." Glen re-ignited his torch and started forward.

Setting her jaw, Kora rolled Paul and continued down the street. Hank was the last one to follow.

By daybreak, their muscles ached. Stinky sweat soaked their clothes. Kora's boots squeezed her feet. Her greasy hair tumbled down the sides of her gaunt face. Her stomach made strange noises, and her tongue clung to the roof of her mouth.

Glen told them to stay back while he checked the gas station. The front door was locked. His eyes landed a chunk of broken asphalt by one of the pumps. Without hesitation, he pulled it up and hurled it at the glass. The impact sent shards of glass flying.

"Bon appétit."

It was a feeding frenzy once they got inside. Kora chugged two bottles of water before loading up on peanuts and beef jerky. They got grocery bags full of candies, snacks, and drinks.

An RV on the shoulder of the interstate was their shelter for the day.

At the little table, Katie tucked her hair behind her ear and said, "Since we're going to spend a lot of time together, maybe we should learn some things about each other."

"What would you like to know?" Dr. Lambert sipped a warm beer.

"How about first love?" Katie asked.

They chuckled.

"We're going there, huh?" the doctor replied and took a large swing. "All right, I'll start. Dr. Kimberley Swann, my professor in med school. She asked me if I wanted to earn some extra credit, and the rest is history."

Kora chuckled. "That sounds like an erotica plot."

"Now you know why I'm all screwed up," Lambert replied.

Katie asked, "Do you still talk to her?"

"Not really. Work became all-consuming after I graduated. She moved to Maine. I stayed here. A lot of my life has been standing around an operating table. Clark, before you get all sad about the people you let down, I can't tell how many surgeries I botched."

Hank said sarcastically, "Wow, Doc. Glad we can count on your expertise."

"Anytime. Who is next?"

"I'll go," Katie said. "My first love was a boy named Avery in grade school. We dated for two months before he accused me of eating bugs. He was just one in the long line of failed romances."

"Did you do it? Eat bugs?" Hank asked.

A coy smile grew on the waitress's pretty face. "A girl will never tell. You're up, Hank."

"Whelp…" the old patriot got comfortable. "I met my wife Angela when I was trucking out of El Paso. I was nineteen/twenty at the time. My friend of mine introduced me to her at church. A year later, we were walking the aisle. You should've seen her in that dress. She was the most beautiful girl in the world. The happiest day of my life."

"Aw," Katie said.

"We were married twenty-three years. We tried having kids, but it just wasn't the Lord's will, I guess. One night, she was coming home from grocery shopping and, uh, she saw this kid playing in the street. A car coming, some young guy not paying attention. My wife pushed the children out of the way, but… the EMTs said it was quick. She didn't feel a thing, they said."

"I'm sorry, Hank," Kora said.

"Yeah, well, you know, what can you do?" The old patriot finished his snack and left the RV.

Katie got up. "I'll go talk to him." She left.

Kora asked, "Any lost love, Glen?"

The prepper shook his head. "I was never good with women."

"Really? A resilient guy like you?" Kora teased.

Glen nodded. "I guess I wanted to work out my own issues before I dragged someone into my life."

"You have no one at all?" Lambert asked curiously.

Glen shook his head.

"I'd be lying if I said you weren't missing out," the doctor remarked.

"The cocaine-snorting doctor has dating advice for me. My lucky day," Glen replied.

Lambert glared at him.

Kora broke the awkward silence. "Paul and I have been together some time."

She squeezed Paul's hand. His one visible eye watered. Only a shallow groan escaped his lips.

"My parents didn't want me dating growing up," Kora explained, looking at her boyfriend. "However, when I met Paul a few years ago, I'd already moved out of the house. I remember him being so nervous when he asked me out. I'd never had that effect on someone before and thought I must really be someone special." Kora kissed his forehead. "Our story isn't that exciting. Just two people who like each other and seeing where the wind takes them... Well, that has not been the case since the EMP exploded."

Kora left out the part about considering leaving him

for the sake of the "cause." *If I did, he might've avoided these scars.*

They traveled by night once again. The vast Texas countryside was a welcome change. On the third morning, the group voted to travel by day going forward. They might have a higher probability of encountering strangers, but they'd move faster, and the major threats of the city were behind them. Paul was walking again, too. Lambert kept his bandages fresh from what little first aid they scavenged from various gas stations.

Mid-morning on the fourth day, they discovered a horse farm. The owners appeared to be missing.

"Have you ever ridden before?" Glen asked.

"A few times as a kid," Kora answered.

Katie and the rest shook their heads.

"I'll show you," Glen said.

Over the next two hours, he taught them the basics. They laughed, screamed, and had a blast trotting around the field. They snagged four horses for the six of them. Kora and Paul shared a white and brown spotted American paint horse, Glen grabbed a black Mustang, Dr. Lambert mounted an ash-gray thoroughbred, and Katie and Hank rode together on the chestnut-colored American quarter horse.

Kora felt guilty stealing the animals, but who knew when or if the caretakers would ever return. *Stealing is still stealing.* Her conscience annoyed her. She chose to ignore it.

It was their best day of travel so far. Despite the chaffing, Kora was getting used to their well-trained mounts. They crashed in a mansion late in the evening. The small towns in the surrounding area had imploded. The locals that didn't self-isolate were hostile, looting and attacking anyone they saw as a threat. Kora's crew chose to stay far away from any strangers. People were dangerous and unpredictable.

On the fifth day, they reached the woods.

Glen guided them to an unmarked dirt road. "The farm is a couple of miles inward. Tread carefully. We might not be the first one here."

"What do you mean?" Kora asked.

"Just keep up your guard, okay," Glen replied, not willing to share any more information.

Unarmed, they ventured into the unknown.

In the heat of the day, they reached the outskirts of Glen's property, and it was not what Kora was expecting. Marijuana plants extended as far as the eye could see. Security cameras—which were dead—were attracted to tall poles. Hunter's nests had been built into various trees but were currently unmanned. The wavy terrain was enclosed by woods. A few hundred yards past the millions of dollars in weed was a two-story cabin. By the size, it likely had three or four bedrooms. A clogged well, a broken down meat-curing hut, and a nearly collapsed shed occupied the area by the residence. Two men stood on the cabin's balcony.

They were too far away to make out anything more than their plaid shirts and cargo pants.

Glen gestured for the team to fall back into the woods. When they were out of sight of the cabin, he said, "As long as the property is occupied, we're not going to be able to secure it."

"You know those guys?" Dr. Lambert asked.

"My old crew," Glen replied. "I narked on them to cut a few years off my sentence. They must've been hiding out here when the bomb went off."

"I thought this was a prepper's hideout," Kora said, hands on her hips. "You never said anything about a weed farm."

"It's just a business," Glen replied.

"And I'm a cop."

"Not anymore, and I don't smoke my product," Glen said before addressing the party. "Even after the fall of civilization, those leaves will become a major bartering tool…. We just have to take it back. I have food and weapons stored up inside, too."

Katie fidgeted nervously. "Can't we just ask them to leave? It's your land, right?"

Glen answered. "It's no one's land…. Now, I know the area like the back of my hands. We can hunt wild deer, turkey, and more in these woods. The well, when we get it working again, will get us a fresh supply of water for drinking and showers. The hunting towers make for excellent lookouts. And lastly, only those men and I know the location of the property. If we act smart, we can spend the winter here without any issues."

"I don't like it," Hank complained. "We can go anywhere and have a lot fewer issues."

"I don't know *anywhere*; that's the problem," Glen replied, stroking his graying beard.

Lambert said, "Let's vote on it: who wants to stay and stop the brigands?"

Glen and Katie put up their hand.

"And who is opposed?"

Hank and Paul put up their hands.

Lambert and Kora exchanged a look. "I'll leave it up to you; I'll vote whatever you do," the doctor said.

Kora looked the way of the farm. She thought of all of her failures. Her actions had led to a series of losses she never thought possible. The world continued to spin on its axis indifferently. Hidden anger bubbled in her heart. It was a disdain for the world. For her life. *Screw it all.* "We'll take the farm," she said. "Tonight."

"That settles it then," Dr. Lambert said.

The party went off trail and hitched their horses by a small creek. Glen had Katie fetch sticks. He had intended to sharpen them into spears. Bitter but silently, Hank opted to survey the area. Dr. Lambert joined him. Kora stayed back and helped set up camp. They didn't have many supplies, so she had to use the natural elements to make a shelter and a small fire.

Paul assisted her, though he moved slowly and

couldn't do much. "Why?" he asked, his voice soft and broken like an old man.

Kora was surprised to hear him speak. She placed rocks in a circle around the soon-to-be firepit. "Just because…"

Her boyfriend's said eyes lingered on her.

She said more, "Paul, we need to look out for ourselves. If Glen is right about this place, then I might be able to get some rest."

"But you'll have to hurt people."

"Just scare them away," Kora replied. "It can't be worse than what I did at the police station."

"That was necessary."

"Was it? Knowing how things turned out, was anything we—I—did justified? Say that to the dead fathers and mothers, to the kids from your halfway house, and to all the others I lead to their deaths."

"You did your best," Paul said, falling into a coughing fit.

"It wasn't good enough," Kora mumbled spitefully.

Lambert and Hank returned in the late afternoon. They counted only four men, and all hung around the house. Though they were armed, it didn't seem they were diligent. Hank believed the party could sneak in the early morning without being seen.

"I like that plan," Glen replied. "Once we're inside, we disarm them as fast as possible."

He gave them each a spear.

"Very primitive," Lambert said, his dark sense of humor starting to shine.

Glen taught them all about how to hold and thrust the weapon.

"Keep it close to their squishy parts. Groin. Neck. etc. A quick kill is much better than a lingering injury."

"Debatable," Dr. Lambert remarked.

"Trust me, we don't want to be spending all of our medical supplies treating the people who are going to want to kill us," Glen replied.

Kora was reminded of a vague rendition of her father's words. *The way you treat your enemies is the judge of your character.* She had pushed it into the back of her mind since she had taken the police station. Reminded of the values she had lost, she opened her mouth but did not have the courage to protest Glen. *You've gone too far already. What difference will it make?*

Stuffing her hands into her pockets, she took a walk through the woods in hopes of clearing her mind. Her principles waged war against her the moment she was alone. It was easier to make morally gray decisions in a position of authority. Ends-justifying-the-means and all those other traps everyone thinks they'll never fall into. Feeling alone, abandoned, and in the wilderness, what excuse could she make to give her soul peace? What pretty cause could she conjure to hide her lust for vengeance against the world? Light-headed, she steadied herself on the coarse bark of a tree.

She wanted to vomit. She wanted to scream. She wanted to kill. She wanted to hide. She wanted to cry. She wanted to hear that things would be okay and believe it. *Where is my faith?* Her soul was in a cave. Paul could not help her. She had ruined the poor man. Katie was aimlessly following them like a living ghost without purpose. Hank had still believed they'd return to the fight. Dr. Lambert, the enigma, was their most useful ally and stayed only because his old world was in shambles. And, Glen, as helpful as he was, would forsake them in a heartbeat if they proved to be burdensome. Kora's perception of these people convinced her that none would aid her in overcoming her sorrows.

We're a team, but we aren't family. Kora ground her teeth. She hated that Martinez was right. She hated it even more that the gangster had robbed her blind.

The morning came, and with it, fog. Spears in hand and moving like panthers, the rugged band of survivors passed through the marijuana fields. The moon was still visible, and the sun had barely awoken. Upon reaching the house, they split into teams of two. Paul and Kora moved around the back. Hank and Katie moved toward the side window. Lambert and Glen headed for the front door.

Now out of sight from the rest of their team, Kora and Paul tried the backdoor. It was unlocked, much to their surprise. The door made a sticky sound as it popped open and quietly creaked as they parted it just enough to slide through. The inside of the house was a pigsty. Drugs, clothes, empty bottles, and trash littered the floor. Navigating the kitchen was like walking through a minefield. Her fingers curling around the wooden spear's shaft, Kora stayed behind Paul. Despite his slower speed, he insisted on going first. They peered into the living room.

A husky man wearing baggy clothes snored loudly on the couch. His face was down in a pillow with drool pooling around his plump lips. He had a farmer's tan to rival any old good ol' boy.

On the recliner, a dark-skinned man was passed-out, hugging a bottle of liquor. Kora couldn't account for the other men Hank had reported.

Paul moved to the one on the couch while Kora went to the one on the recliner. Meanwhile, Glen and Lambert were sneaking upstairs. Hank and Katie stuck to the halls, searching their various rooms and basement.

Kora moved the point of her spear against the man's tattooed neck. The tip caused his skin to crater slightly, and the man opened his groggy eyes.

"Don't. Move," Kora warned softly.

The man's eyes widened as far as they would go, and no sound escaped his slacked jaw.

Paul awoke the other man by prodding his throat. Both of the thugs stayed silent.

A few moments later, Glen and Lambert were marching a prisoner down the steps while Katie and Hank brought one up from the basement.

"Glen," the husky man said in his low, gravelly voice.

"Carver," Glen said, smiling. "You thought you'd never see me, huh?"

"You slimy bastard—"

Glen interrupted and commanded the party. "Get them downstairs. There is a cell waiting for them."

14

SPECIAL

$\mathcal{T}$he four prisoners were locked into a small storage cell in the prepper's basement. Kora felt as though she were re-living San Antonio all over again. Back upstairs, she suggested to the party that exiling the captives would be the easiest course of action.

"They will return," Glen replied. "And though you don't hear them complaining now, they are a vengeful bunch."

"I'm not going to repeat the same mistakes. He releases them today," Kora said.

The party devised a plan. Using pillowcases and ropes, they covered the prisoner's heads and bound their wrists. Kora became numb to their pleas as they marched the strangers deep into the woods. Glen took them down a series of unmarked trails seven hours away from the property. Though it was a grueling hike,

Kora couldn't fault Glen for being too careful. He threatened his old running mates, saying that if they returned, then their heads would sit upon the spears.

They reached the edge of a soft cliff, loosened their ropes, and kicked them down. Shouting, the men tumbled into the wilderness. Quickly vacating the area, the party took the long hike back. Glen concealed their tracks from the rear.

"Do you think they'll survive out there?" Katie asked.

"They're going to have to learn," Kora replied.

Paul kept his opinion to himself.

A wry smile grew on Lambert's face. "Look at us now. From heroes to bandits."

No one laughed at his joke.

At nightfall, they arrived at their conquered home.

Apart from the storage cell, there were shelves loaded with supplies in the basement. Canned foods, MRE rations, ammo crates, and more were there for the taking, and with the six of them, it wouldn't be hard to ration when needed.

That night, they had pre-packed stew around a little campfire. Seated in a circle, they basked in their victory. Glen brought out a guitar and played a little tune. Katie sang along, revealing her hidden talent. Kora could imagine the woman on a large stage, over-looking thousands. It was another future gone.

"Kora," Lambert said, breaking her stare. He handed her a joint.

The former cop refused.

Lambert handed it to Hank. The old patriot shook his head.

"Wow, no one but me?" The doctor took another drag.

There was a strange calmness tonight, one Kora didn't trust. Over the last few weeks, her constant busyness had made her forget what it meant to rest. Her mission to reach the cabin and remove its occupants was strangely easy. Now what? *Just listen to the music*, she told herself.

Katie sang of large pastures, fading suns, old lovers, and new beginnings. There was a rhythm to the music, but words seemed to only mean something to the waitress. The rest of the party nodded along until it was time to sleep.

Early in the morning, Kora arose from her bed upstairs, walked quietly through the hall, and opened the balcony door. Glen was seated on a rocker overlooking the farm. A carbine rifle rested across his lap. It was the few weapons he had in the basement.

"I thought I'd be the first one up," Kora remarked, hoping to spend the morning alone.

Glen gestured for her to approach.

She reached the balcony railing and saw where the prepper was pointing. A family of deer walked through a patch of the grassy field by the sea of pot plants. The eight-point buck, two fawns, and a beautiful doe ate from the earth.

Kora saw Glen mindlessly wiping his gun with a white dust cloth. "Are you going to shoot them?"

Frowning, the prepper shook his head. "Not if I don't have to. As much as I enjoy hunting for sport, I only kill what I'm going to eat. It would be cruel to the young ones to take down their father just because."

Kora envied the simple animals. They didn't have to worry about tomorrow. The earth provided everything they needed. As long as they stayed out of sight from predators, they'd enjoy a pleasant life in the quiet woods. An aching pain shot through Kora's fingernails. She realized she was digging them into the railing, almost breaking her short nails.

"Glen, I'm... I'm sorry," she said, not turning to face him.

"What did you do?" The man asked suspiciously.

"I didn't listen to you. Back in the city," Kora replied.

"Oh," Glen relaxed. "There's nothing to be sorry about. I'm just happy we made it out."

"I shouldn't have dismissed you," Kora admitted. "I thought I could control everything. I thought that if I just did the right thing and said the right words, every-thing would work out."

"Now you feel unrewarded for your labor?"

Kora nodded. "Yeah, something like that."

"Punished," Glen said, strangely friendly.

Offended, Kora twisted back to him. "Why do you say it like that?"

"You're trying to make sense of it all. *Why me? I thought I was doing everything right? Look what happened.* You make it seem like this world owes you something. It doesn't. The same rain that falls on you is the same rain that falls on Martinez, kind old ladies, kid-diddlers, and saints. It's just how nature works."

"If that's the case, why do anything? Why does anything matter?"

Glen shrugged. "Don't know. Ask a priest."

Kora pinched the bridge of her nose. "I had plans. The supply lines. The people. Yet, how could any of that stand against an army of trained killers?"

"Exactly," Glen replied. "You bet against the odds."

"I tried. I really did. I was even ready to die for it."

"You still bet against the odds. Look at this from a logical standpoint: they have better guns, better people, better supply chains, and better skills. You could not have won."

"There could've been some way to overcome. I'm sure of it."

"Not logically. You gambled, Kora. It was a hell of a gamble. Something heroic. Something most people would be too terrified to even attempt. But still, it was a bet, and you lost. So, you can cry all day, or you can learn from it and move on."

"Okay. I'll just move on. Great. Easy. Wow, thanks," Kora said sarcastically.

Glen replied, "Don't get all in your emotions. None of this is personal."

"It's the future of our nation. It affects all of us."

"Not out here. We're alone. If the Chinese win, they have a million other problems than finding this place. If the rebels win, the same story. We get comfy, crack a few beers, and live like that happy buck down there."

Kora directed her gaze back at the deer, but they had already left.

Glen groaned as he adjusted his posture. "Have a seat in the other rocker."

Shoulders slumped, Kora did so.

Glen locked into her eyes. "You're special."

Kora raised a brow. "Are you hitting on me now, Glen?"

"Let me finish," Glen replied. "You're special, but in the same way that everyone is special. Unique fingerprints, eyes, story. But that doesn't mean you're the center of the universe. Your little actions in your little city in your little nation are just one of the billions of stories playing out all around us. It's the same thing for the foreign army that rained on your little parade. And one day, someone bigger than them will come in and do the same. That's just the way it works. Sure, you can fight against the machine like the few who make it into the history books. Or you can focus on your own crap, carve out your little spot on this world, and die old and content."

"But is the second option really living, or is it just survival?" Kora asked.

"To me, it's living. But to you, it might be hell.

You've got too much ambition. You find your reason for being in shooting for greatness. Most people find it in security and simple things."

"What's your point?"

"You gotta figure this stuff out yourself. Everyone will give you their opinion, but only you are in charge of your actions."

Kora pondered his words as she rocked gently. Unsure what she wanted, she left Glen alone and started cleaning the house. Yesterday's long hike made her realize just how weary her body was, but she wanted to do something to occupy her thoughts. As she filled up trash bag after trash bag, the rest of the team rested. It was the first day without some grand adventure or clearly defined goal. Kora couldn't bring herself to settle.

She walked the property at midday. Despite the copious amounts of marijuana, there was no vegetation garden. She happened upon a plot of ground that appeared to have been one years ago, but she'd need to clear out the stones and till it if it were to them any good.

The well was partway collapsed and full of dirt. If they didn't want to live off rations from the basement, they'd need to fix up the place.

In the later part of the day, when everyone decently rested, Kora gathered them around a table. "I don't know a thing about farming," she started. "I can shoot, but only been hunting once as a kid. What I'm trying to get at is that I have a lot of learning to do if we're going to thrive here. What about the rest of you guys?"

Hank said, "My cousin owns a ranch. I've done a little animal husbandry during my time with him, but working the ground is a different story."

Kora replied, "Okay, great. We'll put you in charge of the horses unless anyone has objections."

Dr. Lambert chimed in. "Why don't we take the week off before we start assigning jobs to everyone?"

"If we want this place to work for us, we have to work on it. We'll have ample time to relax when the daily chores are taken care of."

"You sound like my mother," Dr. Lambert pulled out his little vile of cocaine.

"And that has to stop," Kora added.

Dr. Lambert snorted anyway. "Sorry. It was an accident."

Kora decided not to press him. His supply would run out soon enough, and then he'd have to learn to cope.

From her consensus around the table, no one had great survival skills outside of Glen. He considered himself a jack-of-all-trades, master-of-none. He offered to teach people, but it would be up to them to hone their skills.

Paul, still injured, was given lookout duty. It was the most boring of all the jobs, but necessary if they did not want to be ambushed.

Katie was placed in charge of supply management and cooking. Her first job was to label every item in the basement and make sure they knew what they lacked. Once they started getting vegetables, she'd have to make sure they were cleaned of dirt and stored someplace where they wouldn't go back.

"I'll show you how to package our product, too," Glen said.

It took Katie a moment to catch on. "But, why?"

"Future transactions."

No one protested. Anything and everything was a tool now. Kora chuckled inside. *What is life? How did I turn from police chief to drug dealer?*

Dr. Lambert's medical expertise was invaluable but not needed daily. He'd look after the marijuana plants and help out when major projects needed to be completed, like the well. The doctor was not satisfied with his role, citing he should stay free in case one of them were injured. The party did not approve of his laziness and put him to work.

Glen took on a teaching role but was primarily going to be their hunter. He knew how to track wild game and shoot better than all of them.

Kora was put on gardening duty. She would also be a project manager. Believing that a good leader leads, she would be working on multiple tasks at one time. Kora was fine with that. It gave her somewhere to channel her ambition. The others didn't like the idea of having a centralized authority. That was until Glen decided to step up. Though he wouldn't be spending much time around the house, it seemed everyone was more comfortable having him lead from afar. Kora didn't try to change their minds. *Don't take it personally. He has more supplies more skills, and this is his home.* Her ego was bruised, but she forced herself to be humble. Her contribution to the party's good would not change. She had only lost having the final say in various matters. *Get over yourself, Kora. You blew your chance in San Antonio.*

Glen made the rules simple: stay honest, work hard, and look out for each other.

"And no petty crap. I won't tolerate it," he added.

Settling in to their task over the next couple of days proved to be challenging. The tools were old and fragile. Glen had used them for years, but wear and tear made basic tasks harder than they needed to be. The supplies in the basement would only last them three months before they'd need to be replenished. Even the seed bags were low. Despite Glen's stockpile, he had not intended to feed six full-grown adults and four healthy horses.

The simple truth was that even the most thorough preppers had their blind spots. He also only had only a few boxes of ammo. Training would burn through most of it. They'd have to rely on Kora and Glen if they entered combat.

After doing some work, they realized that the well was unsalvageable. They'd have to transport water from the nearby streams until they figured out a solution.

Hank was bitter about everything, constantly reminding Kora in private that they should be in the real fight. He also wanted a stable and fence for the horses. Having them walk free was too risky. There were a few mornings he had to go a few miles to find and bring them back after they had run off.

As for Paul, he despised lookout duty. He spent most days in one of the many hunting nests and felt completely useless. Without security cameras, he was the next best thing to a security system. Thankfully, his wounds were healing.

Dr. Lambert ran out of coke and entered into withdrawals. On top of that, his attitude devolved into bitterness and depression. The mood swings made him a pain to be around, and as the party ignored him, it only worsened his attitude.

Katie was prone to having panic attacks when she thought about bringing her child into this world. She worked hard, but once the supplies were fully counted and labeled, she started to slack on her housekeeping tasks and cooking. Hopelessness was the unseen killer.

Glen told everyone to get over their personal issues. He spent most of the days in the woods. He would return whistling. Some days, he'd bring back edible plants and dead rabbits. He one time brought back a coyote he'd shot. No one had any complaints against him, but he wasn't leading.

"I taught you what I know. Now, do something with it," Glen would say. "If you want to live free, you have to work hard."

Kora kept her head down and her hands busy. She spent hours removing weeds, rocks, and breaking up tough dirt. In her downtime, she'd read about gardening in one of Glen's survival books.

In the evenings, the party played cards or reminisced about their old lives.

Hank had some of the best stories. The trucking career he had mentioned previously was just the tip of the iceberg. The old patriot had had a wild youth. He was a high school prankster, a wheeling, dealing used car salesman, and one time spent a whole year traveling the country in a rugged camper.

Paul tried to draw nearer to Kora. She smiled at his jokes and listened to him talk, but she struggled to look at him after the bandages were removed. The tissue on one side of his face was coarse and distorted. The explosion had caused the corner of his eye to droop and put a permanent grimace on his lips. It wasn't his ugliness that intimated her, but the fact that she was the cause of it.

On the ninth day, late in the evening, Kora awoke to the sound of the creaking floor.

Keeping her covers pulled up to her chin, she listened. Slivers of moonlight spilled through the window blinds. The soft glow hardly illuminated anything in the dark room. She sensed the presence of someone moving through the bedroom door.

"Paul?" she whispered.

Silence.

Kora reached for the matchbox on the nightstand. She pinched the little stick and struck it twice before the fire ignited. In a moment, the husky man was upon her. She yelped, but the stranger's dirty palm silenced her cry. The knife's cold edge kissed her throat.

"Hey, beautiful. Miss me?"

15

THE BEAST INSIDE

*K*ora's heartbeat rapidly, and goose bumps rose across her body. The husky man—Glen's old partner she'd pushed off a cliff —held her life in his hands. He reeked of sweat and mud. His scrappy beard matted around his fat jaw and fatter neck. The weight of his body crushed her.

"You're going to be as quiet as a mouse. Can you do that for me?"

The white of her eyes showing, Kora nodded. The blade scratched against her throat.

The man removed his hand from her lips and wiped the spit on the thigh of his dirty jeans. "Is it still just the six of you?" he asked.

Kora nodded.

"Thought as much," the husky man said. "Get up. Slowly."

Kora sat up. Her covers fell away, revealing her

tank top and boy shorts. The husky man kept the knife on her as she slowly scooted out of bed. A firearm had been stored in the side table's drawer, but she wouldn't be able to reach it without slashing her neck.

The soles of her feet touched the cold floor as her mind came to terms with the harsh situation. The moment she stood, the husky man violently twisted her around and placed the knife against her neck.

Leaning against his obese figure, she was slowly directed out the bedroom door. There was a second bedroom upstairs that belonged to Paul. The door was sealed, and a chair had been placed under the doorknob.

"One step at a time," the husky man whispered, his soul breath assaulting her nose.

Trembling hand on the stair's handrail, Kora descended. The front door was wide open. Everyone else in the house was asleep or dead. She had no way of knowing.

There was an expectation that Glen would pop out and stop the guys or that Kora would find the leverage she needed to escape her capture. It was all fantasy. The man had the upper hand in every way, and screaming would cost Kora her life.

He led her out to the marijuana field. She walked a skinny dirt trail. The chilling air brushed against her thin figure. The man kept breathing down her neck.

Kora mustered the courage to speak. "Your name is

Carver, right? That's what Glen called you when we arrived."

The husky man stayed silent.

"I'm Kora. Listen, I'm a cop and—"

"Shut it." The husky man's crude voice silenced her.

She attempted to steal a peek at the house, but the man kept her focus forward. The house must've been half a football field's length away when they entered the woods.

Sharp twigs and little stones pierced Kora's soles. Prickly branches scratched against her arms. The knife was still closely held against her throat. The edge of the blade had nicked her, and the smallest teardrop of blood trickled down her chest.

A mini-campfire flickered in the distance. Faint whispers sounded behind the breeze.

"Please," Kora tried one final attempt to beg for her release.

"You're annoying," Carver groaned. "Keep walking."

Kora entered into the twenty-foot clearing where the campfire burned. The three other dealers from Glen's past life stood nearby. Dirt and sweat had ruined their clothes. They wielded old knives and hammers. It appeared to be stuff they had stolen from a tool shield. Katie was bound to a tree by an old rope.

"You got back quick," Carver said to his skinny, black companion.

"In and out, baby, that's how we do it," he replied.

Carver stomped the back of Kora's knee. She yelped as she collapsed to the forest's floor. Her knee struck a rock. Throbbing pain shot up her entire leg. She lifted her watery eyes and saw the men flanking her from all sides. The fire bounced off their weapon's tarnished metals.

Carver asked the others, "Do we have any more rope?"

"No, we're gonna use something else."

"Then find something," Carver replied and directed his attention to Kora. "Here is how this is going to work: you stay put and keep your mouth shut. Come morning, when your people realize you're gone, we'll make a nice trade. If all goes well, you and your friend will walk away."

"And if they refuse to give up?" Kora asked.

The man's eyes darkened. "Then we take you far, far away."

One of the men left and returned with a bundle of thorny vines. "Will these work?"

Carver glanced over them. "Just make sure they're tight."

"Hands behind your back," the man told Kora.

She did so as the man tightened the binds around her wrist. One vine was thin enough to break, but he had a couple of dozen. Their sharp points bit into her skin. She muffled a cry behind closed lips. When her wrists were bound, the man grabbed her from under the arm and dragged her to Katie.

"Move from that spot, and I cut you," the man warned. "I don't want to hear a peep, either."

The women exchanged worried looks. Katie was hopelessly stuck. Kora felt she could break the binds if she tried hard enough. Every movement, however, drove the thorns deeper into her skin.

Carver kept his eyes on them as the men gathered around their fire.

One of the thugs said, "We could've killed them when we were inside."

Carver slapped the back of his head. "And damn ourselves to hell? We want the property and the stuff. That's all. Hear that, copper! We don't want any problems. If you respect us, we'll respect you."

"They already left us to die once," the black man groaned.

Carver said, "We have leverage this time. If anything goes wrong, nothing is off-limits."

Is he bluffing? Kora wondered. Leaning against the tree, she pulled at the vines. She felt her skin shred and had to stop before the pain contorted her face. If they discovered she was trying to escape, only God knew what they would do. *Two defenseless women. Four men with criminal histories.* Kora's imagination took her to horrible places.

"Kora," Katie whispered.

"Hey," the black man shouted. He rose from his log seat.

Katie stammered. "Sorry, I—"

Smack!

He struck her across the cheek. The pregnant woman started crying.

"Waterworks don't work on me," he said.

The fourth man walked over to them. He was a burly fella with a thick drawl. "Let me teach her a lesson."

By the tone of his voice, everyone knew what he was implying.

"Screw you, man." the black man shoved him. "We ain't going down that road."

"And who's going to stop us?" the man replied.

"Almighty God," Carver warned, holding the hilt of his now-sheathed knife.

"Whatever," the fourth man returned to fire. He sat in the way to watch Kora. She knew the type of thoughts going through his head.

The black man turned to Carver. "You need to cut it out with that God crap, man. You've been non-stop about it since the blackout."

"It's more than just a blackout," Carver replied. "It was a wake-up call. A grand reset to separate saints from sinners. God told me so."

"Yeah, after you took some LCD."

Carver didn't deny it. "He works in mysterious ways."

The men bickered for another hour before taking turns sleeping.

The fourth man and Carver stayed up first. Carver

pulled up a log and faced the girls a few yards away. The fourth man kept his eyes on the woods. Occasionally, he would turn back to face the girls and smile, showing his yellow teeth. The other two were in sleeping bags with their weapons nearby.

Kora would not take her gaze off her captors. Slowly, she twisted her wrists to and fro, slightly loosening the binds. Her palms and forearms were wet from sweat and blood. She reminded herself of her previous battles. *You survived that. You'll get out of this.* She forced herself to face the pain.

Meanwhile, Katie snored softly. The stress had knocked her out. Kora could see Carver was starting to nod off. If he were truly a heartless bastard, he would've already killed the people in the house and had his way with the women. *He held a knife to my throat in the dead of night.* Hatred brewed inside of her. Moral or not, the man was a threat. They all were, and Kora was a cornered animal.

The embers slowly died, and an unspecified amount of time had passed before Kora noticed Carver lowered his head. His rotund torso rose and fell in a steady motion. His hand fell from the hilt of his knife. *He's asleep.*

Kora pulled her wrists apart as hard as she could. She gasped in pain as a few of the threads broke. It was not enough to get free. However, the slippery blood made it possible to almost slide out though. *Just a little more.*

The fourth man glanced back, noticing her struggle and Carver's lack of response. He stood and drew out an old carving knife.

Kora froze.

The man playfully twirled the knife between his fingers as he softly approached.

One of her Kora's hands slid from the binds and then the other one. She kept them behind her back.

The man approached her with the knife pointed at her chest. He put a finger over his lips and knelt before her.

Kora hid her fear behind a fake sultry look. "I see… the way... you look at me."

The man brushed the point of his knife down her shirt. "Shh."

Inwardly terrified, Kora said, "Don't wake them."

"You little freak," the man whispered. The man glanced over his shoulder before moving closer to Kora. "Show what you can do."

When he was two inches from her face, she head-butted his nose as hard as she could.

Crack!

Letting out a cry of pain, the man recoiled.

Kora seized the knife from his hand and punched his throat a few times with it as the rest of the capturers jerked awake. The man gargled and spit blood as the others screamed curses.

"Are you crazy?" Carver swiped at her, missed, and took the knife in the eye.

He shrieked and tumbled into a tree, the hilt of the blade sticking out of his face.

The other two men watched in horror.

Blood soaked and feral, Kora grabbed Carver's knife from the ground.

"You're freaking psycho!" The black man sprinted into the woods while the other man swung his hammer at her.

She took steps back, narrowly avoiding his blows. Everything was instinct. All she could see was red. One mistake would be instant death.

The man swung at her head and hit a tree. Kora used the opening to stick the knife into his ribs. Howling, he dropped the hammer. She pulled out and stuck him multiple times in the belly before running after her final target.

Only able to see branches in the black of night, Kora had to guess where he was running. She could hardly hear anything over her raging heart and loud breathing.

"Aah!" the man screamed, followed by a splash of water.

Kora upped her speed. Raw adrenaline pushed her forward. She found the black man limping out of a little creek. The fall must've twisted his ankle. His back was toward her, but he heard her approaching.

"Just let me go!" he shouted as he continued his escape.

Kora leaped over the little stream and went after him.

"I swear, I want nothing to do with you," he said as he limped.

Kora drew back the knife and flung it at him. It twirled through the air before sticking in the back of his thigh. She was aiming for his back, but it worked. The man went down to his hands and knees.

Lifting a large tree branch nearby, Kora ran at him.

"Wait!" He turned back just in time to get hit in the face.

The hard impact caused Kora to fall next to her captor. She quickly scrambled to her feet.

Wheezing breath escaped his busted lips. "P-please…"

The darkness obscured the damage.

"M-m-mercy." He hacked up a few teeth.

Kora thought of all of her failures and mistakes and channeled them on this stranger. Taking the log, she hit him repeatedly until he no longer moved. She gazed at his corpse, a blank look on her crimson face. Katie's scream snapped her out of her daze. Kora followed after it. She arrived at the dwindling campfire a moment later

Katie sobbed. "Oh, my Lord."

Carver and the other dead men had driven her to panic. Silent, Kora walked around the tree and undid the ropes.

"I can't breathe," Katie said.

"You're in shock," Kora replied. "Stay calm." She got the ropes off her and extended a hand.

"Get away from me," Katie stood on her own and ran in the direction of the house.

Kora stomped out the fire and went after her.

Having heard the noise, Glen and the other men were out in the fields, armed and yelling their names.

"She killed them all," Katie shouted as she grabbed hold of Hank.

Glen and Paul rushed to Kora.

"You're covered in blood!" Paul exclaimed.

Glen locked eyes with her. "Let's get her to Lambert."

"Kora, you have to tell me everything," Paul said.

"They won't be a problem anymore," Kora mumbled. Her legs suddenly felt like jelly and tumbled.

Paul and Glen each caught an arm.

"Lambert, we need you!" Paul shouted.

"I can't do anything in the dark. Get her inside!" the doctor yelled from the porch.

Glen asked Kora, "How many are left?"

"None," Kora replied before passing out.

NEW LIFE

*K*ora saw the men she had killed standing around her bed. Then she awoke in a cold sweat. Her bedroom was cleaner than before she was abducted, and warm sunlight shined through the open windows.

She brought her fingers to her neck. A scab sealed the small knick. She held her wrists out before her. Gauze and bandages covered the torn flesh. It must've been worse than she thought, but none of her motions were impaired. There was just a stinging, hot agony she had to endure.

She faced the windows. Deep within her, she felt hollow. All of the principles her parents had implanted into her life from her earliest memories died in the woods. The hero cop, the bright-eyed rookie, the benevolent leader... she wasn't anything of those things now. She was not a survivor, either. She could have spared her enemies. She had done it before. She could've run, but she didn't. Despite her rage and despite the hopeless situation she had found herself in the night prior, she knew she was fully in control of her actions. She wanted to kill them. She wanted to feel powerful again. However, now that the moment was over, there was only bitter shame.

I am a killer. A hunter. A predator. She wanted to find strength in her new, self-imposed titles. Reality was a lot more complicated. These new names were brands on her soul. No amount of good deeds would wash them away. Her conscience wanted to help her escape. It told her that the men were going to violate her and Katie, and all Carver's talks about trading them for the property was a lie. The husky man had stopped his partner from raping her, though, and might've done so again if she had just screamed instead of breaking the man's nose.

The bedroom door creaked open.

Kora pretended to be asleep. *Paul, don't look at me. I'm not the woman you fell in love with.*

Footsteps stopped by the bed. "I know you're not asleep."

Kora rolled to face Glen. He was alone and wearing a camo outfit.

He handed her a water bottle. "How are you holding up?"

Kora took the water and chugged it down.

The prepper sat at the corner of the mattress. "Are you going to tell me what happened?"

"It doesn't matter. It's over now." Kora tossed the empty bottle aside.

"I mean to you."

"What about me?"

"You took down four guys two times your size. Katie thinks you must be a serial killer."

"I did what I had to do," Kora said.

Glen nodded respectfully. "You did the smart thing. Now the only people who know about this location are us. We'll be safe. We'll be able to build. Paul won't have to be on lookout duty every day."

"Whoopie," Kora said dryly.

Glen put his hand on her shoulder. "Get some sleep, Kora. You earned it." He lingered a moment longer before exiting the room.

Kora curled into a ball. She closed her eyes but didn't sleep. A few hours later, Paul came to visit. He was naïve enough to think she was resting. He kneeled by her bed and prayed. His words were too soft for her to hear.

Don't pray for me, Kora thought sorrowfully. *I'm not worth your time.*

The next three days came and went in a blink. Everyone but Katie visited her. The pregnant woman had seen "Kora, the killer" and couldn't scrub it from her mind. While she was tied to a tree, the supposed good cop was gutting men before her eyes without a hint of hesitation. Crimes of passion often put the killer in a state of blind rage, but Kora was cool, precise, and merciless. Also, Kora was completely silent and moved from victim to victim without a change in focus.

Growing tired of lying around, Kora returned to her gardening duties. Paul worked alongside her. He'd bring up old memories and ask her about how she was processing everything. Kora gave him short responses. After a week of him lurking around her, Kora told him she was going to help Glen hunt.

"Are you sure? There is still a lot of work around here. You were going to help Hank with the horse stable, too, and we've hardly even started getting the wood," Paul said.

"You two strong guys can figure it out," Kora faked a smile. She stood up from the garden.

"Kora," Paul replied sadly. "I'm on your side. Just let me in."

"I've already made up my mind." Kora left him by their barely spouting crops and asked Glen if she was around to hunt with him.

"We don't need two hunters," the prepper replied.

"If I'm going to survive long term, I need to know how to get my own food."

Glen could see through her BS but didn't say anything. He grabbed a hunting rifle from the stash in the basement.

"It's an old Winchester. If you take care of it, it'll take care of you." He handed her the scoped weapon.

Kora handled the weapon with care. She looked through the scope.

Glen put his hand behind her back. "C'mon. We'll get it sighted in the back."

He showed her the ins and outs of the weapon. They practiced shooting a few old tin cans before he gave her the tour of the woods.

The next two weeks went by quickly. Kora had hoped to have spent more time alongside Glen, but he didn't see the use of them both in the same nest. Two hunters meant they could cover two times the ground. He recommended only shooting small game. If they brought home too much meat, it would go to waste.

Hours slipped by as Kora moved through the woods. She'd listen to the sounds of birds singing and would sometimes spot a deer she was forbidden to kill. At night, she'd help Katie prep the meat as an excuse to stay away from Paul. He finally got the hint and hardly pursued her. Glen would sit next to her when they ate around the campfire. He would not talk much, especially about his past life as a criminal. Kora liked that about him. When he was around, she didn't feel that she needed to justify her actions or boast about her principles.

One morning, as they walked into the woods, Kora asked him, "You want to team up today? You could teach me a few tricks."

"You're doing fine on your own," Glen replied, walking a few paces in front.

Kora caught up to him. Her thumb held the rifle strap slung over her shoulder. "Aw, don't be like that. We could have a lot of fun." She playfully pinched his arm. "Are you afraid you'll be outdone by a girl?"

"No, there's just no practical reason for it," Glen said.

"It's only one day, and then I'll be back in my neck of the woods," Kora said, trying not to sound desperate.

Glen stopped walking. He turned back to the house that was many yards behind them and signed deeply. "Let's be honest here: it's not going to work."

"What? Hunting? We won't get as much today, but we've not been starving so far, so I don't see the—"

"You know what I mean."

Kora averted her eyes.

Glen crossed his arms. "We don't need a bunch of unnecessary drama. Yeah, it has been a few good weeks, but we're nowhere near where we need to be come winter. If we start forming a bunch of little love triangles, we'll lose sight of the bigger picture."

"Or maybe you're just afraid to get close to anyone? Afraid you won't be able to control it? Life is more than just stability," Kora replied.

Glen replied, "You're a beautiful woman, Kora, but this will cause more harm than it's worth. And unlike me, you and your boyfriend have a future outside of this blackout."

"In the old world, you might be right, but things are different now. I'm different."

"For a season, but not forever."

"You don't know that."

"I know you think we are alike, but we're not." He glanced at the sunrise. "We're burning daylight. See you tonight." He patted her back and went his own way.

Kora tasted gall. *What do you mean we're not alike? We both just want to survive and live free?* Annoyed, she traveled to her portion of the hunting ground.

A lot happened over the next few months.

The garden flourished and wilted as November's weather chilled the nation. Lambert, Hank, and Paul finished the horse stable and fence. It was built like a cabin with large interlinked logs and had a stall for each horse. Through a lot of hard work, the well had been repaired but only had a little water. They still relied on spring water for their daily needs. They'd also boil it first and then let it cool before using it.

Once packed with food, the basement shelves were now the storage place for thousands of pounds of marijuana. They were down to a measly few cans of soups and a stack of military rations. Ammo supplies got so low that Glen and Kora had to resort to bow hunting.

They carved their own arrows, which were insufficient at long range. Kora trained herself to move silently toward her prey and take them out from a couple of dozen meters away. Spending most days alone in the woods, she had perfected her craft.

Katie's belly was as big as a balloon. She was open about wanting a relationship with Paul, but he refused her, still having feelings for Kora. She gravitated toward Hank, who viewed her more as a daughter than a potential lover. The old patriot still spoke of going back to San Antonio to finish the good fight but never made any effort to do so. He mostly looked after the horses and played cards when anyone was willing.

Dr. Lambert smoked weed most days and read Glen's survival books cover to cover. He became a well-spring of useful survival knowledge but was a lousy worker. After suffering a minor wrist injury while building the stable, he said he needed to "pre-serve" his surgeon's hands. Despite being the highest qualified, he took the longest to complete anything.

Glen seemed the most comfortable in the daily rhythms. He had reached his goal of living off the land completely and had no intention of aiming for more. Just like the buck they saw when they had arrived, the prepper was living his dream and happily weathering the seasons. It appeared he had no interest in love, and finding a wife and kids was something he never spoke about.

Paul made many attempts to draw near to Kora. Unfortunately for him, she felt very little for him or anyone else. Instead of becoming the family she had hoped the party would be, everyone treated each other like old roommates. They'd all bicker about little things, but there were no life-threatening conflicts or disagreements that couldn't be worked through. No one mentioned leaving, either. As winter neared, they all knew it would be beneficial to further unify. Katie was desperately looking for someone to help her raise the baby when it arrived, and Paul's kindness propelled him to become a de facto caretaker. They expected the birth to happen at the start of spring. He made it clear to Kora that there was nothing between Katie and himself.

On Thanksgiving morning, Kora woke up before dawn. She put on her worn-down jeans, an old T-shirt, and one of Glen's oversized hunting jackets. Her boots were caked in mud, and the rubber at the bottom was about to peel off. She put her long hair into a ponytail, grabbed her bow and quiver, and headed outside. Her features were lean like a coyote. A strict diet gave her sunken cheeks and keen eyes. It didn't help that she dreamed of dead people every night.

Glen was waiting for her on the porch. His camouflage outfit had faded. The darkest shade of green was as light as olive. His bushy beard covered most of his face and formed an edge at his collar. He had shaved his greasy brown hair a week ago, and now light stubble covered his crown. He had lost weight but increased his muscle mass. The trials of nature had sculpted him into a hunter.

A chilling breeze swayed most of the dying crops and marijuana plants.

"Today is a special day," he said, blowing into hands.

"I guess so," Kora replied. She wondered how her parents were faring. This was the first Thanksgiving she had spent away from them.

"Chin up," Glen said. "Let's hunt something big today."

"I thought you said that we only kill what we can save and eat."

"Normally. But I think a little competition is in order. You know, to prove who is the better shot."

Kora smiled slightly. It had been months since she had fully grinned. "What does the winner get?"

"Bragging rights."

"Deal." Kora shook his calloused hand.

"See you tonight." Glen grinned. "Oh, one last thing. You hunt on my side of the wood this time. I'll hunt on yours."

"I imagine this part where you tell me all your secret spots."

"Not a chance.

"Worth a try. Good luck," Kora winked.

Stepping into any woods was like stepping into her home. She had grown used to trees, odd noises, and isolation from other people. Walking deer trails and following creeks, she had a hard time missing the city. The world's wild beauty was nothing compared to mankind's concrete jungles. The ecosystem was rich with diversity, and there was always another secret to be found. She had discovered smooth rocks and strange bugs, little caves and tall trees, and even an eagle's nest. She had trained her feet to move in silence and her senses to pick up the slight detail. A smell, a sound, the glimpse of movement at the corner of her eyes were what separated a full belly from an empty one. Her ambitions had shifted away from grand things to the daily hunt. She was more of an animal than a woman, it seemed.

Deer droppings pointed her deeper into the woods. The unknown always frightened her. She continued forward, alert and ready. She drew her bow and kept an arrow notched on the string. She expected to find a person out here someday and was ready to do anything to keep their little home safe. She'd even practiced the different lies she'd tell the others after she'd eliminated the unfortunate soul. No strangers had entered her woods, though. It was for the best.

A buck appeared between distant trees. Kora stayed low and out of sight. The large animal chomped on the grass. It was unaware of her presence, but that could change with one mistake. Kora traveled from tree to tree until she could see the animal clearer.

It had beautiful fur and a regal appearance. Its tall antlers silhouetted against the rising sun. Kora recognized the animal. It was the first she had seen when she arrived. Its family was elsewhere. Now was the time to take the shot.

Kora pulled back her bowstring. She focused on its heart. In the past, she would've hesitated. Not now. She loosed the arrow. It struck the large beast. The buck ran a few yards before collapsing. Kora slung her bow back over her shoulder and pulled out Carver's knife.

She hurried to the animal. She wanted to ease its suffering. The deer breathed rapidly. Fear reflected its gentle black eyes.

"Sorry, bud."

She put the knife into the animal, killing it quickly. Despite the great prize, it didn't feel much like a victory. The adrenaline rush was nothing like killing a man. She lifted her eyes, seeing a doe and her two grown offspring. The animals seemed stunned. Flashes of the Alamo echoed in Kora's mind as well as her old words. *"I did everything right."* The invaders were merciless, nonetheless.

She moved slightly, and the deer fled.

What if this was my final moment? She wondered. *One moment, sitting on the grass and the next dead. Was my survival so valuable that I should kill others to keep it? All I've built, how I trained, does it mean anything? Does it have any value outside of "bragging rights?"*

Kora leaned on her palms. The last few months had helped her embrace what she had done, but instead of moving forward with this acceptance, she was stuck. She had no goals, no children, no love, no faith, nothing to keep her going forward but the hunt. Now that she had her biggest win but what she had was more of the same: a hollow pit.

These were feelings she couldn't express in the old world. Where so many found their identity in value in their doing, what about just existing? Was that valuable? Was that worth killing for? Supposed Kora survived to a hundred years old living how she was living now. What was the point? Was it God's grand design for her to hide in the woods the rest of her days? When her father preached on the purpose, was this what he'd had in mind? What about helping people? Making a difference? Building something that lasts beyond her? Is that possible now?

"Jesus," she mumbled as the existential walls shattered around her.

I have to get up, she knew. *Even if I fail, I must move forward. I cannot—I will not—stay here.*

She stood to her feet. It was a sense of purpose that drove her to fight for San Antonio, and she thought that her drive would be enough to see her through. It was not. But now, she could be smarter and use her limits to her advantage. This time she would not fly by the seat of her pants. She knew the price she had to pay: a life lived for something bigger at the cost of safety, comfortability, and her ego. Tonight she would tell the others… even if it meant going alone.

17

THE SEARCH FOR SOMETHING MORE

*I*t was a chilly night, so they sat in the dining room. A hodgepodge of candles was squeezed together in the center of the table. Their multicolor waxes dripped and pooled around their base.

"I have to commend Kora," Glen said as he bit into the fresh meat. "She not only got the bigger buck but got it in half the time as me. I think it is safe to say that she is the better hunter. At least for now."

The table clapped.

Kora replied, "I just got lucky, that's all. If we never switched sides, I would've been the one congratulating you."

Hank snipped a glass of cool water. "Seeing how it's Thanksgiving, I say we go around and say something we're thankful for. Who wants to start?"

No one replied.

"You start," Paul told the old patriot.

"Hmm," Hank rubbed his chin. He had kept his goatee short. "For that little one." He raised a glass to Katie's belly. "He's going to be a strong man one day, just like his mother."

Katie blushed. "How do you know it is a boy?"

"Call it a gut feeling." He chuckled as he patted his belly.

"Okay, I'll go next," Lambert said in his monotone voice. "I'm thankful for family, friends, this dinner, and all the other generic stuff people say every year. And no, you are not allowed to copy my answer."

Paul replied, "That was weak. Say something you are genuinely thankful for."

The doctor groaned. "All right. Not having to care about bedside manners."

"We wish you did," Paul said.

"You wanted honesty." Lambert returned to his plate.

Paul lowered his fork and looked into Kora's eyes. "I'm thankful to be alive and for God's plan to get us out of this mess."

Glen said, "And I'm thankful *for* the mess. Otherwise, I'd be in a six-by-eight concrete cell. Also, I'm thankful for Kora for letting me out… even though she locked me up in the first place…"

Katie smiled innocently. "And I'm thankful to be safe. Kora saved me… twice. And, both times, it was…

what matters is that the baby is safe. So thank you, Kora, for showing up."

Time must've washed away her bad perspective of Kora.

Paul looked at her. "You're the last one."

The table waited for Kora's reply.

She cleared her throat. "I'm thankful for you guys and our time together. But... I don't think there is an easy way of saying this... I'm leaving soon."

"*Leaving* leaving?" Katie exclaimed.

"Where to?" Hank asked, ready for the next big move. "San Antonio?"

"Maybe not the city. Just somewhere I can make a difference," Kora replied.

"But you make a difference here," Paul reminded her.

Kora said, "There are a lot of people in pain, and with winter coming, the death toll will be astronomical."

Dr. Lambert remarked, "We have to focus on ourselves. That said, I believe opening up a few trade routes would be beneficial to all of us."

Kora continued, "Finding a bigger community with ambitious goals is what I had in mind."

Glen said, "You assume such a place exists."

"And why not? I can't be the only person who wants to see our country restored," Kora argued.

Glen replied, "You underestimate mankind's selfishness. The harsh cold coming in the next couple of

months is going to further exasperate their desperation. There will only be three types of people out there:
the prepared, the hungry, and the dead. And the hungry
will be more dangerous than any gangbanger or soldier
you'll ever meet. History shows us that mothers will eat
their own babies to stay alive."

The thought sickened Kora. "I know it seems like
the timing is bad, but…" She realized she didn't have
much of a logical argument. Her heart and complete
lack of purpose were driving her. "I just need to get
out," she completed her sentence. "And to make sure
I'm not leaving you guys stranded, I'll help you out
with a final supply runs. That will give me a good look
at the surrounding area, ya.

Hank said, "Count me in."

Katie lightly grabbed his arm. "Are you going to
leave with her? What about helping me raise the baby?"

The patriot's countenance sank. "I'll… I'll just go on
the supply run."

"And you, Paul?" Katie asked.

"I don't know yet," he replied. "This is a lot to think
about."

Kora addressed the table, "Listen, staying here is
probably our safest bet. I know this. You know this. So,
please, do not follow me unless you want it as badly as
I do."

"There is something you're not considering," Glen
said.

"And what is that?" Kora asked

237

"If someone follows you back here, all of our lives will be in danger. You need to be careful," Glen warned.

"We'll do a supply run first, just to see. If we don't find a lot of people, I'll reconsider my leave," Kora promised.

"Fair enough," Glen replied and returned to his meal.

After dinner clean-up, Paul pulled Kora aside and asked if they could talk privately. She invited him into her room.

"You should stay," Kora said preemptively.

"I promised I would support you wherever you went."

"What we have is over, Paul. You understand?"

Paul said, "I've noticed, but I still don't get what I've done wrong. You've been dodging me for months. I never knew that there could be such a lack of communication in a small house. Can you at least tell me what I've done wrong?"

"Nothing, it just won't work."

"Is it my face? The scars?"

"No."

"Then what?"

"You don't want me, Paul. I'm not the girl you asked out anymore."

"You look like her. You talk like her. You're still you. Nothing has changed."

"Everything has," Kora raised her voice. "I ruined your life. I've killed people."

"We've been over this many times before. It was for survival," Paul justified.

"I wish that were true, but I choose my path. And I have to live with it, not you."

"This journey is not just about you, Kora. No one's journey is. You made mistakes. I forgive you." He took his hand in his. "Let's just go forward. Together."

"Paul…"

His eyes watered. "I'm tired of being alone, aren't you? You know I'll be loyal. You know I can provide."

Kora withdrew her hand back to herself. "I'm a dangerous person; you deserve better."

"Who says I want better? I want you."

"Please, it won't work. I know it won't."

"Tell me what I need to do to prove to you I'm serious."

"Your seriousness is not in question. You need a good woman. Someone who won't drag you down. I'm not her," Kora replied sternly.

"Like it or not, I'm coming with you."

"Why? I just said we have no future."

"Because I love you," Paul said.

You foolish man. Kora sat on the corner of her bed. "Look, I gotta get ready for tomorrow."

"Crack of dawn?" Paul asked.

Kora nodded.

"Okay, I'll see you then… I love you."

"Goodnight, Paul."

Sorrowful, the man left.

Kora wanted until she had locked the door before letting her emotions show. Crying silently, she sat at the foot of her bed and hugged her knees close to her chest. *What does he see in me that is so good? Is he stupid enough to think love can change the past? I led you into a death trap, Paul. I'll do it again, most likely. You'd be better off staying as far away from me as possible.* She wished she could've been this concise with her thoughts when they were arguing.

Lying awake into the late hours of the night, Kora still could not process why he would love her. If the roles had been reversed and he was the one who led San Antonio to its grave as well as scorching half of her body, would she still stay loyal? Logically, no. From a place of love, though… maybe.

Kora's father had taught her there were different types of love in Greek.

Eros was romantic love. It was the type most people associated with the word. Kisses, stomach butterflies, and the general attraction to another person. The greatest issue with eros was that it could easily be considered lust. Maybe great people have said they *loved* someone but were just sexually drawn to them. They then wondered why their marriage lost steam after they grew older.

Philia was a friendship love. It was purely platonic and chosen freely.

Storge was a familial love, like a brother to a sister or father to son. It came from a familiarity.

Lastly was *Agape*. Unconditional love. God's love.

Kora did not know which she felt for Paul. At one point, eros. Now, a weak form of philia. He seemed to show agape to her. *Is there even such a thing?* Kora believed there was at one time. Now, her failures blinded her to it. The walls of the room seemed to close in. She wanted to run away to people who didn't know her. She wanted a fresh start. Tomorrow could not come fast enough.

She was already dressed and armed with a pistol and bow before first light. The gun was one from Glen's collection. She only had one spare magazine. Relying on archery would be the play if she entered combat. The arrows could be retrieved, and she was confident in her marksmanship.

Hank, Dr. Lambert, and Paul were waiting for her downstairs.

"Wishing me goodbye?" Kora asked.

"Joining you for the supply run," Hank corrected. "After you went to bed last night, Glen offered to stay back with Katie until we returned."

"Make sure your backpacks are light. We'll try to get as much as we can in one trip," Kora explained.

Glen and Katie stayed behind. They were apprehensive about the trip but knew they could not sway the soon-to-be scavengers.

Hank, Lambert, Paul, and Kora mounted their respective horses. The early morning wind nipped at their noses as they exited the property. By mid-morning, they were out of the woods. It was not long before they reached the first neighboring farm. They rode the horses up its gravel driveway and knocked on the door. Without a reply, Paul used a pry bar he had brought along to bust open the entrance.

The room reeked of death. An elderly couple dangled from nooses on the rafter's beam. Below their feet were tipped over bar stools and an envelope.

Covering her mouth, Kora opened it and read the contents within. She glanced over her shoulder at her shaken team and gave them a summary. "It's to their children and grandchildren. They apologized and said they did want to starve to death."

Hank grimaced. "The bodies don't look that old."

"A week and half-ish," Lambert said objectively.

"God forgive them," Paul mumbled.

After all the death Kora had witnessed, she felt numb. *Dead is dead*. She thought she could not get conditioned to such horrors, but repetition has a way of making the unnatural natural.

They searched the cabinets, pantry, basement, and attic. There was no food, water, or weapons. The dead husband had a nice toolset in the garage, but it was not practical to tote all that dead weight around when their journey was just beginning.

The next two farms were occupied by dead elderly people, too. Lambert said they had been dead for months. Though was hard to determine an exact cause of death, it was likely a heart attack, a lack of medication, and starvation. Their farmland was largely undeveloped. Despite having acres, most didn't have even a modest vegetable garden.

The average rural dweller was no prepper. Unlike the people who traveled the Oregon Trail, most modern landowners had land just for the sake of it, instead of using it for survival or leaving an inheritance for their children. In return, when society collapses, children have little incentive to seek out their parents. One of Kora's greatest fears was to grow old without a purpose. If she was not using her life experience to help the following generations, what activities would consume her time? Games, TV, useless debate?

One of her father's greatest lessons was always bringing value to people, even if it was unrewarded. One act of kindness or one word of wisdom could alter a person's entire existence. It first produced a snowball of change in their personal life, then close friends and family, then to colleagues, and into the community. When the community was disrupted by a valuable idea and unhypocritical action, the change could be nation-wide. *This is just another reason I need to get off of the farm. I will not waste any more of my short life cooped up in hiding.*

The fresh zeal carried her to the nearest town. It had a simple name like *Limebrook or Lemmings*. Kora didn't pay much mind to sign as the place was a ghost town. The few convenience stores and gas stations had been gutted of all their wares. Business and houses alike were abandoned.

Hank found old shell casings on the sidewalk. "Looks like something drove everyone out."

"Where are the bodies?" Paul asked.

"Found something!" Lambert shouted from behind a building.

Still, on horseback, the others followed to the baseball field and piles of charred corpses within.

"There are dozens!" Paul exclaimed, galloping closer.

Lambert looked over the disfigured bodies. "It's old. Probably from last month. See, most of the remaining flesh is nearly gone."

Paul trotted around the pile. "I don't see any kids. There are not a lot of women, either."

"Modern-day slavers," Hank growled.

Paul's scarred face turned ghostly pale. "You really think so?"

"Yeah, son. Evil is universal. It could be bikers or gangsters. Maybe even the Chinese army."

"But why didn't they come to the farms in our area?" Paul asked.

"If they're following a map, they would know there are no towns that way," the old patriot replied.

Dr. Lambert looked at Kora, "I know it's noon, but we should head back. I'd rather not meet whoever did this."

"We haven't found any supplies," Kora replied. "What about establishing trade routes?"

Lambert replied, "If our options are Pol Pot or no one, I say we ration our way through the winter."

Paul said, "If they took the children, we have to do something."

Hank nodded stoically. "I agree. Hard justice is the only way forward."

Lambert replied, "Cool it, Rambo. This fire was set weeks ago. They could be halfway across the state. The weather has done away with any tracks they have left behind. And say we do find them? If we aren't shot on sight and managed to save the starved children and their impregnated mothers, what food can we give them? Do we bring them back to the farm for the winter? Even if we had the space, Glen would never approve of that."

Hank and Paul were silent.

Lambert continued, "If we all learned one thing from our time in San Antonio, its heroism is great until it's put into practice. Say a little prayer for them, Paul, and then we'll move on with our lives."

Paul ground his teeth. Hank cursed under his breath, knowing the doctor was right.

"We'll keep point anyway," Kora declared.

Lambert sighed deeply.

Kora squeezed her horse's reins. "Not for the slavers, but to find supplies and settlers as we originally planned. We have plenty of daylight to reach the next town over. Mount up, Doctor, and let's go." She turned her steed around and started down the road.

The men eventually followed after her.

They visited a few properties along the way. The houses were ransacked, and owners were either dead or gone. It was difficult to imagine that less than six months ago, everyone here was just going about their normal lives.

Kora and her posse froze at the sight of the next town. As if scorched by napalm, every building, car, and street were blackened by fire.

They traveled down the quiet roads, finding charred bones and the remains of a survivor settlement. Vehicles had been pushed around a hotel to form a blockade. Wooden sniper towers lay in ashy heaps. The various hotel entrances were sealed by melted chains. The arsonists had trapped the residents inside and set the place ablaze. They did the same to the whole town.

Hank said, "It's a warning to everyone around here. *If you build, we will burn you down, too.*"

Lambert glared at Kora. "You still think coming out here was a good idea?"

"If this is the country, imagine what must be happening in San Antonio?" Kora thought aloud. She thought about the children Paul used to look after. Their paths would never cross again.

"You ignored my question," Lambert said.

Kora's shoulders slumped. "Fine. We'll do a final

sweep through the town and look for a place to camp out for the evening. I don't want to travel back in the dark."

The team agreed. They slowly combed through the various buildings, but everything that wasn't looted was burned beyond recognition. Whatever faction had done this must've been large. How else could they have swept the place so clean? Near sundown, they moved into a small home a half-mile from the town. It had been previously looted but not set ablaze. They shut the blinds and sealed the front door. For dinner, they sat around the table and ate what few rations they had brought from the base.

The small meal reminded them of how desperately they needed supplies. Sure, they could survive through the winter by intense rationing, but no one enjoys an empty stomach.

Kora let the men have the rooms and took the first watch. Using a candle for light, she drew her arrows from her quiver and whittled their wooden points. After each arrow, she plucked the point against her finger to make sure it was sharp enough to kill.

The floor creaked in the hall. Kora jerked in that direction and aimed her bow. It was Paul.

"You don't have to stay up alone," he said as he joined her on the couch.

"I wouldn't get much sleep anyhow," Kora admitted.

"Nightmares?"

"Always."

Paul put his arm around her shoulder. "It's not always going to be like this. People will rebuild. China will need to do something if they want to profit off their plundered land."

"Maybe. Defeating the American empire was enough to put every other nation in submission. They could keep us in the stone age as a warning to the rest of the world."

Paul groaned. "I hope not… Anyway, I just want to commend you for coming out here."

"We didn't accomplish anything."

"Not yet."

Suddenly, there was a noise in the restroom. The two of them stood. Armed, they moved through the hall and pushed open the restroom door. The window was open. Paul went to the closed shower curtain while Kora headed for the towel closet. She put her bow aside and drew her pistol. Readying herself to shoot, she pulled open the door at the same time Paul scooted aside the curtain. The towel closet was empty.

"Kora." Paul had his gun aimed at a kid's head.

The boy had bug-like eyes and a sunken frame. A horrible stench hung to him like a cloud. His sweater was tattered, and dirt marred his sweatpants. A backpack was slung over his shoulder. In his right hand was a small knife.

Paul lowered his gun. "Kid, are you okay?"

The boy froze in terror. His legs shook lightly. Fear

and trauma oozed behind his horrified countenance. His mouth hung agape.

"Kid?" Paul gently pried the knife from his fingers. "It's all right. We're not going to hurt you."

"F-food?" the boy pleaded.

Kora grabbed an MRE bar from her back pocket and handed it to Paul. She asked the kid, "Are you alone?"

The boy nodded as he consumed the bar like a ravenous animal.

Kora turned to the window. *It could be a trap...*

"What's your name?" Paul asked softly.

Still chewing, the boy dropped the wrapper. "Water?"

"Kora, could you?"

She shut the window and grabbed a bottle from the living room. She returned to find Paul speaking comforting words to the child, but the boy seemed not to answer any of his questions. He gulped down the bottle in seconds and tossed it aside.

"How old are you?" Kora asked.

"S-seven."

Paul asked, "And why won't you tell us your name?"

"Cause, if they find you, they'll find me," the child replied. "Do you have more food?"

"They?" Paul asked.

"The bad men," the boy replied. "The others said they would stop them, but they've not come back."

"The bad men burned down the town?" Kora asked.

The boy confirmed her theory. "They took the other children. Mom, too."

The news turned Kora's stomach.

Paul said, "And you've been alone this whole time?"

"Sometimes a stranger gives me food, but no one wants me," the kid replied.

Paul's heart broke. "That's horrible."

Kora stayed on task. "Who are the others you mentioned?"

The kid's eyes lit up. "They have guns. And a base. I wanted to follow them. They said they would send someone to me."

Kora stroked her chin. "And that was how long ago?"

"Days, I think." the kids said, unsure. "Can you take me to them? I won't cause you trouble. I promise. Please? Pretty please? It's so cold out here."

The fact that the boy had survived this long defied logic, but it was for this very reason Kora left safety. She agreed to help the boy. Paul was glad. They let the kid sleep on the couch. Kora and Paul took turns watching him. The extra food they had given him had knocked him out. Being so malnourished, it was a shock he kept anything down.

The next morning, Kora persuaded the others to help the boy find the survivors. She assumed that whatever home camp these strangers had created was not far away. Eating the remainder of the rations, they left the house and the burned town behind. The child rode on Kora's horse. His little arms wrapped around her torso as she galloped into unknown territory.

The surrounding farmlands had been abandoned, and the remaining livestock was forced to fend for itself. Hank had suggested bringing a few cows back to Glen's place. If they could keep the animals alive through winter, they'd have plenty of milk and meat come springtime.

Chilling wind and an iron-gray sky gave their trek a dower tone. Kora, though wishing to be alert at all times, was entrapped by her worries. Caring for the skeletal child could prove to be her greatest challenge. She'd have to make sure to feed him, clothe him, and keep him from getting sick. A serious cold could ruin them if they were not hygienic. Speaking of which, Kora was glad that Glen had a stockpile of toothpaste in his basement. If she weren't brushing and flossing daily, her teeth would've been yellow, black, or rotted like the little boy.

Paul pointed to the road up ahead. A blockade made from junk wood and crashed cars barred the journey forward. Spray painted across a plywood sheet nailed on the front of the makeshift wall was the phrase: "Shiner Territory: Trespassers will be Shot."

"What's a Shiner?" Hank asked no one in particular.

Dr. Lambert stopped his horse. "I'd rather not find out."

Kora glanced back at the boy. "Does that name sound familiar?"

The kid shook his head. "I-I don't think so…."

Paul said, "I say we investigate."

"And get ourselves shot or enslaved? Brilliant," Dr. Lambert replied.

Hank grumbled. "There's no way of knowing if they're the ones who burned down the town."

"If we want trade routes and supplies, this is our best shot," Paul added. "Kora, are you up for it?"

Kora was glad to see Paul taking the initiative. "Lead the way." She gestured.

They got ten feet from the barricade before seeing the line of armed men poke their heads out from behind the wall of junk. Wearing matching black ski masks and armed with a mix of rifles and shotguns, the strangers stopped them dead in their tracks.

"We're not here to cause any trouble," Paul said with his hand on his weapon.

The armed men stayed silent. Their fingers rested gently on their weapon's trigger. A single miss-said word or the slightest sneeze could cause a blood bath.

Kora carefully removed the police chief badge from her belt, not taking her gaze off the masked men. She held it up. "My name is Kora Clark. I was acting chief of police in San Antonio. We're just looking for this kid's parents. Can you help us?"

The boy peeked his head out from behind Kora.

The armed men seemed alarmed at the sight of the boy but kept silent.

Heart racing, Paul said, "That's Dr. Lambert, MD, to

my right and my good patriot friend Hank to my left. I was a youth counselor before the collapse. We're not bad people, and we're not asking for any handouts, either. We just want to find the kid's parents. If you can't help us, then we'll—"

The masked man spoke in a slow, menacing tone. "Turn around and go home."

Paul said, "Listen, we saw what happened to the last town over. We're not those people, okay?"

The stranger's weapon stayed trained on Paul's heart.

Lambert joined the conversation. "If you're injured, I can look after you. If you need supplies, we can trade. The kid's parents are just a plus. That's about as transparent as I can be. Interested in business or not?"

"As trade partners?" the masked man asked. "You don't have much on you."

"We have hundreds of kilos of cannabis and other basic survival stuff, but I'd be an idiot to lug that along with me. Let us talk to your leader, and we'll work something out."

"Wait here." Three of the masked men vanished behind the wall. The other two kept their eyes on Kora's posse.

The tense silence was something Kora would never grow used to. Thankfully, she had become adept at hiding her worry behind a natural expression.

The masked men returned and presented their terms clearly: only Kora and the boy were allowed access behind the wall. The other men would have to wait by the barricade until they returned. Also, Kora would have to enter unarmed.

Their reply annoyed Lambert. "I'm the one in charge of our team's trade and negotiation. It should be me going."

"This is the way it is. Take it or leave it," the masked man said.

Kora gave her weapons to Paul and dismounted her horse. "Stay on guard."

"I know," Paul replied. "If you're not back soon, I will come for you. I swear on my life. Hear that! If even one hair on her head is missing, we're going to have a big problem!" The burn scars on his face added to his intimidation factor.

The masked men, though silent, heard his warning and nodded soberly.

Taking the child's hand, Kora climbed the barricade and followed one of the armed men toward whatever their base may be.

"I'm Daniel, by the way," the boy said.

"About time you told me your name," Kora smiled, trying to appear brave.

"I wanted you to know in case the bad men get us."

Kora's heart sank. "Stay close to me, okay? I'll protect you."

It was an hour-long walk to the ranch's dirt road. The wooden cattle fence surrounding the *Shiner's Ranch* had been extra fortified with scrap wood, barbed wire, and wood spikes jutting in the direction of any would-be climbers. Twin sniper towers flanked either side of the large wooden gate at the property's entrance. Whoever had designed the security had been pretty long before the EMP. For such precision craftsmanship to be completed in the last couple of months took people with tested skills and keen knowledge of guerilla warfare.

"Are you army?" Kora asked the gunman.

He gave a strange gesture to snipers. A moment later, the gate opened. Silent to Kora's question, he signaled for them to enter first.

Inside was paradise.

18

THE CALVARY

*F*amilies gathered around bonfires, hardworking men raised the walls on a new barn, children played tag across the vast fields, and people buzzed around the small village of campers far in the distance, enjoying simple lives.

Kora had not seen a community so amazing since visiting Martinez's neighborhood. *There must be at least two hundred people living here.*

"What is this place?" Kora asked,

"Home," the masked gunman replied.

There has to be a catch. No place can be this perfect. Where are the skeletons buried? Where is the id *to the* ego? Kora squeezed Daniel's hand tighter.

The starving boy was enthralled by the other children's mindless games. Kora pulled him along. *Sorry, kid. No fun. Not yet anyway.*

Suspicious gazes followed them to the mansion's

front door. Museum paintings covered the entrance hall's walls. The guards inside asked them to take a seat in the vast visitor lounge. The antique furniture was well persevered and clean. Pleasant warmth radiated from the fireplace. Kora was a peasant in a king's castle. Her clothes were mismatched and worn for practical purposes while everything around her screamed luxury. The owner was clearly a collector of the finer things in life.

Footsteps thumped in the hall. Kora sat at the edge of the couch. She replayed her close-quarter-combat training in her mind and prepared herself for anything. A familiar man entered.

Kora stood immediately. "No way! Shultz!" She ran and embraced the short and stocky cop.

"Whoa, at least buy me dinner first," Officer Shultz replied jokingly in his gruff tone of voice.

Kora pulled away from him but kept her hands on his upper arms. Her eyes darted up and down the clean-shaven man. "I can't believe it's really you."

"Likewise," the grumbling cop replied, a small smile appearing on his face. "Have a seat."

"Right, yeah." Kora lowered herself next to Daniel. "Seriously, man, what the hell happened? I mean, what are the chances?"

"The world grows smaller every day, Clark."

"You can say that again."

Shultz explained, "After I left the station the day of the collapse, I got the hell out of San Antonio."

"I remember." *You abandoned me, but it was probably for the best,* Kora thought, still having no peace from her past failings.

"I have some relatives that live in the area, so I made the hike. My family and I ran out of supplies in the first two weeks, so we started a little scavenging party with our neighbors. About three or four weeks ago, we found *Shiner's Ranch.* They needed able-bodied men. I was willing to work. That's the long and short of it anyway. How about you? How did you end up here?"

Kora sighed deeply. "I tried to fix things in San Antonio, but it backfired. One of the inmates I was holding, believe it or not, had a place just a few miles away. I've been there for months."

"And where is your place exactly?" Shultz asked.

"Oh, it's just—" she stopped herself. *I'm saying too much.* "Well, it's not far."

Shultz's eyebrows narrowed. "You don't trust me?"

The masked man stood at the entrance to the lounge.

"It's not that. Just a lot has changed since that first day. I've changed," Kora replied, mindless rubbing the thorny rope scars on her wrist.

Shultz's eyes glazed over as he nodded in agreement. "Yeah. All of us have." He snapped out of a painful memory. "Who's the kid?"

"Daniel. I found him yesterday in a scorched town not too far from here. He said his mother was taken and some people promised to help him find her. I was hoping it was you guys," Kora replied.

"The ones who burned the town?"

"No, the helpers."

"I know. I was joking," Schultz replied flatly. "But, no. We don't send people that way anymore. Whatever strangers made him that promise are probably gutted on the side of the road."

"Shultz. Please, the kid's listening."

Shultz turned his gaze to the kid. "Gutted, as in dead."

"Dude," Kora nudged him.

"What? No use lying to him." The former cop leaned back in the recliner. "My guy says you're interested in bartering. What do you got?"

It annoyed Kora that he changed the topic so quickly. "We can talk about business later. Tell me what's going on here. What is this place? Who built it? Who are the people that razed the nearby town?"

Shultz replied, "Easy, Clark. I'm not saying anything until I know it's worth our time."

His remark annoyed her. "I didn't know you were so mercenary."

"Comes with the territory. You should be thankful that you even got far. If not for the kid, we probably would've sent you away at the barricade. Forcefully, if necessary. Now tell me what you're offering."

Kora huffed. "Marijuana."

Shultz chuckled before realizing she was serious. "You're just full of surprises."

"It's not what I asked for, but it's what we got."

"I wonder what Garrick thinks of this."

A sudden pain struck Kora's heart. "Garrick's gone, Shultz. All of them are gone. You and I are the only ones I know of who got out of San Antonio."

Shultz cursed under his breath.

Kora said, "My people are looking for a trade alliance. Personally, I'm tired of hiding from the world. I want to do something that makes a difference. That's why I'm here."

"So you want to join us?"

"If what I see is legit, yeah. I can't speak for the rest of my crew, though."

"How many are you?"

Kora replied, "Just a handful. One of our people is a doctor. He's willing to offer his services in exchange for goods. The rest are trained for war as well as gardening—am I making this worth your time yet?"

"A little," Shultz stood. "I'll tell my higher-ups what you're offering, but I can't guarantee anything. The only way to keep things so nice around here is being very selective in who we let inside."

Without answering any of Kora's questions, her old friend left her with the masked gunman.

Daniel sniffled. "I want my mom."

"One thing at a time, sweetie," Kora replied.

The little boy rested his head on her lap.

Shultz and another man returned a little while later. The outline of the bulletproof vest could be seen under the stranger's winter coat. Likely in his sixties, he had professionally cut silver hair, a clean-shaven face, and thick glasses. A Glock was strapped to his hip, and the man exuded a certain "hyper activeness" not seen in many his age.

"Officer Clark. A pleasure." The man extended a hand. His shiny gold wedding ring reflected the fireplace's glow.

Kora shook his hand. "Glad to be here, sir."

"My name is Mitchel Gray Shiner. What you're looking at is my family's ranch."

"It's an amazing place, sir."

Mitchel smiled proudly. "Made it from selling pillows of all things. One of God's great ironies is that a guy like me would become the refuge for hundreds."

Very humble, Kora kept her sarcastic remark to herself.

"We're supposed to use our unrighteous mammon for the good of all. So the last, gosh, twenty-two years I've been storing my *grain* quote-unquote for such a time as this."

"Your preparations paid off," Kora flattered him.

"Shultz told me about your product," Mitchel said, switching into a business mode. "I'm not interested. God smote this country down for tolerating such vice once. I'm not going to put Him to the test again."

"I see..." Kora said, disappointed.

"*But*, a doctor's services are always needed, and I'm more than happy to take in an officer of the law if you adhere and enforce our rules."

"Which are?"

Mitchel met his eyes with hers. "What I say is the law."

"Rather intense," Kora laughed nervously.

"I'm a fair man. That's why I was chosen for this righteous assignment. Mind you, I would never tell someone do something morally apprehensible. Let me rephrase that: I won't have you do anything that compromises your integrity or the integrity of others."

"Good to know." The man's ego made Kora uneasy.

"It *is* good. And goodness is in short supply these days. So if you, the doctor, and the kid are interested in joining, I'll let you, but only under the conditions that you fulfill the roles you are assigned, and you surrender your goods."

"Just give up all my earthly possessions, and I'm in?"

"When you say it like that, it makes me look like the bad guy. I'm not the one in search of a home. That's you, and if you pay the price, you're welcome."

"What about the rest of my crew?"

"How many do you have?"

"Just a few."

"Give me an exact number."

"Ten," Kora lied. "But not all are interested."

"Too many. I'll take one aside from you, the doctor, and the boy. And that's it."

"What about your *righteous assignment*? I would think you need all the people you could get if your neighbors are burning down villages."

The comment caused Shiner unease. "So you've encountered *them*?"

"*Them*?"

"The godless marauders who came up from the south a few months ago. At first, they were just high-waymen, but now I hear they're building an empire. Hence, why we can't allow everyone inside. They could have spies."

"Did you ever encounter them yourselves?"

"I spotted a large band of them a few weeks after the EMP. They were recruiting bad men, enslaving the children and women, and killing anyone who got in the way. It takes a special type of person to commit such atrocities, so I'd have to say whoever is in charge is fully demonized. I keep my territory well-guarded enough. That deters any attacks."

"You have the means to stop them if it came to that, right?" Kora asked.

"The best war is one you don't have to fight," Shiner replied. "I will not kick that hornet's nest unless there is no other option."

Daniel spoke up. "They have my mom."

The air was sucked out of the room.

Shiner looked at the boy with pity. "There is nothing I can do."

Kora bounced her gaze between Shultz and Shiner.

"As long as these marauders run free, more women and children are going to get taken."

"It's not our fight," Shiner replied.

Shultz nodded in agreement.

Kora felt a righteous zeal burn inside her. "Someone has to stop them. They can't be allowed to continue."

Shultz said, "Clark, you came here to make a trade, not start an unnecessary war. Why don't we work out our business arrangements and leave this mess for someone else?"

"Like you did in San Antonio?" Kora replied. "People needed us, Shultz. We were public servants. Cops. We failed there, but that doesn't mean we need to fail here."

"You're being emotional," Shultz replied.

"Yeah, I am! This kid's mom is being violated as we speak! And you have the means to stop it, but instead, you collect stupid art and hide inside of your perfect ranch."

Shiner repeated sternly. "It's not our fight."

"Then whose? You think help is coming? Our nation is occupied. We, the normal everyday people, are the cavalry. No one is fighting for us. If we don't act, these monsters will continue raping, killing, and burning whatever they please."

Schultz glared. "Is this the real reason why you came? To persuade us to join a crusade?"

"No, I sincerely wanted to trade and find this kid's mother and a home for myself, but the longer I stay in this perfect comfortable place, I can't help but think of all the people who are suffering because of our inaction." Kora turned to Shiner. "I believe they call that a sin of omission, Shiner."

The rancher stood in silent conviction.

Kora got to her feet. "I'll get my people, and you get yours, and we take the fight to the devil. When it's finished, we can rebuild together."

Schultz seemed confused. "Why on God's green earth would we risk our lives for a war that doesn't affect us?"

"Have you listened to a word I've said? You're a cop. If this injustice doesn't burn in you like in me, perhaps it was best you left behind the uniform."

"Careful, Clark. I can be short-tempered," Schultz warned.

"Good, channel it toward the enemy." Kora then addressed Shiner. "I'm going back to my people now. Enjoy your holy huddle; I'll be finding a way to prevent this evil from spreading."

The rancher said nothing.

Kora took Daniel's hand and left the mansion and its fancy furnishings behind. Stepping out of the ranch was like leaving heaven. Security, safety, and community were within her grasp, but she couldn't accept. Her convictions were too great, her need to help the helpless burned too bright, and the hollow pit in her dark soul cried out for redemption.

She found her posse waiting anxiously by the barricade. They had questions, and Kora gave them answers. She told them the place was good and had a lot of long-term stability. She also told them that the leader would only accept Dr. Lambert and the kid. The rest would have to find a way to earn their trust.

"Whelp, I guess that settles it," Hank replied. "Back to Glen's."

"Not me," Lambert said, smiling coyly.

"You're going with the Shiners?" Paul asked.

The doctor nodded. "And I can't say I'll miss you guys. Good luck with everything. And, Kora…"

"Yeah?" she asked.

"In case I don't see you again, please try not to get yourself killed," the doctor responded.

Kora hugged him and wished him the best.

Paul said, "I guess it's time to get home, then."

Hank agreed.

They mounted their horses and began the slow trot back to the cabin. They took a longer route home, hoping to discourage anyone from following them.

Glen was stationed in one of the hunting towers when they arrived. He yelled at Katie to get dinner going. By the time the horses were stabled, their little vegetable and venison stew was bubbling in the pot above the campfire.

Glen eyed Kora suspiciously. "The doctor is gone, and you've brought back a kid."

"Very astute observation," Kora replied sarcastically.

"I trust you know what you're doing," Glen said.

Kora addressed the rest around the fire. "I'm not staying."

"Did you find a place?" Katie asked.

"I found an enemy. The people who took this kid's mother seem to have this area in a vice. I aim to stop them. I don't expect any of you to join me. I only ask that you watch over Daniel until I return."

"That sounds like suicide," Katie replied.

"Maybe, but I'd rather die doing what is right than to sit around while time wastes away," Kora answered.

Hank asked, "Why didn't you tell us your plan when we are on the road?"

"Because I didn't want to involve you in something you didn't believe in." *I made that mistake in San Antonio.*

Paul lowered his soup bowl and took Kora's hand. "I promised you I'd go wherever you go. Frankly, I'm terrified, but if you want this, I'll be by your side."

Kora was amazed the man would still stand by her after everything she'd put him through.

Katie said, flustered. "No, not me. I can't. Not be with the baby. Paul, please stay. We need helpers around here."

Hank spoke up before Paul could answer. "Cheer up, girl. I'll stay with you and the baby."

Katie hugged the older man. "Thank you, Hank."

Hank gave Kora a look. She could see in her eye that the old patriot wanted to join the fight.

"You're making the right decision, Hank. This

nation will need men like you when it is time to rebuild," Kora replied.

Hank said, "If—sorry, *when*—you get through this, and you decide to take the fight to the Chinese, I'll be by your side."

"If this works out, we'll go. I promise." Kora smiled at him. *I guess it's just Paul and me.* "How about you, Glen?" she asked.

The prepper's eyes watered. It was his first real show of emotions Kora had seen in him. He said, "You have everything you need here."

"I know. And I'm grateful you allowed me to stay," Kora replied. "As well as everything you taught me."

"You don't know the enemy's numbers."

"My only goal is to cut off the head of the snake," Kora replied. "I'll rescue the prisoners after. Once I have them, I'll return them to Shiner's Ranch to get help. I will figure out where I want to be after that."

"You make it sound easy," Glen replied.

"You don't think I can pull it off?"

"Not many could," Glen said honestly.

"Will you help me, then? Katie and Hank could look after the cabin and Daniel while we're gone."

Glen thought about it. Instead of answering, he took the leftover dishes from everyone and headed to the wash bucket. "I'll let you know in the morning."

Paul said, "I'll get our supplies packed. Glen, do you mind if we have a few weapons?"

"Take what you need."

With the prepper's blessing, Paul headed to the basement. Kora spent the final night with Daniel, Hank, and Katie. They laughed, prayed, and said their final goodbyes.

The howling winter winds kept Kora awake. At sunrise, frost crystallized the window and grass. Just leaving the bed felt like stepping into a tub full of ice. Sleepless and cold, Kora thought about forsaking her mission and going back to bed. Life would be easier, Paul could relax, and Daniel could acclimate to his new home. *What are the chances his mother is still alive anyway?* Kora stopped that train of thought before it went too far. She had spent months doing nothing but hunting and living for the sake of it. Not anymore.

She dressed warmly and re-sharpened the arrows in her quiver. She regretted not having brought back any supplies from their scavenging trip, but without Lambert, Paul, and herself, the party would be able to extend the rations much further.

Stepping out onto the balcony, Kora looked over the property a final time. The woods had taught her their way. She could hunt animals as well as man, and it would be needed as she searched the countryside of the marauder's base. Stealth and shadow were her greatest allies. And, unlike San Antonio, she would not have the burden of caring for others during this venture. Destroying evil was her only directive. She made an agreement with herself not to rescue anyone until she'd decapitated the snake. *As long as the weed lived, it would continue to grow.*

The door opened and closed behind her, and Glen joined her by her side. Bearded and scruffy, the prepper eyed his frosted fields and the trees beyond. "I know I won't change your mind," he finally said.

"Sometimes, I wonder why I continue to choose the hardest path possible," Kora admitted.

"It's because you don't see what is. You see what can be. Most people don't let themselves dream. It's much easier to be preoccupied with the self than to focus on something greater. Being self-centered also gives them a guilt-free excuse to say *no* to the call of greatness…. I know because that's how I am," Glen replied honestly.

"I just want to be happy, but no matter what I do, there is this… this… emptiness to everything I do. Living here, on the farm, it's good. But the emptiness is stronger. And, when I'm honest with myself, I don't think stopping these slavers is going to change that."

"Yet, you run into the fire anyway."

"And, I'll keep going until I drop," Kora declared. She looked at her friend with sorrow in her eyes. "What else is there in life but to do good and suffer for it?"

Glen met her gaze. "We can start a family together. Teach them how to survive and build. Live long lives out here."

"That's not the most dashing marriage proposal, Glen," Kora said half-jokingly.

"I was never much of a romantic. And we fit together like fire and ice, but the more I think about it, the more value I see in such a relationship. Our nation is screwed; that doesn't mean we can't leave behind something beautiful."

"This is not what I suspected on my final morning here," Kora answered, not sure if she felt honored by the proposal or horrified by the suddenness of the moment.

"Fortune favors the bold. You taught me that," Glen replied.

"I'm not the best example…. Also, I don't have the best track record of success."

"But you reach for it. That's what I saw in that jail cell, and that's all I could think about when you were off on your scavenging hunt. I don't want to lose you again."

A family. A future. Safety. The offer is appealing, but… "I'm going to storm the gates of hell. My future be damned; someone has to go. You coming or what?"

Glen frowned. He thought for a long moment. Then, shook his head. "It's not for me. I wish you the best, though."

19

HEART OF DARKNESS

Glen, Hank, Katie, and Daniel waved Kora and Paul goodbye as they trotted into the unknown. Holding onto her reins and her only ally on horseback beside her, Kora severed her ties to security, her new family, and a long life. She thought she'd feel terrified, but instead, there was a resolute calmness in her soul. Her mind was set, and her fate sealed. Whether she succeeded or failed, she was glad to be on a worthy journey.

By the perplexed expression on Paul's face, he did not share the same conviction.

"Hey," Kora said when they were off of Glen's property.

The burned man turned to her.

"If we manage to stop these slavers, I'll marry you," Kora promised.

Paul's eyes lit up. "Wait. What? I mean—I-I'd like that. What… What changed your mind?"

"I've never met anyone as loyal as you, Paul. Even with all the crap I put you through—I still don't get it. I wouldn't marry me."

"When you were distant over these last few months, I tried to change the feelings in my heart, but…" He shook his head. "I'm convinced you're the only woman for me."

Kora steered her horse next to his and kissed him. She wished she could feel something, anything, for the man who gave everything for her, but aside from zeal, her emotions had been mostly deadened since she had killed the men in the woods. Nevertheless, having a loyal companion at her side was worth much more than butterflies in her stomach. She made a deal within herself to give Paul the affections he desired, even if she felt none of it.

An abandoned house near the scorched village was their shelter for the night. Kora dreamt of a void as black as death. She awoke at daybreak, cold and shivering. Snow blanketed the grass outside her window. Winter was here. She did her morning stretches, relieved herself behind the house, and ate a protein bar for breakfast.

They spent the day scouting for the marauders. The snow made the already difficult task even more strenuous. She found leftover trash at the start of the main road and followed it. Looted houses and the occasional frozen corpse littered her path. It was like ascending deeper into the bowels of a frozen hell. At sundown on the second day, she found her destination.

Headless corpses were impaled on wooden spikes. Black botches spotted the rotting bodies. The "stick men" continued in a far-reaching horizontal line extending through thick, leafless woods beside the main street. The display seemed to slightly curve, forming what Kora believed to be a circle around the unseen property hidden within the trees.

"Dear God," Paul mumbled. "How... How could this happen? The EMP was only a few months ago. People are doing this much evil so soon. I can't wrap my mind around it."

They have a dark messiah, Kora thought. Shiner was right about removing the snake's head. If there was no HItler, no Stalin, no Mao Zedong, then the face of the movement and the movement itself would wither and die. At least, she hoped so.

Kora inched her horse closer. The barren branches seemed to wave at her like skeletal hands. Crows took flight in the distance. "Start praying, Paul. It's just God and us now."

Paul mumbled a prayer as the two of them crossed the threshold of the dead. They steered their horses down the first branching trail and hitched them to a tree as far away from the main path as possible. The night came upon them almost suddenly.

A cold breeze bit at Kora's head nose and put an

ache in her bones.

Paul suggested camping until daybreak, but Kora refused. Without knowing the size of their opponent's force, they needed to use the shadows to their advantage. They moved back to the path and let the pale moon guide their way. The darkness was heavy. Even after their eyes adjusted, they couldn't see more than a few feet and woodland's crude silhouettes. The asphalt road took them toward large flickering lights in the distance. Hundreds of yards away, obscured by trees, huge bonfires reached the stars.

Brushing aside branches, the couple melded into the forest. Being spotted on the main path was a risk they were unwilling to take, but navigating through the wild proved troublesome. Roots snagged Kora's boots. Thorns raked across the burned half of Paul's face. Kora's many months of hunting had prepared her for such a journey.

Closing the distance between themselves and the bonfire, they heard a cacophony of noises. Screams of terror and hysterical crying. Curses and commands. Through a weave of bushes and branches obscured their vision, the sounds of hell plunged their imagination into Satan's court. Screams. Horrible, horrible screams. Human, yet so in so much pain it sounded like butchered beasts.

Paul grabbed Kora's scarred wrist. She looked over her shoulder at him, unable to see his shrouded expression. She could guess his intention, though. *Last chance to turn back. Last chance to live with my head in the sand.*

The underworld and its demons were real. The shrieks clawed at her soul. Where was their savior? Who would help them? There was no knight in shining armor, only damaged little Kora and her disfigured lover.

Fear was palpable in them both. She was going to vomit. No, cry. No, scream in rage.

She took Paul's hand to reassure him. He intertwined his fingers with hers as an eternal ally. Hand in hand, they pressed forward together.

The cries grew louder, the screams more brutal. Kora's heart clashed against her chest. It was worse than all she had felt in San Antonio. *You don't have to do this,* she reminded herself. She scrubbed the doubts from her mind and reminded herself that her cause was righteous. If there was any good in the world, it was on her side. She forced herself to believe this more than a choice. It was destiny. She was the liberator. If she could not see herself completing the job, she would lose heart in an instant.

Twigs broke beneath her boots like little bones. The stench of death and cooked meat wafted through the air. She could now see the shapes of people around the bonfire. Naked women were tied to poles. Wicked men in heavy winter clothes drank, snored, and violated everything and everyone.

Kora's reality twisted upside down. *This is our world.*

Something in her mind and soul broke, never to come back again. She was peering into the heart of darkness, feeling herself erode by simply being in its presence. She gnashed her teeth so hard they hurt. Hatred coursed through her veins. *I will kill them all.*

Paul pointed ahead.

There was a mansion in the distance, not unlike Shiners. With amber candlelight in its windows, the multi-story structure overlooked the unholy mosh.

Who was the man ruling within its halls, and how fast could Kora end him?

Unwilling to release each other, Kora and Paul left the evils behind and traversed the woods until they found a way to the mansion. Instead of finding guard patrols, they were just a handful of armed men indulging in drugs and drinks around small fires.

Kora spotted a second-story window without candlelight and concluded it would be the best entry point. She and Paul stayed out of sight as they moved to the wall lattice and began their climb. Taking a screwdriver from his backpack, Paul jimmied open the window and allowed Kora to enter first. The restroom was fitted with a toilet and shower. Both hadn't been used since the EMP. With their infiltration complete, it was just a matter of finding their target.

They peered into the hall. Unlit and unguarded, they stepped inside. Kora drew out her bow and notched an arrow. Paul pulled a knife from its sheath. They tried the doorknobs on the first two bedrooms.

Locked. The last was not. Paul gave it a twist. Kora stood back with her bow raised.

Slowly, the door opened into the master bedroom. Standing by the window and sipping a glass of red wine, the silver-haired man loomed over his empire of sin. Candles on different nightstands and dressers gave the room an amber glow. Kora slipped inside while Paul shut the door.

"What is it now?" the man asked without looking back.

Kora gasped. "Turn around. Slowly."

The man stopped mid-sip. "Fate must have a sense of humor." Setting the glass on the windowsill, the man faced them.

"Martinez," Kora gasped.

"Officer Clark," the kingpin replied. "I can recognize your voice anywhere."

"No, this can't be—you're not the one in charge of this, are you?" Kora said, trying to process the revelation.

"*This?* Oh, the mess outside. They're animals, Clark. Beastly men. Heartless. Cold. Just the kind of people you want on your team when every institution has failed."

Kora trained her arrow on him. "You started this gang? You captured those women? You burned down that town?"

Jose trained his predatory gaze on her. "Don't escalate things. I'll talk if you want to talk."

Paul growled. "Kora, don't entertain this monster."

Kora kept the bow aimed but eased up on the draw. "We could've done something amazing in San Antonio, but you left when it mattered most."

Jose crossed his hairy arms. "I bought into your idealism once. It was infectious and almost made me think there was more to this world than kill or be killed."

"There is," Kora replied.

"No," Jose said sternly. "On the streets as a kid, I knew it. When the Chinese attacked us, it further reinforced the truth: there is no justice in this world, just the hunter and prey."

Kora ground her teeth.

Jose continued, "Sometimes, the hunter is merciful, but there is no place for that anymore. These men outside are the soldiers that keep my little corner of the world under my heel. I get security and kingdom among the ashes, and they get whatever their wicked heart desires. Like Genghis Khan, Alexander the Great, and the other great conquerors, we're expanding our reach. The strong will join us. The weak become our property. It's not complicated. It's simply the nature of the world."

Furious, Paul took a step forward.

Jose held his ground. "Try it and I'll have my entire army up here in a moment."

Kora replied, "Yeah, but you'll be dead, and your people scattered."

Jose chuckled. "Do you think that killing me is going to stop anything? These people have tasted true freedom. Wherever they go, they will rape and kill until someone bigger puts them in the grave."

"You're evil," Paul hissed.

"And you're the knight in shining armor coming to stop me? Please, you don't have the balls. That's why you follow around your woman like a little lost puppy. If not for her, you'd be nothing. When you die this winter, you'll be just another nameless statistic among the millions of insignificant people who fell when the nation collapsed. Not me, though. The world will know what I've done."

"Shut up!" Paul charged forward in a burst of rage and jabbed the point of the knife at his chest.

In a quick motion, Jose deflected Paul's wrist, grabbed the back of his jacket, and hurled him toward the window.

"*Gawk!*" Paul broke through the glass and plummeted into the snowy darkness.

"Paul!" Kora loosed her arrow.

Its point punched into Jose's inner shoulder. Cursing, he bull-rushed her.

Kora reached in her quiver for another arrow.

Too late.

Jose's large fist decked her across the cheek. She staggered and took another hit, putting her on the ground. She reached for her gun, but Jose put his boot into her stomach and tossed it away. Screaming, she pulled her knife—her final weapon—stabbed the point into his calf muscle.

"Aaaaah!" Jose ripped away his leg, the blade still lodged in him.

Fighting for her life, Kora snatched an arrow that had rolled from her quiver and lunged at him. Jose swung his limbering arm, missed, and took the arrow to the gut. Kora's body smacked against his large chest, forcing the arrow in a few more inches.

Shouting obscenities, Jose grabbed the side of her head and slammed into the nearby dresser.

Slack!

Blackness for a split second.

She returned to reality before getting her head smacked into the dresser a second time. Weakened, Jose released her like a rag doll. Nearly lifeless, she dropped to the floor. Her skull throbbed. The pain was excruciating. Blood leaked from her lips from a bit tongue. Paralyzed by agony, she watched Jose stumble to his bed.

Stuck with two arrows and a knife, the silver-haired man lowered his rear to the corner of the mattress. He steadied his breath. A few tears rolled down his cheeks.

"You really messed me up." He grimaced and grabbed the arrow in his belly. The pain was too unbearable to pull it out. He quickly gave up.

Crimson stained the bedsheets and hardwood. With heavy-lidded eyes, Jose looked over the woman. "I should've killed you in San Antonio."

The bedroom door burst open. Tako, his teenage daughter, Abigail, and a handful of goons rushed inside.

"Dad!" Abigail rushed to his aid.

Jose swatted away her hand. "Get me a doctor."

Tako trained his pistol at Kora. "What do you want me to do with her?"

"Put her with the others," Jose said through his teeth.

Tako marched over to Kora, said something in Spanish, and stomped her face.

HOWLING WINDS

A stench hovered in the cellar's stale, cold air. It was the stink of people, sweat, and living decay. Stripped down to their underwear and packed in the dark, Jose's captives were treated worse than cattle. The only time they saw light was when Tako opened the cellar doors to toss scraps of food inside or when he demanded a few women for entertainment. This sort of evil had no rhyme or reason. It wasn't justifiable in any sense and served no greater purpose than to fulfill the men's darkest desires. The slaves who refused were beaten, killed, and thrown into a ditch behind the mansion.

When Kora was dragged inside four days ago, she attempted to start an uprising. "If we wait until they open the door…" Kora said before laying out a plan.

In complete blackness, the captives silently listened

to her. Her words only stirred greater despair. One woman told her to shut up before they all got killed.

"Death has to be better than this," Kora replied, getting quick flashes of Paul's final charge.

The woman replied, "And what if the underworld is worse?"

After many hours, Kora gave up on trying to convince them. Trembling, she hugged her knees close to her chest. Her tongue touched the place where her front tooth once was. Tako's boot had knocked it out.

Lowering her head, she thought of her mission. Surely, it was righteous. Surely, there was some eternal reward for her efforts. *Maybe Jose's right. Maybe this world is only kill or be killed.* She refused to believe it. There was good in people. She'd seen it at Shiners. Why couldn't she calm her ambitious heart and choose a safer life? Why wasn't there ever any satisfaction in her efforts? Was this her punishment for wanting more to life, for rushing headlong against the tsunami of evil and men's useless complacency? Was her crusade destined to fail, or were her failures the workings of her unskilled hands?

Her heart sank to her stomach. If only Tako had shot her…. If only she could plead her case before God…. If only she could rest…. Yes, sleep would be good.

She slowly shut her eyes. She dreamed of San Antonio, but in this timeline, she'd won the battle at the Alamo. People were rebuilding. A new culture of community and life was springing forth. The dream changed to Shiner's Ranch. It was the same scenario: peaceful and unified. It was a world that could've been.

Kora awoke at the sound of the cellar door opening.

Flanked by two men holding torches, Tako pointed at her. "You. Hurry up."

Her thin stomach grumbled as she stood. Four days with nothing but scraps, and her head was spinning. The other women shamefully looked away from her. She moved lethargically, knowing what was in store for her. If there were ever a moment for divine intervention, now was the time.

"C'mon. Quicker," Tako snapped.

Defiantly, Kora lifted her head and faced her captors. She screamed internally behind her hardened expression. Her courage was front. Fear and dread silently constricted her. She considered falling on her knees and begging the men for mercy. *If they showed no mercy to other women, why would they do so for me? Am I more special? More beautiful? No.*

Reaching the cellar's entrance, Tako bound her scarred wrists together with ropes. The knot was so tight that even the tips of her fingers tingled. He shoved her in front of him.

Snow crunched beneath her dirty, blackened soles. Screaming wind whipped through the dark woods. Out of sight, she could hear the horrible howls of women. Tears welled in her eyes. Her gaze fell upon a scarecrow among the trees. She was confused by the odd placement before she noted it was not a scarecrow but a headless man with old burn scars on his naked body.

Paul... She lurched over and vomited what little was in her stomach.

Tako pushed her. "Keep walking."

Like a ghost, her hope lifted from her. All that remained was a submissive husk. Eyes glassed over and her mind far away, she walked to a side entrance of the mansion. There was no more fight in her. No more zeal. No more life.

Multiple fireplaces burned, but none could keep the house warm tonight. Death's cold chill was in every room, hall, and corridor. Kora blinked, and she was upstairs. Tako opened the doors to one of the bedrooms and pushed her inside.

The room was tidy. Expensive jewelry rested on the dresser and desk, fancy dresses clothed various mannequins, and there was a canopy bed made for a princess.

Kora stopped a few feet into the room, and the door was shut behind her. She didn't move. Her gaze fell on the closed window. Would jumping from two stories be enough to end her miserable life?

"You're that cop," Abigail said as she entered from the shoe closet. A large fur coat covered her thin, tan frame. Gold chains hung around her slender neck. Diamond rings sat snugly on her fingers. "You really hurt my dad, you know?"

Kora stayed silent.

Approaching, Abigail recoiled at her smell. "Eww."

She pulled a little glass bottle of perfume from her pocket and spritzed Kora. The aroma was intoxicating. Kora felt she was going to be sick.

Though chapped lips, Kora asked, "What do you want from me?"

Abigail said, "To talk, mostly. I'm sure you've noticed how horrible things are around here. Everyone has lost their minds. I feel like I'm the only sane person left."

Kora looked like a dolled-up teenager incredulously. "Then leave."

"Like my father would allow that. He's a control freak. I was kind of relieved you put him in his place. The doctor says it'll take weeks to recover." The teenage girl smiled to herself.

"He deserves to die," Kora said coldly.

"This world needs strong men. Just think, what would happen if we were subject to the Chinese?" Abigail shuttered.

Kora balled her fists. "Have you seen what he does with those women?"

"Yeah, it's messed up, but what choice do I have? I won't survive out there. Besides, look at the stuff he got me? I'm a lot better off than most people." Abigail gestured to the room.

The girl's shallowness flabbergasted Kora.

Abigail was offended. "Don't look at me like that. I'm just trying to stay alive like everyone else."

"Right, and that excuses you from all responsibility?"

"Uh, yeah, because what good is the responsibility if I'm dead? God, you're stupid."

Kora glanced around the room. "Why did you bring me up here? Really? I know it wasn't just to talk."

Abigail replied, "Remember when my father wanted you to mentor me? I think that would be pretty cool. Besides, I need a friend who is a girl. All the guys around here are pervs, and the women are so weak and stupid, it's embarrassing."

"They're enslaved," Kora replied flatly.

Abigail brushed over the comment. "I can put in a good word for my dad, but he won't release you until he knows you are on our team…. I get it if you don't want to be friends. I can always put you back in the cellar."

She's just as bad as Jose, Kora thought.

Abigail tilted her head slightly, asking. "Well? Friends or what?"

"Does your father trust you?"

"A little," Abigail said. "That's why you have to prove yourself. Go talk to him, and do what he says. I'm sure he'll forgive you for your mistakes if he knows how useful you can be."

My mistakes? Kora wanted to go off on the girl, but

dying in the cellar would do her no good. "Take me to him…."

"Awesome, but if you try to do anything, I'll tell Tako to no longer protect you," Abigail replied.

Kora nodded. *If I'm going to die, I might as well bring Jose down with me.*

Abigail led her down the hall. "You know, if not for me, the guys around here would've had their way with you on the first night."

An armed thug stood outside of Jose's room. He let them enter at Abigail's command but followed them inside. Jose was on his bed with his back against the backboard. Bandages wrapped around his leg, torso, and upper shoulder. Wearing glasses, he read a book by candlelight.

"Father, I would like to talk to you about Kora—"

"Silence, girl." Jose snapped and set the book beside his painkillers.

Abigail shut up and lowered her head.

Jose glared at Kora. "You should be in the cellar."

"Abigail said there was a way I could earn your trust," Kora replied.

Jose grinned. "Really? That's funny. I should have you both beaten for your foolishness."

"But, Father—"

"Did I say you could speak?" Jose shouted.

Shuttering, Abigail hurried out of the room. Jose, the guard, and Kora remained.

"The girl is an idiot," Jose remarked. "Her mind has

been screwed up since San Antonio. I buy her gifts to keep her occupied, but her stupidity abounds…. These drugs make me talk too much."

"What can I do to make amends?" Kora asked.

"Four days in the darkness, and you've already broken. No, Clark. You have a stronger will than that. Did you deceive my daughter so you can avenge your boyfriend? I'm sure you saw my display when you left the cellar. Tako said he went down fighting. I was honestly surprised. I didn't think he had it in him."

"We knew what we were getting ourselves into," Kora replied.

"He loved you, didn't he? And all you have to say about his death is something trite like that. You were always cold, Clark. Don't be ashamed of that. It takes a certain ruthlessness to get the job done," Jose replied.

Kora felt sick. She masked her feelings behind her sunken eyes and pale face. "You and I made a good team back in the day. Let me help you get this place organized."

"I already have everything I need."

"If you have hope to expand, you'll need structure. Fear and pleasures will only get you so far. When your people realize that they don't need you to live out their dark fantasies, they put you and your daughter into the ground. Let me help establish some rules. We can even put the women to work."

"You're desperate."

"I can be an asset to you."

"No. You're a threat. You always have been." Jose gestured to the guard.

He grabbed Kora's upper arm and started to pull her out of the room.

"You're going to regret this, Jose. I promise you," Kora threatened. "You may throw me away, you may kill me, but you will reap what you sow eventually."

Jose smirked. "I've survived this long."

Gunfire erupted in the distance.

"What the hell was that?" the guard exclaimed.

More shots fired. There was an exchange of gunfire near and far.

Jose's eyes widened. "Get Tako, and find out what is happening out there!"

"What should I do with her?" the guard asked.

Jose cursed. Wincing, he pulled open the drawer to his nightstand and pulled out a revolver.

A smug grin grew on Kora's face. "You're scared. I can see it."

Bam!

Like a bolt of lightning, the sharp pain hit her gut, and she dropped to her knees.

"Find Tako. Now!" Jose shouted.

The guard released Kora and ran from the room.

Head down, Kora watched the blood leaking from her abdomen. The corners of her vision blurred. She put her bound hands on the bullet wound, hoping to staunch the crimson flow.

Jose lowered the revolver. "A lot worse than an

arrow. Are those your people outside? Did they follow you?"

Kora tried to speak, but she was still in shock.

"I could shoot you again, but such mercies would make me look weak. I'll give you five, ten minutes tops before you leak out. I think I'll leave the stain as a reminder of what happens to those who strike a king," Jose gloated.

Shouting and gunfire surrounded the mansion. Whoever was attacking had a sizable force and an arsenal at their disposal. Fighting beside bonfire fires, Jose's army was hopelessly shooting in the dark. The attacks had the advantage, but only if they were willing to push forward.

On her knees, Kora stayed perfectly still. She pressed hard against the wound. As much as she thought death would be a release, everything in her was fighting to live another day. She attempted to control her breathing. *Not today. Not like this. Not by his hands.*

Jose attempted to leave the bed, but the simple act of sitting up was too much to bear. Bedridden, he slammed his fist on the mattress in frustration. "I should be there with them. You did this to me."

A little smile formed on the corner of Kora's taut lips.

"Laugh all you want. My empire's not falling today."

"Pride... comes before the..."

"Oh, spare me," Jose replied.

Tako rushed inside and yelled something in Spanish. Jose replied in kind and sent Tako out.

"Whoever these people are, I'm going to impale them on sticks," Jose seethed.

Kora felt the room sway, and she plopped to her side. Blood seeped between her fingers. *Is this it, God? Did I fail? Was it worth it, this little life of mine?*

Machine guns roared outside the mansion.

"That a boy, Tako," Jose said with a wicked grin before turning to Kora. "I have to thank you for one thing, Kora. What you did in San Antonio made me who I am today. Without you, I'd be licking the boots of our invaders. Now, I can live like a king. You told me to seize my destiny, and I did." He chuckled.

Kora squeezed her eyelid as her body became lighter. Cold chills raked her exposed body. *I made this monster.... No, he chose to use his liberty for evil. I'm a good person. I am... right?*

Bam-bam-bam! A few bullets shot up through the window.

Jose cursed as icy gales ripped through the room. "Why aren't these people dead yet?"

He tried to sit up once again but only managed to open the wound in his gut. "Aaaah! C'mon!"

A burgundy stain grew behind his bandage. "No, no, no!" he yelled and cursed.

Kora thought of Kensley, Garrick, Paul, and all the other people who had died around her. *Was it all in vain? God, I'm a failure. I'm sorry. Forgive me. Please, forgive me.*

She rolled to her back. Her sticky blood smeared over her torso and the floorboards around her. *I never found Daniel's mother. The poor kid. Glen, look after him. Hank, stay with Katie. She needs all the help she can get with the baby. Lambert, just... keep doing what you're doing with Shiners. Make it worth it.*

"Kora? Are you still here?" Jose asked. "Say something."

She groaned.

Jose replied, "You didn't give up, did you?"

Kora groaned again.

"Fine. I'll give you the easy way out." He grabbed his revolver and aimed.

Jesus, have mercy on my soul. Kora waited for the end.

Something knocked the downstairs door open.

In the hallway, Abigail shrieked, "They're inside!"

Horrified, Jose grabbed the ammo box from the drawer and loaded in the missing shot. "This can't be happening. No, not after all I've done," he mumbled.

The warfare echoed in the house. Windows broke. Future was upturned. Loud boot prints thumped up the stairs.

Jose aimed at the door, wincing from his leaking wound. The door smashed open, and he fired two shots. Shocked by the sudden betrayal, Tako looked at his wounds before collapsing in the doorway.

"Ah, you idiot. Why didn't you say something?" Jose yelled.

More boots sounded on the stairs.

Jose swiveled his legs out of bed, farther opening his wounds. He spat on the floor. "I'm not dying with you, whore."

Attempting to stand, Jose spotted a man in a ghillie suit in the hallway. He drew up his revolve as fast as he could and—

Bam! Bam!

—took two bullets in the face.

Disfigured, his body flopped onto the large mattress, blood pooling on his silk sheets. Outside, bonfires burned, and the cold wind started to die.

"Kora!" The shooter leaped over Tako's corpse and ran to the fallen cop.

He put his hands on her colorless cheeks. "Hey, hey. It's me. Glen. Stay with me. Kora? Kora!"

PHOENIX

*W*armth.
　　　　　Soft cushions.
Was it heaven?

Kora's eyes fluttered open. Lavish, heavenly inspired artwork covered every surface of the walls. The sun's warm rays spilled through the window and shed a ray of light across her face. Elsewhere in the room, firewood crackled in the fireplace. Kora bent forward slightly, and a sudden pain knocked her back to her pillow.

She delicately pulled away the thick covers and eyed the cloth wrapped around her torso. *Not heaven.*

Next to her, a blood bag hung on its metal post. *They guessed my blood type correctly... I shouldn't be alive. God, why am I still here?*

Fluffy clouds cruised across the blue sky. It must've been around noon.

"Finally awake." Sitting in a rocking chair, Glen watched her.

Kora asked, faintly remembering the night of the battle. "You shot Jose?"

"Not just him," Glen bragged. "All those bastards are gone. Well, we have the daughter in captivity."

"How do you find me?" Part of her was still bitter that he didn't join her in the beginning. Paul might still be alive if she'd had support.

"I followed you after you left my place. The night Jose captured you, I thought about going in, but there were just too many. I fell back and managed to find that Shiner guy you mentioned. I told him what had happened. He rallied up his best men and was at Jose's place a few days later. I would've come sooner if I could've of, but there's only so much I can do as one guy."

"I'm surprised Shiner did anything."

"It wasn't just him. Your old friend Shultz was the first one to volunteer. He was also the one who knew your blood type," Glen replied.

"And the captives? Daniel's mom?"

"Shiner's taking care of them, and yeah, she's alive. I wouldn't wish what happened to them on my worst enemy. Some of them are pretty messed up. I would say they'll get through it, but some things you never really recover from."

Kora leaned back into her pillow. "It's over, then."

"Thanks to you, yeah."

"I wasn't the one who stopped them."

"No, but you paved the way... Most of us are so caught up in our own survival that we reject visionaries like yourself, but in the end, you were right. If we don't take a stand against lawlessness, who will? Without people like you, nothing would change."

Tears welled in Kora's eyes. "There were so many lost."

"Everything worthwhile costs something. With Jose and his band of marauders gone, our little spot in the world will be a much safer place. The victory even inspired Shiner to expand his reach. Once again, because of what you did," Glen replied.

"All right, you can stop buttering me up now," Kora groaned.

Smiling, Glen got up. "I'll let you rest."

"Thank you, Glen. For saving me."

The prepper nodded respectfully and exited the room.

Kora placed her hand just above the bullet wound. Despite everything, she felt some joy. It wasn't perfect closure, but there was a sense of satisfaction for her deeds. She had started the work and saw it through to the end. The people around her were finally doing something with their lives. What else could she ask for? *My friends I lost along the way...*

After a few days in bed, she was wheelchaired out of her room. Perfect fluffy snow blanketed the property. Children ran and played, Daniel among them. Laughing, the adults roasted deer meat over the fire pit. Glen rolled Kora into the lounge where Lambert, Shiner, and Shultz were gathered by the fire.

"Speak of the devil," Shultz remarked.

"Gentlemen," Kora replied, wheeling herself in their direction. "Looking spiffy."

Shiner replied, "I found some great winter coats at Jose's. They were the only thing I didn't want to burn in that God-forsaken place."

"The corpse display was a bit much, I admit," Dr. Lambert said.

Shiner and Shultz glared at him.

"Too soon? Fine," the doctor replied.

Kora said, "I appreciate the stitches, doc. I'm gonna have some pretty gnarly scars after all this. You don't have a spare front tooth sitting around here, too, do you?" She grinned wide, revealing the gap in her upper jaw.

"We'll see what Santa Claus gets ya." Lambert winked.

"Just FYI, I'm not sure if gold is my style," Kora teased.

Shiner warmed his hands above the fireplace. The flames danced in his eyes. "I wish you could've seen it, Kora. The night of the assault, it was like God himself was fighting alongside us."

Shultz nodded in agreement.

"What happened?" Kora asked.

Shiner explained, "We hit hard and fast. They

couldn't see us, but their bonfires made them easy targets. They were so confused, so drugged out of their mind, that they were practically shooting each other by the end. We only suffered three casualties with a handful of injured folk. I thought the battle would take hours, but it was over in minutes. Despite their forces, we cut through them like butter... Providence, I say."

Shultz added, "I don't think they ever expected anyone to fight them on their home turf. You were right to take the battle to their doorstep."

"Have you decided what to do with the daughter?" Kora asked.

"We're putting her on trial tonight," Shiner said resolutely.

"I thought your word was law. Why not just pronounce judgment and be done with it?"

Shine replied, "I'm changing things up around here. Too much power consolidated in one place can easily be abused. We'll decide on these bigger issues as a collective."

"I like it," Kora replied.

Glen spoke up. "Oh, Hank and Katie arrived last night."

Kora was surprised. "I'm surprised you let them in, Shiner."

Shiner replied, "Your friends are my friends."

Kora looked up at Glen. "I'd like to see them."

Leaving the others to their conversation, Glen pushed Kora to the horse stables. Hank and Katie brushed the large animals, speaking comforting words as they did so.

"Kora!" Katie exclaimed. Letting go of her brush, she rushed to hug Kora.

"Easy," Kora replied, feeling her wound.

"I'm so happy you're alive. I thought we'd never see you again."

"I missed you, too. Do you plan to spend the winter here?" Kora asked.

Katie nodded enthusiastically. "Yes! Shiner even set me up in the big house until the baby comes."

"The rest of us are in tents," Hank said neutrally.

"Well, I'm glad you two could make it," Kora replied.

Hank said, "I haven't forgotten your promise."

"Neither have I," Kora replied. "We'll rest up through the winter and then make our move."

"Sounds like a plan," the patriot agreed.

After relaxing for that afternoon, it was time for Abigail's trial. With all Jose's men were killed during the assault—which Kora believed to be intentional—it wouldn't take long. In handcuffs, Abigail was brought about before the people and a large bonfire.

"My father was a monster!" she cried. "He kept me against my will. Beat me when I refused to listen… He even… he even touched me. Please, let me stay. I'm a good girl, I promise! I'll make myself useful."

Kora saw through her crocodile tears. She asked Shiner if she could share her testimony. Shiner allowed it.

Kora faced the crowd. "When I was in captivity, I met with Abigail. Her father had showered her with gifts, and she did nothing to help the captive women. She even threatened to have me thrown back into the cellar if I didn't abide by her wishes."

"That's not true! I would've helped if I could, but I saw what my father did. I couldn't go against him."

"You were the closest one to Jose. At any point, you could've slit his throat and put an end to evils."

"I'm not a killer. Listen to me, people. I was just trying to stay alive. Is that a crime?"

A few of the surviving captives testified against the teenager. They claimed she turned a blind eye every time a man abused her and flaunted their jewelry around the mansion.

When it came time for a final verdict, Kora made a suggestion. "Executing the girl seems excessive. She's not a threat. And imprisoning her, though I believe it is just, would mean wasting our resources on our enemy. I say we will exile her."

"I'll die out there!" she screamed.

Kora replied, "You claim to be a survivor. Time to survive."

The people discussed the case amongst themselves and eventually voted to send Abigail out of the ranch.

Out of the kindness of his heart, Shiner gave her three days' worth of rations. His mercy reminded Kora of her father. She wished she could've lived up to the expectation of showing fairness to her enemies, but

Kora was tired, and the world was a dark place. *Maybe one day, Dad.*

The next morning, Abigail was escorted out of the land and promised death if she ever returned. She left crying.

The Martinez saga was over.

Kora let her wounds recover for the winter.

When spring arrived, Kora and Hank trained the people and marched a sizable force to San Antonio. Much to their surprise, Shultz and Glen joined them. Shultz was in search of redemption, while Glen was set on winning Kora's heart. The previous battle had hardened them all. Now, it was time for the real revolution.

Meanwhile, Katie stayed back to look after her newborn. Lambert acted as the local doctor, and Daniel was taken under Shiner's wing. The ranch would continue to prosper as whatever threats had remained died in the previous season's cold.

Kora was unsure if she would survive her assault against the Chinese, but it didn't matter to her. Her sacrifice and her actions would prompt other patriots to leave hiding and join the fight. Though it was not the happily ever after Paul would've wanted for her, it was a meaningful existence, and that was all Kora really wanted.

THE END.

Made in the USA
Middletown, DE
15 July 2023

35174121R00176